THE NET

THE NET

By
AGNES BLUNDELL

ST. AIDAN PRESS
Harpers Ferry, West Virginia

The Net.

First published in 1937 by Sands & Co. Limited.

Typesetting, layout and cover design copyright 2022 St. Aidan Press.

Cover art by Andrea England.

ISBN-13: 978-0-9719230-6-5
ISBN-10: 0-9719230-6-X

For more information, contact:
www.staidanpress.com
staidanpress@gmail.com

CONTENTS

CHAPTER | PAGE

CHAPTER ONE 1

CHAPTER TWO 9

CHAPTER THREE 16

CHAPTER FOUR 22

CHAPTER FIVE 31

CHAPTER SIX 38

CHAPTER SEVEN 47

CHAPTER EIGHT 58

CHAPTER NINE 67

CHAPTER TEN 76

CHAPTER ELEVEN 85

CHAPTER TWELVE 95

CHAPTER THIRTEEN 103

CHAPTER FOURTEEN 112

CHAPTER FIFTEEN 119

CHAPTER SIXTEEN 127

CHAPTER SEVENTEEN 135

CHAPTER EIGHTEEN 144

CHAPTER NINETEEN 154

CHAPTER TWENTY 162

CHAPTER TWENTY-ONE 175

CHAPTER TWENTY-TWO 184

CHAPTER TWENTY-THREE 191

CHAPTER TWENTY-FOUR 198

CHAPTER TWENTY-FIVE 204

CHAPTER TWENTY-SIX 212

CHAPTER TWENTY-SEVEN 222

CHAPTER TWENTY-EIGHT 230

CHAPTER TWENTY-NINE. 243

THE NET

CHAPTER ONE

IT WAS A DULL, damp spring morning when young Mr. Dicconson disembarked at Rye. The sturdy Lancashire-man had been untroubled by the rough voyage, and was one of the first ashore with his baggage. He had prudently donned an old cloak while the little packet-boat tossed in the Channel, and its worn surface was whitened by congealed sea-spray. It was three years since the lad had set foot in his native land, and the voices of his fellow-countrymen sounded strangely in his ears. He spoke carefully when asking the way to the coach office in terror of betraying a foreign accent. The young man's intention was first to secure his seat in the coach, and then if enough money remained, to repair to the tavern, have a meal, change his clothes and send for a barber. He regretted that he was still wearing his own hair, and hoped that his brother would accommodate him with sufficient ready money to order a full bag-wig while he was in town.

Roger Dicconson had left home at the age of fourteen and, after concluding his schooling at St. Omers, he had proceeded to Rome as tutor to a young Italian of quality, whose elder brother had been his classmate. The Englishman had been a popular inmate of the household of the Duke of San Rocca and an advantageous match had even been proposed to him, but nostalgia for his own country had caused him to throw over all his prospects in the foreign capital. His parents were dead and an elder brother was in possession of the family estates; a brother who had not very warmly encouraged his return.

Roger had not written to claim his share, as he had been able to provide for himself by his own exertions; and William wrote doleful accounts of the financial troubles to which Catholics were being subjected in England, and particularly of his own difficulties in the administration of an encumbered inheritance. Roger was anxious to spend a few days in town; besides a young man's natural desire to know something of London, he had hopes of a meeting with the great hero of his boyhood—one Martin Buckland—who had been the most brilliant boy at St. Omers, and carelessly kind to the youngster, four years his junior. Roger had heard nothing from Buckland of late, and entertained a shrewd suspicion that he was engaged in political activities. He had written announcing his arrival in England but had had no answer. It was an exciting moment. Here he was really entering upon life at last; his own master, personable and of strong health if of small fortune. Roger stepped gaily to the coach office, followed by a porter with his bags and sword-case. He secured his place inside and then, thrusting his hand into his pocket, was struck with consternation—his wallet was gone!

Here was vexation, which was not allayed by the supercilious glances which passed between the clerk and the porter while he vented his wrath. He had a few stray coins in his valise and offered these and the promise of prompt payment at the journey's end without effect. Two or three idlers gathered round to sneer at the rogue who thought to take folks in by such greenhorn pretences.

"You seem to think we're not up to snuff here," remarked the clerk.

"I see you're not used to gentlemen," returned Dicconson hotly, "or you would have been taught manners ere now."

2

Chapter One

"We're used to gentlemen o' *your* sort," retorted the fellow, and the ostlers slapped their thighs and guffawed loudly.

Roger stood fuming, longing to go for his adversary with his fists. He decided, however, that an attitude of good-humoured contempt was more dignified, as well as more prudent. There was some loose silver in his breeches pocket and he took out a shilling and fingered it as he addressed the porter.

"Set down my baggage in the tavern yonder. And you," he added, turning to the clerk, "you will lose the gratuity you might well have gained, had you kept a civil tongue in your head."

"You'll not require the seat then?" asked the clerk, more politely.

Roger shook his head and strode off with as much indifference as he could assume.

At the inn he got out his money—there was just enough to pay for the dispatch of his luggage by wagon and leave a few shillings in hand. He resolved to walk to London rather than pledge any of his clothes. It would be too awkward to arrive in town without his fine shirts, and it would be troublesome also to redeem them. He had asked his brother to arrange for necessary supplies for him at any of his friends in town, or with some counting-house with which he dealt. A letter telling him where to apply was to await him at "The Angel"—the hostelry where the coach route ended.

Roger felt young and inexperienced as he prepared for the journey. He had been robbed at his first setting foot on English soil, and had been mocked to boot as though he were of the same brand as his despoiler. No doubt the roads, as well as the port, would be infested with rogues and cutpurses. He put on his plainest clothes and stoutest boots, and determined to assume the character of a bluff country fellow, such as might be walking to town to seek service with a gentleman of quality. Some natural distaste had to be swallowed before Roger

3

convinced himself that such a person was less likely to be molested than a green young gallant without even a periwig to uphold his birth. Nevertheless there was a distinct spice of excitement in the adventure, and when he presently strolled out of Rye in the wake of the coach which bore his valise and sword-case and paused to cut a holly staff in the hedge, Roger felt his spirits rising.

The little port was soon left behind, the road, still deep with winter ruts, was empty, and there was no sound but the carolling of innumerable birds. The young man's self-esteem had received a rude blow—it was extremely humiliating to have been robbed like any greenhorn, he told himself, but the loss of his guineas did not weigh upon him, and he marched along whistling jovially in time to his strides. Wooden sign-posts loomed through the growing dusk and pointed out the way to London; an occasional packman jogged past on a tired horse, or a ploughman trudging home from the field, but for the most part he had the road to himself. When a milestone informed him that Rye lay ten miles behind, the young man determined to seek lodging for the night, before the April light waned.

The next turn of the road brought him to a little whitewashed tavern close to a toll-bar, which seemed eminently suitable for his purpose. He peeped through the window and saw a snug, sanded kitchen with a bright fire. There was a bar at one end of the room and a row of clean clay pipes on the high mantelpiece. Roger stepped in and inquired if he could be obliged with a bed for the night. The landlord seemed a hearty fellow, but the hardness and shrewdness of his little grey eyes somewhat belied his jovial bearing. His welcome grew cold as soon as he perceived that the traveller had neither horse nor baggage.

"We can give you a bite of food to be sure," he observed dubiously. "But a bed for the night is another thing altogether. Being toll-keeper I do have to be extra careful."

"No doubt, good fellow," rejoined Roger, "but your care ain't likely to suffer from my sleeping here. Doubtless you haven't a spare bed, or a clean one. Give me some eggs and bacon and a pint of beer, as how 'tis!"

"There speaks a Lanky lad!" exclaimed a woman's voice; and a comely, rosy-cheeked dame came in, with some eggs in her hand. "And I'm sorry anyone should speak ill o' my beds, for they're good goose-down, every one of 'em, as I've plucked with my own hands."

"I ask no better than to sample one of them, Ma'am," cried Roger, but the landlord struck in with an oath.

"Damn it, woman, you know well enough the big room is taken."

"What of it?" she retorted. "Can't the lad have our Johnny's little chamber at the stair-head? My lad is at sea, Sir—he was pressed, he were—and there's no knowing how he'll be treated now the new King has ordered flogging in the Navy."

"It's a fine life for a young man, however," replied Dicconson. "And I'll be thankful for Johnny's bed, which I'll engage is as good as you say. And now supper if you please! Some of those good eggs and a rasher or two of bacon, Dame, will be champion."

Wilson, the landlord, had been nudging his wife and frowning at her, but the last word warmed the heart of the North-countrywoman and she shook off her husband's hand.

"'Tis a small room, but you can have it if you're none too particular," she remarked.

"Thank you kindly then," agreed Roger, stifling his qualms.

He felt quite sure that he ought to take alarm at the landlord's mood and his dark allusions to other guests, but he was tired and felt very unwilling to tramp on to the next village, where he might fare worse. His solitary crown-piece was concealed in his stocking and his trifling stock of small silver was not worth robbing. He took possession of an armchair by the hearth and stretched his feet to the blaze.

His ally, Mrs. Wilson, seemed to be having a lengthy altercation with her husband; the angry scolding voices continued the argument in subdued tones in the back premises all the time the rashers were frying. The woman presently entered, looking flushed and agitated, and placed the supper on the large, well-scrubbed table. She answered the hungry young traveller's remarks with monosyllables until a shout at the toll-bar caused Wilson to hurry from the house. Instantly the woman's manner changed.

"My mind misgives me as I let ye stay," she murmured, leaning over the table. "There are ill folks coming—aye, not satisfied with swearing away the life of some poor fool who has snatched a purse or stole a silk handkerchief, they'll set folk on to steal, they will, and get 'em hanged for 't and pocket the reward. Don't let 'em know your name."

"I'll not steal, Mother," said Roger, but his heart quickened its beat. "I'm honest."

"Think you they'll stay for that? So a chap hasn't friends, they'll swear away his life for blood-money. The Judges don't ax for evidence nowadays, so look to yourself, lad!"

She sprang away from him and fell to mending the fire, as horses' hoofs clattered on the cobblestones outside, and Wilson shouted to her to open the door. Dicconson pulled his hat down on his brow and helped himself to the last rasher of bacon; he called out a "good e'en to ye" without turning round, as three men tramped into the room and took their stand near the fire.

"Good evening, comrado," rejoined one of the newcomers in a Cockney accent.

Roger looked up and was by no means predisposed in favour of the group. Two of the men were rakishly dressed in military greatcoats and one wore his own hair. The third man looked like a drunken ostler. The speaker had a sword, and a suspicious bulkiness under the belt warned Roger that his companions doubtless carried pistols. He drained his mug of ale and set it down with a laugh.

"If you're for drinking, good lads, choose wine, I'd advise ye," he said. "This ale is plaguey thin, poor stuff."

"You should pledge the King in his own liquor," retorted the newcomer. "Come, woman—serve us a noggin of hollands! That's the stuff to warm the vitals and make a man of a raw boy. Will you join us?"

"Faith, not I!" cried Roger. "I've had enough of hollands and of Holland too, to last me a lifetime, blast it! But give me another pot, good wife, and I'll drain it to King William and this honest gentleman here."

There was a pause. The horsemen looked at Dicconson askance, undetermined whether to take offence or to play a friendly part. Roger called for a pipe and busied himself in lighting it. He was fully aware of the danger of his situation, but meant to carry things off with a high hand.

"Why, we're four, I perceive," he exclaimed. "Just right for a little game—what say you, brothers?" And he pulled from his pocket the well-worn cards with which he and the Captain of the packet-boat had whiled away the hours while they were waiting for the wind, and which he had carried off by mistake.

A quiver of astonishment ran through the three men on the hearth. Perhaps this innocent-looking youth was not a pigeon to be plucked after all; perchance he was even of their own kind.

"I don't play cards with strangers, Sir!" answered the leader truculently.

"Well, now, you're quite right," said Roger. "'Tis a precept my mother was never tired of repeating. I respect you, Sir, for your prudence."

He got up, and swept an exaggerated bow. The landlord had come in and fidgeted about the room uneasily.

"I'll bid you good-night, then," continued Dicconson airily, and turned towards the staircase. But he was not to be allowed to withdraw unchallenged. The man with the drunken face sprang before him at a sign from his chief.

"Who are you?" he demanded with an oath.

Chapter Two

"**W**HO ARE YOU?"

As the challenge rang out, the landlord slipped from the room and closed the door; he was not going to be responsible for the behaviour of his guests. Dicconson stood his ground, and resisted the inclination to raise his holly staff in a defensive gesture.

"Who am I?" he repeated. "Why, my name is Harding, and I'm a gentleman. And further, my face is my fortune, like the girl's in the ballad—and that is more than can be said of you, friend!"

"What's your game?" continued the other, in the same low, fierce tone.

"Come, come!" remonstrated Roger, with the tail of his eye on the tarnished gallants by the chimney. "I ask you no questions. A gentleman must live, damn it! And live as genteel as he can. If there's little to be had abroad, I'm told there are pickings at home."

"Faugh!" exclaimed the man who had not yet spoken. "'Tis but a common footpad, I believe. He's not worth your trouble, Captain."

A significant glance passed between the pair, and Dicconson was by no means misled. Mrs. Wilson's whisper of horrid doings was still in his ears.

"Nay, lads, I've nought against me!" he said hastily. "Never a conviction," he added with a sly look.

With that he stepped suddenly behind the ruffian and up the staircase, leaving silence in the parlour until he had banged the door of the little attic room. But though he slammed it heartily he had the presence of mind to hold up the latch and leave the door ajar. He groped about in the stuffy darkness, that they might hear his footsteps, but all the time kept his ears pricked in case he should be followed. At last he found the window and drew back the ragged curtain. Through the tiny aperture he could see the lantern on the toll-bar winking but a hundred yards away, but even if he were able to break the thick glass he could not possibly squeeze through so small a space.

Down below they were whispering, and presently steps crossed the kitchen and the outer door was opened. In a moment it was closed again, and the person who had questioned him said with a hoarse laugh: "Safe as a rat in a trap!" Whereupon the other two laughed also, and shouted to the landlord to bring supper.

"Take up the saddle-bags, Diggory," exclaimed the man who had been addressed as "Captain."

Roger had just time to close his door and wedge his stick under it before light footsteps ran up the stairs, and his latch fluttered in a ghostly manner. As the door did not yield, Diggory went into the adjoining room. He was carrying a candle and yellow light glowed under the door. Roger snatched up a piece of carpet from the floor and stretched it against the sill, blotting out the light and hiding his wedge, he hoped. Then he waited with his heart hammering against his ribs, and fantastic pictures teasing his brain. Now it was the fowlers he had seen in Rome offering their wares in huge sieves, covered with netting; he seemed to see the hapless little terrified wild birds fluttering again and again towards the sky, to beat their wings fruitlessly against the cruel meshes. Objects in the room began to take shape in the dimness—a truckle bed, a home-made chest; nothing heavy enough to barricade the door or large enough to be braced between its panels and the wall. He listened intently. Diggory was moving about in the adjoining room. Downstairs the other men were talking and such chance phrases as reached his ears seemed to bear out Mrs. Wilson's warnings.

"There's no risk if you're bold enough," said one. "They'll not ask for proof other than what we'll find on him."

"Mark a coin or two then," said the other.

There was a sound of knives and forks clattering on pewter trenchers, evidently the landlord was in the room.

Presently Diggory descended the stairs and was greeted with a guffaw.

"Look, Dig—a good notion! They'll recognize that clipped crown, for 'twas only paid over on Wednesday."

"Who was it for?" inquired Diggory.

"That half-witted fool at Canterbury. The justice was easy enough and will swallow another tale of a slit wallet," returned the Captain. "Trade is good, my jolly men; and there's no need to be particular, especially when we're working with a keen thief-taker like George here!"

There was a renewed clinking of glasses, evidently George's health was being drunk; then someone muttered, "He'll hear!"

"No matter, he can't get out," retorted his comrade, not troubling to lower his voice.

Roger felt a freezing dew break out upon his forehead. The net was over him it seemed; in vain he told himself that he could establish his identity. His head was worth forty pounds to the vile creatures at the stair foot, and once in their clutches who knew if he could ever communicate with his friends? Judges were prompt, he had heard, and no doubt some of the thief-takers' blood-money adhered to the Messenger's fingers. Gaolers and pursuivants alike fattened on the traffic in human life and divided the spoils. Judges were as careless as callous.

A slight noise close at hand made him turn his head—a rustling, then a tiny scratching. A rat perhaps? He listened again, and this time was amazed to hear whispered words.

"Wake up, lad. But make no din."

"I am awake," he returned. The scuffling sounds appeared to come from the bed, but he could see well enough now to make sure that he was alone in the room.

The voice, which sounded like Mrs. Wilson's, continued:

"There's a way out into the stable by a hole under the bed. Creep down and push against skirting, but keep mum as you value your life."

Roger dropped on his hands and knees and crawled under the bedstead; the wainscot did not yield under his hand, but Mrs. Wilson bade him feel for a bobbin. The wooden shutter opened into the room, and there was no means of securing it on the farther side. The young man had some difficulty in forcing his broad shoulders through the hole, but he came out at last into a sweet-scented hay loft and found Mrs. Wilson waiting with a horn lantern screened under her shawl.

"The master'll give me a rare thumping if he guesses I've meddled," she observed. "There's a gap i' the hedge on the left of the gate. Better keep off the road, I'd advise you, and leg it to Bodiam as fast as you may."

She led the way down a home-made wooden ladder and softly unbolted the stable door, while the horses moved uneasily, disturbed by the light.

"Ye'll be mum, lad, for my sake?" whispered the woman, as Roger tried to express his gratitude. "That's all the thanks I want."

"I'll not go if 'tis to bring you into danger," declared the young man.

"Nay, nay; no one will know. The gaffer is drinking wi' the other chaps. Good-bye, lad; and sitha—keep honest!"

"I will that," promised Roger, and flinging his arms round her neck, he imparted a hearty salute on her lips.

"That's a son's kiss," she murmured with a little laugh as he disappeared into the night. "Thou's not tasted love yet. God grant thou pick a good 'un."

Roger stood for some time in a clump of bushes close to the house, for fear his evasion should be discovered and revenged on his hostess. But there was no sound, and as his eyes became accustomed to the darkness, he made out the gap in the hedge and, crossing it, stumbled along in the wet grass. As soon as he was out of sight of the toll-gate he climbed over the bank into the road where he could walk more rapidly. The night was full of delicious scents, and owls were wooing each other with elfish trills—quite different from their winter notes. He smelt cowslips sometimes, and there were whiffs of sweet-briar. His blood tingled through his veins and he felt conscious of life and youth as never before.

The little village of Bodiam was virtuously asleep. There were no lights anywhere, save in the tap-room of the solitary inn. A laden wagon stood before the door drawn by a pair of stout grey horses, but the wagoner was refreshing himself indoors.

Roger quietly unhooked the curtain of sailcloth at the rear and managed to climb up and force himself between the heavy sacks of flour which filled the wagon. The driver presently came out, wiping his mouth on his hand, mounted to his seat, and gathering up the reins, sent his team jogging on their way with a jolly jingling of harness bells. In spite of the jolting and his cramped position the stowaway slept a good deal and contrived to slip out unperceived when the wagoner stopped next morning to bait his horses.

Roger stepped on merrily to Sevenoaks, where he disposed of a solid breakfast. Gigs and post chaises soon began to pass him on the road, and he overtook the heavy drays of country produce and left them behind him as he strode along. Sundry queer-looking folk sought to engage him in talk, but Roger was on his guard. In the early afternoon he began to enter into London, and in another hour, tired and footsore, he reached "The Angel." To his surprise and indignation there was no packet awaiting him from his brother, and he had considerable difficulty in persuading the folk at the coach-office to render up his baggage. But Roger now considered himself an old campaigner. He pawned four of his best shirts and gained twenty shillings. This paltry sum enabled him to engage a room at "The Angel," to send for a barber, and to order a meal. His indignation with brother William grew every moment. The fact that he had not hitherto drawn upon his inheritance seemed all the more reason that William should accede to his very modest request now. There were tenements of his well-let of which William had enjoyed the profits undisturbed for the last two years! There was no chance of his letters having gone astray, for he had sent at least one of them by a friend and had heard that he had delivered it in person. But fortune favoured Roger. At the coffee-house in the Strand, to which he presently repaired, he met the father of a school-fellow, who, hearing of his plight, offered to be his banker to the extent of a handful of guineas. Mr. Courtney informed him that he believed Squire Dicconson to be still in town; at any rate, he had met him at the play a week agone, and he and his lady were putting up in Vere Street.

Roger determined to seek them out forthwith, even before he ordered the peruke which he so sadly needed; and it was not yet seven when he was vigorously plying the knocker at Squire Dicconson's lodging.

To his surprise the door flew open instantly and disclosed an agitated group of ladies.

"Well," screamed one. "What's happened? Speak, man! I know they have come to some accident!"

"Oh, la! if ever I let the minx out of my sight again," screeched another, whom he fancied he recognized.

The third, a very stout matron in an extremely high head-dress, after two or three hysterical bursts of laughter, sank bodily into Roger's arms.

"Is Madam Dicconson here?" he cried, bearing up his burden with difficulty. "Faith, Ma'am, I know no ill tidings of anyone or anything! Is there anyone here," shouted Roger desperately, "who hasn't got the vapours?"

CHAPTER THREE

"'T IS ALL THE FAULT of that bold hussy, Lady Abigail." "And you'll see, my dear, we'll never hear the end on't."

"Bridget, too—a chit but just out of school. I'm sure I don't know what my respected father will say, when he learns the lass has been on such a wild jaunt. La, how well I remember the day he told me of her birth: 'Another daughter,' he wrote. 'We have called the thing Bridget.' I was already abroad at school."

They were all standing just within the parlour door, the ladies' billowing furbelows filling all the space and their agitated voices chiming together so that poor Roger gazed helplessly from one to another without being able to make head or tail of the business.

A tea equipage stood in the bay window, and as the delicate porcelain cups had spoons standing in them, Roger saw at a glance that his arrival had interrupted the repast.

"My dear Sophia," he murmured, "do persuade your friends to a little refreshment. Now, Madam, let me assist you to a chair."

He had already hoisted the good dame up a short flight of shallow stairs and she still clung to his aching arm.

"To be sure!" exclaimed Sophia Dicconson. "I was just about to count spoons when we heard the knocker. The urn is hot and I will infuse a second pot while I explain what has happened."

"If only Mr. Dicconson were at home," wailed the fainting lady who was watching eagerly the amount of bohea her friend was measuring out in a silver scallop shell.

The three matrons all began to speak at the same time, but Roger at last made out that a certain Lady Abigail Beaulieu had called in a coach with a gallant and had induced Madam Towneley's sister Bridget, and Madam Dicconson's daughter Elizabeth to go a-junketing with her to the May Fair.

"'Tis most improper that any young gentlewoman should be seen there!" exclaimed Madam Dicconson. "Though indeed they say the Queen set the fashion. To think of my Lizzie in that crowd where all the bold town minxes will be flaunting about."

"Why, sister, I'll soon set your heart at ease!" exclaimed Roger, making good an unexpected chance of escape. "I should know niece again by her likeness to you. I'll go to the Fair and escort the ladies home—if I can find them."

"Aye, do, Roger. And doubtless Dicconson will be here by the time you return. He never came in to dinner, and where he is I can't say."

"The Fair is held on Hay Hill, you know," interrupted Mistress Towneley. "On the open space just before my Lord Berkeley's new house—just on the old spot, indeed."

"And the girls are in a yellow chawyot, with a pair of blacks, and the footmen wear black and yellow. But, bless the man, he'll never find them—there'll be a monstrous crowd, I warrant you."

"I'll find them, never fear!" answered Roger, and bowed himself out of the room with more haste than grace.

It was still light when he reached the famous old fair-ground which had fallen from its original good estate and was now the haunt of roughs and rogues of all descriptions.

Some of the stalls were already illumined with smoky torches, and from the demeanour of many of the company it was plain that there were no lack of drinking-booths; yet the vulgarity and coarseness of the gathering were less in evidence than a certain jolly good-humour. Here were 'prentices buying ribbons for pretty pale little seamstresses and gipsies with wheedling eyes and great gold ear-rings, and whole families taking their pleasure, with toddlers clinging to their mothers' skirts and babies in their fathers' arms. Every now and then a running footman beat a way through the throng for his master's carriage, and it was thus that Roger identified Lord Macerfield's livery, as he stood on the wheel of a stationary cart to raise himself above the crowd.

Yes, there was the yellow chariot a little way off—drawn up before the stand of a Punch and Judy showman who had just concluded his performance.

Dicconson pushed his way through the audience which was now dispersing. He felt suddenly diffident, especially when he perceived that all the ladies in the carriage wore loups or black velvet masks which made it quite impossible to identify his niece.

The coach-load of elegantly dressed women had already attracted the attention of the bystanders, and had indeed aroused the ire of one of them. This was a shock-headed yokel, evidently fresh from the country; he had just picked up a toad from the dirty ditch which marked the boundary of the fair-ground, and he stood staring first at the reptile in his hand and then at the velvet visors, through which eyes sparkled provocatively, with equal disfavour.

"You and your black faces!" he shouted out suddenly. "You do all look so ugly as my toad here!"

And so saying, he hurled the creature through the open window on to the ladies' laps.

There was a shrill outcry and wild agitation among the billows of flowered velvet and shot grosgrain. Roger rushed forward and knocked down the countryman without more ado. The doors of the coach flew open and screaming ladies burst out on each side. One only remained in her place; her hood had been pulled off in her companions' hurry to escape, and a crown of red curls waved triumphantly under the disordered black *fontanges*. But Roger had little leisure to observe the ladies, for the yokel, abetted by his friends, had promptly risen and returned the attack. Folk began to run up from every direction; here was a better show than lads grinning through a horse collar or catching a greased pig! The ladies' screams added to the fun, for the Fair folk resented the arrogance of the nobility who caused such a commotion with their coaches and yet had an air of despising honest folks' amusement. Roger's sky-blue coat split in all directions as he sparred at his adversary. The countryman was no novice at the game, and he felt himself backed up by his friends while the young gentleman had apparently no supporters. The fight was a signal for further rudeness which young Lord Macerfield and his servants were powerless to check.

"Get into the coach, ladies, I implore—get in and we'll drive on!" he exclaimed.

Lady Abigail had flung herself on his arm so impetuously that his peruke was knocked awry. Elizabeth clutched him on the other side, while the red-headed damsel plucked up the poor toad which sprawled on the cushions and replaced it in the ditch. On her return she found herself seized round the waist.

"Don't be alarmed, lovey," hiccuped a drunken voice in her ear, "I'll take care of you!"

The lout was surprised by the swiftness and strength of the fine lady's answer, delivered in the shape of a smart blow in the face. He relinquished her with a curse and the crowd applauded uproariously. The girl flew back towards the coach to hear her friends exclaiming in disgust:

"Faugh, the coarse creature! She positively touched the foul thing!"

"I vow she shan't sit next me!"

The footmen were struggling with the crowd, and for a moment the girl stood alone.

"Give her a kiss, Jack!" shouted a blowzy female, who feared the unexpected entertainment would come to an end before the pride of the fine folk had been chastened.

"Get in, Bridget, quick!" shrieked Lizzie Dicconson. "He's coming after you!"

"Oh, help!" screamed Bridget, seeing her tormentor close upon her once more.

Roger glanced round at the cry; the yokel seized his advantage and struck him a blow which sent him rolling in the mud. The oafs sent up a yell of delight, and the victorious countryman thus encouraged, aimed a kick at his fallen foe.

"Jump on him, lad, jump on him!" cried some. "Teach him to keep his hands off thee."

But Roger found an unexpected ally.

"Fair play!" shouted the red-haired young lady. "Aren't we in England? Form a ring and fight fair if you must fight."

She accompanied her words with a vigorous push which sent the surprised yokel reeling in his turn. Lord Macerfield came up, stammering with annoyance.

"Get into the coach, Madam. For heaven's sake do not make an exhibition of us all before this vulgar rabble! Shame, Madam!"

"Shame yourself!" retorted Bridget. "This man struck in our behalf, and if you are coward enough to leave him to be murdered, I'm not. He is stunned, I believe—open the door, Lizzie! Now, you men, lift him in—make room, ladies! Make room, you fools, I say!"

The chariot seemed already somewhat overcrowded by the ladies, but they shrank back so precipitately before Bridget's vigorous gesture, that there was space for the half-stunned man. The crowd had now taken sides, and while the footmen hesitated two or three respectable-looking men came forward.

"The little spitfire's in the right of it," cried one. "Come on, man, take his feet. Your beau's none the worse, Miss—hop into the coach and we'll put him next you."

"I don't know the fellow—I'll give you a guinea to get a hackney coach for him," expostulated the young nobleman.

But nobody heeded him, and Roger's large, muddy person was propped up on the seat. Bridget climbed in, followed by Macerfield, now helplessly swearing, the door was slammed, the horses sprang away, but at the last moment the window was lowered, and a red-haired chit of a girl tore off her concealing mask, and called out clearly:

"Thank you."

CHAPTER FOUR

ROGER STARED in astonishment at his own broken and bleeding knuckles, then at the bright silks which seemed to encompass him on every side. As he straightened himself and looked round, the women's voices which had been contending strident with wrath, suddenly ceased.

Into the silence fell a girl's soft speech.

"Why, he is quite a pretty fellow, after all!"

The young man laughed uncertainly and strove to pull himself together.

"I'm sure I ask your pardon, ladies! I scarce know how I come to be cast among you in such sorry plight. But there's one here should call me kinsman—is Mistress Elizabeth Dicconson here? She may own me as her uncle."

"Oh, Uncle Roger, how could you go brawling so? And then to come to London without even a peruke!" exclaimed Lizzie, scarlet with vexation.

"I came to fetch you home, my dear, for I must tell you, ladies, that my sister is in a proper taking at the notion of her daughter being seen at Hay Hill Fair. I must ask your forgiveness," he repeated, "for being thus thrust upon your society."

"Indeed, Sir, you are scarce in a suitable state to be seen abroad with ladies," observed Macerfield. "Mr. Dicconson, I believe? Permit me, Mr. Dicconson, to set you down at my friend Lord Berkeley's, whence you may send a man for your own coach."

Roger laughed, 'twixt anger and scorn.

"I'll not trouble my Lord Berkeley," he said. "But you may set me down if you will, my lord, on the understanding that you escort my niece and her friend, Mistress Thornleigh, straight back to my sister's lodging."

"Do you presume to dictate to me, Sir?" cried Macerfield, his suppressed ill-temper bursting forth.

"Why, certainly, my lord, if 'tis necessary, for I promised my good sister-in-law to assuage her anxiety at the first possible moment."

"Oh, Tom, don't anger the creature!" screamed Lady Abigail in mock alarm. "And you, good Sir, pray don't let fly at my poor friend here as you did at Hodge just now! Nay, do not glower so, Macerfield! The young man was far quicker to put up his hands in our defence than you were!"

"Madam! Your ladyship!" stammered the young man.

"Pull the cord, my lord. I'll alight here!" interrupted Roger. "Lizzie, tell your father that I'll present myself tomorrow. Ladies, I kiss your hands!"

The phrase was intended to be a pure formality, but Abigail pulled off her glove and extended her plump, scented fingers.

"Ah, do," she sighed. "I dote on a brave man."

Dicconson obeyed with zest. Then as he stood leaning through the doorway, still holding the tapered fingers, his dancing eyes caught the brooding glance of Macerfield.

"Where do you lie, Sir, if you please?" inquired the beau.

"At 'The Angel,'" returned Roger promptly. His heels clicked together as he bowed, tossing his battered hat and flinging it on to his disordered hair with the most debonair flourish in the world.

"Well, your fame is made, Mistress Bridget," exclaimed Abigail, with an acid titter as the coach proceeded. "Sure, you'll be the toast of the town."

"Hush!" cried Bridget sharply. "He doesn't know—he doesn't remember." She broke off, catching her trembling lip between her teeth.

"He soon will then," retorted the other. "Unless Tom, here, spits him tomorrow morning. Tush, never look so glum, man! The tale will be round all the coffee-houses ere eight o' the clock, I vow. Is it to be swords or pistols, Tom?"

"Lady Abigail, I dislike your notion of a jest very strongly," quoth Bridget suddenly. "Pray, girl, forget your folly and act the woman for once. Lord Macerfield, I see now that our junketing had danger as well as folly in it, and I ask your pardon for my share."

"Spoke like a Dean at the very least!" interposed Lady Abigail.

"I do beg you both," insisted Bridget, "let our foolishness end here. Lord Macerfield, you do not speak! Pray assure me that there will be no quarrel—no ill results? Promise me to blot this silly escapade completely from your recollection."

She spoke with a certain youthful dignity, and the young man was touched at her appeal. All might have blown over had not Abigail again interposed, inspired by the very spirit of mischief.

"Nay, but I'll not consent to that! I vow I mean to thank your uncle prettily, Lizzie! Pray tell him to wait on me."

"I'll bear your message, Madam!" exclaimed Macerfield. His eyes glittered feverishly as they searched her mocking face.

The coach drew up at this moment. Mistress Thornleigh and Lizzie alighted, and Lord Macerfield escorted them up the steps to the door grimly enough. Bridget tried again.

"Pray, Sir, be not guided by my Lady Abigail; she speaks with such heedless freedom as she scarce knows what she says. You won't fight, my lord, I trust?"

"Fight, Mistress Bridget? What put such a notion in your head? Unless *you* need a champion, indeed!"

"Nay, Sir, do not mock me. I'm young and inexperienced, but I'm no fool. I'll never forgive myself if there's an ill consequence of our outing."

"I vow you have no cause for alarm—" he began.

"Alarm! Speak not of fear to a female who can touch a toad! Faugh, she's past all fear, I warrant you!" screamed Abigail from the coach. "Come, are you to escort me home, my lord, or must I leave you here?"

With a hasty bow Macerfield left Bridget's side. She thought her cause won, and entered the house with a lightened heart. Court ladies such as Lady Abigail Beaulieu were heartless, odious hussies, she declared, and she made a proper show of repentance to Madame Dicconson and her own sister, Susan Towneley, and deemed the matter ended.

Meanwhile Roger returned to his lodging in a hackney coach, and ordered supper to be served in his room. Though he had embraced Lady Abigail's hand with apparent ardour, she herself had small charm for him. The damsel with the red curls had made a much deeper impression, and having a gift for catching a likeness, he presently made a drawing on a blank page of the copy of Metastasio's poems which he carried in his pocket. The remainder of the evening was spent in colouring the spirited little head while supper cooled on the table. He was about to retire to bed when two gentlemen came to wait upon him. They were, they announced, friends of Lord Macerfield, and they bore a letter from his lordship.

Both were monstrous polite, but there was something hard and sinister under the smiling glances. Roger knew as he held the paper in his fingers that he must decide without the slightest delay. Every young man of parts was prepared for the exigency of being called out: his first feeling was one of exultation, and he glanced vaingloriously at his beautiful new Roman rapier which lay across the table. Then his kindling gaze fell on the cross-shaped hilt and he stepped back as though he had received a blow. The Church forbade duels under pain of mortal sin, but here was honour to be considered. God's law or man's law?

Roger's face was flaming but he spoke with assurance.

"I don't fight duels, gentlemen," he said bluntly. "But I am accustomed to walk every day in Lincoln's Inn Fields. I carry my sword by my side. I'll not forbear my walk for any man, and any as wishes can find me there!"

"This is most unusual, Sir. A gentleman must give satisfaction, Mr. Dicconson."

"And so I will, Colonel Leveson, if anyone comes to ask it of me."

"Lord Macerfield cannot permit the lady he honours with his attentions to be annoyed. Lady—"

"No names, I pray, Mr."—he glanced at the card on the table—"Mr. Hilton. If my lord has any explanation to ask or make—no doubt he will take occasion to meet me in the fields. Your servant, gentlemen."

"You are a very young man, Sir," began the officer. "And I should be loath that any promising youth should lose his honour over some damned puritan scruple. Are you a Quaker, Sir, or a shaker, Sir?"

"Neither, Sir. I am a Catholic, however. And I wear a sword and know how to use it. Or pistols, either."

He broke off; it was all very difficult.

"And at what time do you walk, Sir, may I inquire?" observed the younger visitor suavely.

Roger was tripped up by the laughter which often burst forth uncontrollably, just when he wanted to be solemn and dignified.

"Indeed, Sir, whilst I have this swollen eye, it must needs be betwixt six and seven in the morning," he cried gaily.

The two men bowed and withdrew, and as they crossed the street Colonel Leveson said to his companion:

"That is a pretty fellow, I warrant you. Damn women! The jade will have a life to feed her vanity, and then she'll fling Mac aside like a squeezed orange."

The dawn chill was still in the air as Dicconson marched up and down beneath the mulberry tree; for a time he had the place to himself, but on the stroke of six a little party of gentlemen came into view, strolling towards him. Roger's lips tightened: he walked on, humming to himself, until Macerfield and his friends blocked his path.

No time was wasted.

"Mr. Dicconson, I believe?" cried Macerfield. "Stand away, gentlemen—on guard, Sir, at your peril!"

In a second two swords were quivering in the sunlight; no word was spoken and after the first few abortive clashes of metal on metal, Roger began to feel quite equal to the occasion. He pressed his adversary hard, and then with a carefully executed twist of the wrist, learnt in the fencing-school at Trastevere, he sent Macerfield's sword flying into the bushes. In his inexperience he scarcely knew what to do next, and stood with his point dropped to the earth, as though waiting on the tan for Messer Vittorio's praise or blame.

"Are you satisfied, my lord?" inquired Hilton, retrieving his patron's weapon.

"By —— no! Are you ready, Sir?"

Roger nodded.

"Though I have really no quarrel with you," he said with a little laugh which proved his undoing.

Lord Macerfield conceived himself to be patronized and flung himself into the fray with fury. Roger stepped back before the onslaught, but his foot slipped on the dewy grass: the ground seemed to smite the back of his head, while a sickening pain blazed like fire in his shoulder. He was conscious of anger at the futility of the whole affair; voices roared indistinctly in his ears, one of them seemed to be his own, loudly asseverating that he was not out yet. A peaceful period of inaction followed, and then the sense of struggle began again with growing indignation at the pain to which he was being subjected. At last the trees which had seemed to be reeling about steadied themselves, and an impatient voice exclaimed:

"I hate these irregular affairs—a gentleman should bring his own friends. Can't you stop the bleeding, Leveson?"

"I told you we should have had a surgeon, my lord," exclaimed another voice. "By gad—look here! Why, Mac, blast me if you weren't on the wrong tack after all. 'Tis a faithful Corydon, split me, with his Amaryllis's red head carried on his faithful heart."

Roger made an inarticulate exclamation of rage, and heaved himself up by the simple expedient of grasping the dangling neck-scarf of the gentleman who bent over him.

"My lord—my private papers!" he protested again angrily, for the little vellum book of Metastasio's poetry was open in Macerfield's hands.

Waves of nausea swept over him as he struggled impotently in Leveson's arms, and though the Italian verses with the tell-tale portrait and his slender pocket-book were quickly laid aside on the grass, he had a confused sense of catastrophe. Macerfield stooped over him and seemed to be uttering words of apology—till Hilton dragged him away. He heard the phrase "Only pinked through the arm," and renewed the effort to command full consciousness.

"That is well," cried the soldier encouragingly. "Let me help you to the bench yonder, and fling this cloak round you, in case anyone should come by. You're cold now, but I've sent my servant for brandy—you'll be your own man in a moment."

Dicconson clenched his teeth and rose unsteadily to his feet.

"Your first affair, I think?" remarked Leveson. "You are a pretty swordsman, Sir," he added hastily, seeing that his observation was distasteful.

"It's all most monstrous inconvenient!" exclaimed Roger ruefully. "Your damned friends have spoiled my only two coats! Lord, London is no place for a younger son."

Strangely enough, the dram of brandy entirely deprived the wounded man of the strength which he thought to have completely recovered.

"Colonel Leveson," he stammered, sinking down, "I must trespass on your kindness to have me conveyed to my lodging."

But Roger eventually found himself not in the dismal inn chamber, but on Colonel Leveson's own bed in a comfortable apartment in Birdcage Walk.

"Younger sons, my dear Sir, must stand by each other!" answered Leveson airily, as the younger man strove to thank him. "No doubt you'll be all the rage! Sensations are all too rare, and your fame is being noised about already. Of course the amazon gets the first place."

Roger had been leaning back on the pile of frilled pillows, listening with youthful complaisance. His wound had been neatly dressed by a surgeon, and he was feeling comfortable and pleased with himself. But the last phrase spoiled everything, and his new friend was aghast at the sudden change in his face. He sat up, his brow beaded with sweat, for being pinked hurt confoundedly.

"Look here, Leveson—you must find my brother for me. Oh, blast it all—don't tell me they have got hold of the—the—the lady's name?"

"Have they not? Fair Abigail will die of envy to see a country chit the toast of the town." He spoke soothingly, and laid a restraining hand on Roger's sound shoulder. "Lie still—there'll be a touch of fever, I don't doubt."

29

Roger swore again in helpless exasperation as his head reeled.

"Colonel Leveson, forget you are a man of the world for a moment," he besought. "Advise me. This lady—her father is the most perfect, punctilious gentleman in the world—'tis a mere girl fresh from school—she's been scarce a week in town—'tis unthinkable that a child like that should suffer in reputation from a prank she doubtless thought as innocent as going to see the maypole dressed on the village green at home."

"Well," returned Leveson unconsolingly, "you can't stop folks' tongues once they start wagging. The wits will make a story out of the meeting this morning too, no doubt—but isn't that just what you gay Lotharios aim at?"

Roger groaned. "I have but twelve hundred pounds to my name," he said. "And Lord knows if I'll ever squeeze half of it out of my brother's clutches. What is the honourable thing to do? To offer marriage or no?"

"'S death! she'd jump at it, my lad! Or her friends will! But perhaps that will not displease you since you carry the lady's portrait next your heart?"

"You'll be pleased not to jest on that subject, Sir!" Roger answered hotly.

He blamed himself as an insufferable young puppy for having exposed Bridget Thornleigh by his carelessness. He clung to bachelorhood too, now that it was in jeopardy. Perhaps the girl was a shrew! He knew nothing whatever of "the thing called Bridget," except that Fate seemed determined to throw them together.

William Dicconson was duly sent for, and the ensuing interview was stormy. But before sundown a new ready-made peruke was requisitioned, Roger struggled into brother William's second best coat, and, with his arm in a sling and his mouth set in grim lines, he was hoisted into Colonel Leveson's *calèche* and departed to his wooing.

CHAPTER FIVE

HEN BRIDGET Thornleigh awoke, she could not at first remember where she was. She lay bewildered, listening to the wagons rattling over the pavement in the street below her window. This was not the hard school pillow beneath her tumbled red curls, and Sister Scholastica would certainly have jangled the rising bell before folk were astir in the streets!

Then, at last fully awake, she realized with a pang which was bitter-sweet that school was over for all time! Never again in all probability would she catch even that fleeting glimpse of Mother Abbess, or hear that dear voice—now grave, now gay—from behind the grille. She had bid farewell to the Convent with its icy passages, and laughing girls, and the nuns, and the little whitewashed, cell-like dormitories. Bridget was grown-up—turned seventeen—and Life was before her! She remembered with a little self-pity how blithely she had jumped out of bed on the previous day, after the luxurious dish of chocolate which kind Sister Susan had had served to her among her pillows. Now there were clouds in the sky, which she told herself impatiently were all of her own making.

What would her father say if the story of yesterday's imprudence came to his ears? And Grandfather? Mother would take her tone from the men-folk, and it would indubitably be better for the story to be told to Grandfather, with due expressions of repentance by Bridget herself. As she reviewed her own conduct, sipping the foaming bowl of delicious chocolate and biting into the crisp French roll which accompanied it, Bridget was in anything but a contrite mood. After all, Madam Dicconson had not forbid the outing, she and Lizzie had slipped out of the house without asking leave. But they were accompanied by a gentleman, who should, in her opinion, have been able to protect his fair companions from the rudeness of the crowd. She was not dissatisfied with the part she herself had played—how it would have thrilled the girls at school to hear how she had championed the young gentleman who had been assaulted in their defence. Here was some news to write to Alethea Carew and Margery Anderson, her special cronies! But what of Mother Abbess? Nay, on the whole she would reserve the recital till the girls left school at Christmas. Somehow at the thought of Mother Abbess Bridget's elation began to evaporate a little: she knew exactly what the nun would say.

"Of course, Bridget, you told your sister everything?"

But she had not. She had told kind Susan Towneley as little as possible, and had escaped importunate questioning on the plea of fatigue. No use going back upon it now, the girl decided. Probably these were everyday excitements to townsfolk—they would think her a fool to give so much thought to them. Today perhaps the Towneleys would take her to the play!

She got up presently, pulled the curtain, and then turned to consider her reflection in the mirror. She saw a tall, lissome young thing in a voluminous white night-shift, ruffled round the throat. Her curls rose crisply from her forehead, like a cockatoo's crest—and luckily high dressed heads were the fashion. It was a pity that red hair was so much looked down upon; she thought it rather pretty herself, especially if one had dark eyebrows and was careful to keep down freckles with applications of buttermilk and rosemary water. They would come though—there was one now at the tip of her impertinent little nose.

The old mirror had a tarnished surface, and only parts of it held a reflection. Bridget turned it to the right angle and nodded approvingly. A white skin and darkish eyebrows were an advantage—if her eyes had only been brown instead of the colour of the succory flowers in the kitchen garden, she would have been quite satisfied. She would like to have been smaller also, with a tiny little waist like a fashionable London young lady instead of the buxom young countrywoman she was, with a rounded figure and a soft dimpled neck like a baby's!

Her father had not been able to come to meet her, but luckily Mistress Towneley was in London, and Grandmamma also had come to town to inspect the youngest of her daughter's large family. What delightful presents they had showered upon her! And Susan had remarked aside to Grandmamma Eyre that the chit's looks were not amiss—of course Bridget had overheard! She gave a little quiver of delight as she thought of the charming new clothes and wondered if she could ever make her hair stay up stiff and straight over her brow without a frontal? Susan declared that she was too young for a frontal.

When Bridget went downstairs Madam Towneley was reading a letter.

"'Tis a note by hand from Madam Dicconson," she remarked. "The poor lady was in such a state yesterday that she forgot to tell us that young Roger was straight from Rome and brought news of our brother Joseph at the English college. You must know the Dicconsons are our neighbours in Lancashire, Bridget—but indeed she is vastly imprudent to put so much in writing. And while I think on't, sister, take heed and guard your tongue, child. You are not now on the Christian side of the sea, as the saying is!"

"Burn the paper, wife," said Mr. Towneley.

"Aye, directly I have deciphered it," returned his wife.

Bridget looked on in wonder.

"Do you have to practise such caution in your own household?" she asked. "Are not your servants Catholics?"

"Aye, maybe, but they are only hired, and their fidelity is strangely tried. Plot-mongering is a trade which brings a rich return and little danger to the promoter."

Bridget's bright blue eyes widened.

"La, brother! Plot-mongering! What may that be? Are the folks going to rise for poor King James after all?"

She spoke gaily and was frightened by Towneley's sudden change of countenance; what sinister menace could give a brave man such an ashen look? Her sister was moved to anger.

"Be silent, both of you! Bridget, do you want to ruin us all?"

"I didn't know," faltered the girl. Then she added with a toss of her bright head: "'Twould be safer if you told me all frankly, and I'll promise never to speak heedlessly again. *Are* Catholics in hourly danger? Are there plots brewing? My father says nought in his letters."

"Nay, and good reason for it—he has seen his father imprisoned too often, good man, to risk it for himself." Towneley glanced at his wife, and she nodded. "Well, Bridget, know ye that Catholics are considered fair play. And Doctor Oates, who wrought such havoc before you were born, still lives, and has many imitators. The King is short of money, and his friends strip him of what little he has."

"But I thought there were scarce any Court functions nowadays," protested Bridget. "Lady Verney, who visited her daughter at the Con—I mean the school—a year ago, declared that the King sits below stairs swilling beer and smoking a pipe like a coachman, and the Queen is left alone knotting cotton yarn into fringes, without any company."

"H'm, that may be. But King William has friends who need posts, you see, lass. So he makes 'em colonels, forsooth, and they draw colonel's pay, aye, and pay for a regiment which don't exist! 'Tis all open robbery in the army nowadays. The storekeepers make fortunes."

"But that's dishonest!" cried downright Bridget.

"Oh, aye! So one of his Majesty's servants remarked a while ago—'twas Van Torp, they say, a Dutchman. 'It seems there's not an honest man in England,' says he. 'You're wrong,' says the King, 'there are many, but they're no friends of mine.' And recusant's fines and seizures of property fill up the King's empty coffers so—"

"Stay, Towneley—here's something strange!" Susan laid her hand on her husband's arm and thrust the letter before his eyes. "What can this mean? 'Dicconson is but just come in with the news. Lord, what an ill-natured town! And what must we do about it?'"

"The woman is a fool!" commented her husband, but Bridget coloured up guiltily. "I'll look in at the 'Cocoa Tree,' my dear, and find out if there's any stir! Doubtless 'tis nought—why cannot she send word what's to do if she needs must send at all?"

He settled his peruke, took his gold-headed cane and best town hat and strolled forth, nothing loath. In order to avoid any questioning, Bridget slipped upstairs to the nursery, but within an hour she heard her brother-in-law calling for her.

He wore a very long face as he beckoned her into the parlour and closed the door. The town, he declared, was ringing with her name, and the best he could do was to send her home by the first coach that had a seat to spare.

"What made you take off your mask, child?" wailed Susan. "Sure, there are couplets being sung about you in the theatres, and you are being toasted in the coffee-houses, and your name in everyone's mouth! My father will die of shame if this comes to his ears."

"How could they know my name?" asked Bridget, very low. Her face was as white as paper, but her eyes blazed. "I've done no harm, sister, and if my name has got abroad, 'tis through my Lady Abigail Beaulieu."

"The young man comes of honourable folk," said Towneley, but his wife checked him with a sharp glance.

"We'll keep quiet and say no more at present," she observed. "But I must own, Bridget, 'tis the saddest misfortune. La, to think of it! And you but ten days out of the nuns' hands."

"It is no fault of the Convent!" cried Bridget with spirit. "How was I to know the Fair was such a low, vile place? They told me the Queen went, and her ladies and all. Aye, and they got out of their coaches too, and were all through the India houses a-foot."

"'Tis true enough," agreed Towneley.

"And what kind of couplets were they?" queried Bridget, seizing her opportunity at his milder tone.

"Faith, my dear, no stuff for your ears," he returned, trying to look severe.

The girl said no more, but later in the day one of the maids came giggling into her room with a scrap of dirty paper in her hand.

"La, Miss Biddy! Just look what Joe the boot-boy has brought in! And he says there's broadsides, with pictures and all, of you and the young gentleman! And there's a fat, red-faced gentleman in the parlour, Miss—and his name is Dicconson—he's waiting on the master."

Bridget glanced at the verses and colour leaped into her cheek.

> "'Blood from his nose the villain drew,
> Swift to his aid the damsel flew!...'

La, child, what vulgar stuff. 'Mr. R–g–r D–cc–ns–n'—why, that's pretty plain. 'Fair Bridget claims the life she saved.' How dare they! The insolent wretches!"

She crumpled the page in her hand furiously.

"Oh, well, it's all nonsense! I suppose they behave so to everybody," she declared, trying to speak loftily.

"There is another gentleman with Mr. Dicconson," whispered Alice. "A handsome lad, he is, Miss Biddy. He'd his arm in a sling."

She stopped and pretended to be busy folding a scarf, for Mistress Towneley was hurrying along the corridor in her high-heeled shoes.

"Begone, Alice," she cried breathlessly. "Now, Bridget, I have something very serious to say to you."

"I know what it is then!" retorted the girl. "Mr. Roger Dicconson is come to make me an offer of marriage. I wouldn't have him, sister, if he was the only man in the world."

CHAPTER SIX

SQUIRE DICCONSON was much relieved at the failure of his brother's suit. Roger's return was extremely inconvenient in any case, but a single man could "table" with the family without causing additional expense. The lad had a right to his inheritance, but the longer it could remain sunk in the encumbered lands at Wrightington the better. He felt some remorse at having failed to give his brother a better welcome, and to provide the funds he expected to find on arrival. As they returned through the crowded streets he explained his position at great length, but Roger paid scant attention; his thoughts were divided between his smarting arm and wounded self-esteem. That prodigious pause in Mr. Towneley's parlour, while Madam Towneley's voice in the chamber overhead rose ever to a louder and shriller key, had been almost unendurable. It was one thing to sigh for lost liberty and another to have one's offer of marriage refused with mortifying finality. He broke irritably into his brother's discourse.

"Colonel Leveson has kindly invited me to remain with him until this cut heals. And Mr. Courtney has been friendly enough to lend me twenty guineas. How long do you remain in town?"

"Why, it depends on my business," returned William lamely. "If you can content yourself at home for a space, you may go North as soon as you are fit to travel." He thought Roger's expression somewhat sarcastic and added in haste: "I am in hope of getting a post—even a small one in the Customs would be of great assistance to me. And then my wife gave me no peace till I promised to bring her and Lizzie up too—to see the sights."

"Including the May Fair, I suppose?" muttered Roger.

He clenched his teeth, closed his eyes and endured the jolting motion of the vehicle as best he could until it pulled up in Birdcage Walk, and he had to face Leveson's congratulations on his escape from matrimony.

After supper, when the invalid was propped up in bed, flushed and feverish, Leveson proposed a hand or two of écarté to raise his spirits, and Roger agreed, recklessly pledging the remains of his borrowed guineas. He won and won again.

"Unlucky in love, lucky at cards," murmured Leveson under his breath. "You'll clean me out, I swear."

"Nay, I've had enough," declared the other, petulantly flinging himself back on his pillows. "Unless you desire to have your revenge?" he added, mindful of civility.

"Not at all—the run of luck is against me." Leveson was minded to jest upon the subject, but refrained, snuffed the lights and bid his guest good-night.

Roger opened the narrow casement and the fresh air swept into the room, dissipating the stale atmosphere of wax candles and wine, and easing his aching head. He felt forlorn and soured. Life was not such an enchanting adventure as he had anticipated when setting sail for his native land. After a while he sought out Metastasio, and flung the little book unopened into the ashes of the wood fire. The vellum cover curled in the heat and opened of itself, disclosing the provocative face of Mistress Bridget Thornleigh. Roger thought anything but tenderly of his whilom lady.

"Women are full of mischief," he reflected. "The wench might at least have granted him an interview before she discarded him.

The flames caught the leaf and reduced it to a cinder, and Roger blew out the lights and flung himself on the bed. But though her portrait was destroyed, the vision of Bridget still pursued him. Now she was standing over him at the Fair, now she was supporting him in the coach. In vain he tossed and turned, the events of the last two days continually re-enacted themselves before his eyes, and his bandaged arm seemed to acquire monstrous proportions. In the early dawn it occurred to him to count his gains, still strewn upon the table at his elbow. He reckoned up fifty guineas, and felt solace to his injured self-esteem. No doubt gambling was a dreadful vice, but it was mighty pleasant to win! After all, he had found a true friend in George Leveson and had acquitted himself creditably, even if he had been worsted in both fisticuffs and duel. He had acted honourably towards Bridget and no one could reproach him. These comforting thoughts sent him to sleep, just as the milkmaids began calling their wares.

The surgeon, when he came, found the patient very feverish and recommended complete quiet for the next three days. He was anxious to bleed him in the foot, but Dicconson resisted, pleading the amount of blood he had lost already. Mr. Greene smiled at such ignorance.

"We must make a vent for the humours caused by the fever, my dear Sir—'twill escape with the flow of blood. I should not take more than eight or ten ounces."

"Leave it till tomorrow," suggested Leveson, and the good man consented unwillingly.

"The game is in your hands now," declared Leveson.

He had come into his new friend's room in his brocade dressing-gown, holding a glass cone in his hand, the use of which Roger was unable to guess.

"The game is in your hands," he repeated. "While you lie abed the tailor and peruke-maker must work against time. Shoes, too—how are you off for shoes?"

"'Twould be folly to spend much on town clothes when I am going to live in the country," protested Dicconson half-heartedly.

"Pooh," retorted the Colonel. "Now that you are free of entanglements you must at least have a taste of London ere you bury yourself in the backwoods. Powdered wigs are going to be the fashion—not brown meal such as we have used hitherto, but white powder—conceive it!"

"Impossible! We should have coats like millers," exclaimed the invalid.

"'Tis vastly becoming though!" returned the other. "Would it entertain you if my hairdresser serves me here? He'll have the latest gossip, I promise you. Alphonse, set me a chair: call Rackett here."

Roger stared in amused wonder while the French valet spread a sheet on the carpet and adjusted the mirror to the right angle. The dapper little barber came in followed by a boy, bearing the wig on a stand, each silvery curl rolled round a pipe of warm clay.

Meanwhile Rackett conversed eagerly with his patron.

"Bobs are coming in, Sir. The half-bob will be all the rage next week. And if this is the young gentleman that has been mentioned in the news, 'tis of the last importance that he should be to the forefront of the fashion."

"I'm too ignorant of the world to carry it off," protested Roger.

"La, Sir, 'tis the easiest thing if you are properly dressed. Does young Sir smoke, Colonel? If so, to carry a little silver bowl is the new tone. You must sit languidly on a bench, Sir, and set it beside you while you smoke: spit into it once or twice in an elegant way—lord, 'tis the latest!"

"Do you say so? Begad, I'll try it!" Colonel Leveson's voice was somewhat muffled, for he had thrust his face into the cone, and the barber, having delicately poised the wig on his cropped head, was now sprinkling it with perfumed powder.

"A white wig, Sir, and red heels a good inch higher than they were in the winter—long tongues to the shoes too. As to the holland cravat, 'tis as dead as mutton, Colonel. There's nought to be worn this season but mechlin lace.

An animated discussion ensued as to the relative merits of periwigs, perukes, bobs and short bobs, pole-locks or dildos. The gold-headed cane must be carried on the wrist by a loop of ribbon, Roger discovered, and shoe-strings were quite out— buckles were now the thing.

"Do you snuff, man? You must certainly snuff!" exclaimed Leveson at last. The glass face mask had now been discarded and he turned his head complacently towards his friend. The masses of powdered ringlets set off his handsome features, and he leaned back with a weary air while Alphonse stepped forward to tie his cravat.

"Loosely, you fool, loosely—shake out the ends! Nay, take another and try again. Hark ye, Mr. Dicconson, be sure your pockets are cut of the right fashion—and you must wear claret colour—'tis all the rage."

Roger had never before been among people to whom matters of dress were so serious. He felt that he might easily get out of his depth, and he despised Leveson as something of a fop. But there is no denying that the picture of himself as a dashing blade in claret colour, with the newest of dildos—or should it be a single "pipe" hanging down the back?—was vastly pleasant.

Colonel Leveson was a gentleman of leisure. His regiment was a skeleton though fully officered; he was therefore able to devote his full attention to his new friend. Dicconson was soon bored with endless discussions as to the shape of pockets, as to whether the huge coat cuffs should be held in place by two or three buttons, and the like. He declined to carry a muff, but obediently purchased shoe buckles, new stockings to draw over the knee, a white cane and a snuff-box. He liked to fancy himself cutting a splendid figure before the dazzled eyes of Mistress Bridget Thornleigh: the wench must be made to regret her arrogance, and should certainly be shown that other women could appreciate the man she had spurned.

Before the week was at an end Mr. Dicconson's purse was light once more, but his shirts were released from pawn, the fine new coat had come home and was pronounced a perfect fit, and Roger had acquired proficiency in the art of elegantly inhaling rappee or Best Brazil. He wore a dash of powder, and carried his arm in an embroidered scarf. His new hat turned up at one side and flaunted a bit of gold lace, and altogether he felt ready to meet the wit, wisdom and beauty of the town.

"We'll dine with Lord Breconhurst," announced Leveson. "I always dine with him on Thursdays—no need to know him, *mon cher*, you come as my friend."

It was new to Dicconson that rich men and great lords kept open house for all and sundry, but it seemed a good, generous habit and he heartily approved it.

They met Lord Macerfield as they mounted the staircase and conversed for a few minutes with great formality.

"Mac takes it ill that you and I are on good terms," explained Leveson as they forced their way through the crowd towards the dining-room. "But split me, I can't espouse all the man's enmities—he don't offer to share his loves with me! Do not look so much interested, my dear—'tis not elegant. For heaven's sake look bored or prim, a man must be one or t'other to succeed. Your servant, my lord!"

Leveson, however, showed plenty of energy in his successful endeavour to secure good places. He criticized the entertainment freely, which scarcely seemed good manners to the neophyte. "Only twelve dishes in the remove—that's a shabby dinner, I vow. Let me assist you to this sallet, my lord—my friend, Mr. Dicconson, Sir!"

Between bows, nods and glasses of wine, the Colonel kept up a running commentary to Roger.

"That's Churchill yonder—the handsome black man—but it won't do to catch his eye. He belongs to the Princess Anne's set, and she's prodigious out of favour. My lord Nottingham, now—there, in the green coat—is the Queen's right hand, they say. A glass of wine with you, my lord! Dash it, he is looking the other way!"

It was late in the afternoon before the two friends emerged from the throng. Roger longed to breathe fresh air after the fumes of food and wine, but the May breezes were vitiated by the stench from the unswept street. Colonel Leveson was fain to produce a scent-bottle as they strolled along; he held it in one hand and trailed his cane from the other wrist so that it clattered on the cobblestones.

"The latest thing," he explained aside. "All is for extremes this year: a man must be extreme prim or extreme *dégagé*. An absent-minded air would go well with a hat of your cut, Dicconson, and be not over merry, Sir—a smart man must be pensive. Yonder is Lady Abigail's house—her father is in his dotage and the Countess cares for nought but the card-table."

"Let us pay our respects," suggested Roger. "It would be only civil to inquire for her—she begged I would wait upon her."

Colonel Leveson hesitated and then agreed. His protégé was a pretty young sprig, and Mac deserved to be paid out for his insolent demeanour this morning. He, too, felt in the mood for female society, and going briskly up the steps, he plied the knocker. The flunkeys lounging in the hall opened the door and ushered the visitors into the long saloon, at one end of which a quartet of ladies sat at cards.

Lady Abigail was already engaged with two gentlemen, but she rose and greeted them very prettily.

"We'll not disturb the card-table," she observed. "But come into the window, Mr. Dicconson, and tell me how you came to hurt your arm. Colonel Leveson, you know Mrs. Wingfield and my dear Kitty Carey, I'm certain. Gentlemen, must you leave so soon? Now, Sir!"

She laid her soft, warm hand on Roger's arm, and propelled him towards two chairs set obligingly almost behind the heavy brocade curtain.

"You are wounded?" she breathed, when safe in this seclusion. "Ah, you are suffering for my sake!"

She clasped his arm again, this time with both hands, to Roger's great alarm. He saw himself between the Scylla and Charybdis of being "extreme prim or extreme *dégagé*" and steered towards the latter.

"No, indeed, Ma'am! 'Tis but a trifling accident." He took her hand clumsily and conveyed it to his lips, dropping his new hat as he did so. "Who would not gladly suffer for such a kind glance," he added lamely, and got up to retrieve his hat.

The lady hesitated a moment, but her love of mischief decided her to overlook this insufficiently gallant conduct.

"Tell me," she whispered, "why did you propose marriage to that vulgar, low-mannered wench? Was it for my sake—to shield my good name?"

Roger looked at the beautiful rouged face anxiously. There was something greedy about the pouting scarlet lips, the furtive eyes. How was he to escape the inferences this vanity-mad creature would force into any explanation he might give?

"If truth must out, I fought because I was challenged," he admitted, striving to speak merrily, "and I courted where I loved withal. But I seem to have gained a friend and lost the lady."

He met the challenge of her melting gaze with a laugh.

"Never pity a bachelor, Ma'am," he cried gaily. "We shouldn't love the ladies half so well, could we foretell their little caprices."

"Simple creature!" exclaimed Abigail. "You to think yourself a man of the world!"

45

She sprang up from her chair and darted back into the room, leaving Roger relieved but feeling uncommonly foolish.

Before he could move, a young man came to join him. He wore powder and had very piercing dark eyes.

"Your servant, Sir. I must introduce myself and pray you to pardon the informality. My name is Buckland—" He interrupted himself with a joyful shout. "As I live," he cried, "'tis little Rogue Dicconson from St. Omer!"

CHAPTER SEVEN

THE CARD-PARTY had broken up and the room was full of talk and laughter. Down below a great coach was turning in the street; the mettlesome horses plunged and sparks shot from the cobblestones beneath their dancing feet. The group of footmen, waiting by the door, exchanged jests with the coachman and his satellites in voices raised to carry above the din. In the alcove where Roger stood face to face with the hero of his early school-days it seemed strangely quiet: his senses were all alert, he had drawn back a little, the better to gaze at his interlocutor.

"We cannot talk here," said Buckland, and flicking open his snuff-box he presented it. "Pray honour me, Mr. Dicconson—the lid is worthy of your notice." Then in a lower tone and on a note of urgency he added: "Tomorrow—at nine."

Dicconson took a pinch of rappee with elegant deliberation. He noted the card tucked into the box-lid on which an address was written and he raised his eyebrows inquiringly.

"Not a word to Leveson," continued Buckland urgently. "He is not of our persuasion. I am not mistook, I suppose? You are indeed little Rogue Dicconson. These be plaguey times for Catholics and a man is like to suffer for any chance imprudence."

"Bold Buck is greatly changed if he has grown discreet!" cried Roger.

His face was glowing with joy: he could not have dreamed of anything more fortunate than this chance meeting. In an instant the old glamour returned, he felt the old worship astir

47

within him. Had not Buckland fought for him against a bully-
ing French boy, when he was a shy child, fresh from home? He
had been head of the school, and the acknowledged champion
at every sport, brilliant at his books, and a merry, mischievous
young devil withal!

"You need not twit me," cried Buckland, "for your own wisdom is not so great by all accounts! Here's a great stir you have
made already and you scarce three days in town."

He glanced over his shoulder, scarcely attending to Roger's
answer.

"Till we meet! I must go squeeze the hand of the fair fool
Abigail. I'll count on thee, Rogue!"

He went as suddenly as he had come, but the world seemed
quite changed to Roger. As they presently walked home Leveson looked at him in surprise. He imputed his companion's
good spirits to the smiles of their hostess and warned him very
seriously about the toils of the ladies.

His friend answered joyously enough.

"When I marry, I'll choose a country lass," he declared. "But
there are other things in life than women."

Next day he was up and strolling forth before his host had
opened his eyes. He vowed he would explore the town and
strange things he saw and heard before the day was done.

It was not yet noon when Roger found himself in Old
'Change, where goldsmiths now congregated. He had studied
niello work in Rome and glanced at their wares with interest,
noting new designs and richness of ornament; presently strolling down a narrow alley he came upon a window in which pieces
of foreign origin were set forth. In the centre was a salver by
the hand of the famous Frenchman from whom the Czar of all
the Russias had ordered not one but several complete services
of plate at fabulous cost, and pushed into a corner were some
little dishes where Italian fancy had been given play. One held a

charming design of an Italian bird-seller, crouching over his net with his decoy-pipe hanging from his neck. Roger mounted the greasy steps and bent his head to pass the low doorway, and then, instead of making his purchase and commanding it to be sent to his lodgings like a fashionable town gallant, he fell into conversation with the shopkeeper who was a master-craftsman, and was soon deep in a comparison of the methods of foreign and English trade. Mr. Oakley was interested in his new patron's description of the tools used in Rome. He was a true artist and, forgetting to tempt the gentleman to buy, he presently invited him into his workshop. The old fascination stole over Roger; he doffed hat, frogged coat and peruke, and turned up his long, ruffled shirt-sleeves. His fingers itched to draw on the gleaming surface.

"We don't do much niello work now," observed Mr. Oakley. "'Tis quite out of fashion this year: but tea vessels are coming in and there's a call for urns: this here is a sweet, elegant design."

"I do not care for the handles," declared Dicconson. "Since you have chose a classic design it should be classic throughout— the tap too—"

He broke off and groped for a pencil which one of the apprentices obligingly pushed towards him. Roger sat down and began to draw on the first rough scrap of paper which came to his hand. The goldsmith recognized a fellow artist, the gentleman drew with a beautiful line, moreover he had a sense of design, and no doubt he had experience of other countries.

"The feet, Sir, shall it be claws or not claws?" he inquired deferentially.

"Claws, man! With these Corinthian columns!" exclaimed Roger indignantly. "No, no, a plain termination. The drawing of the cornucopia seems to me too ornate—"

He reached for a fresh piece of paper and Oakley regretfully withdrew in obedience to the impatient jangling of the shop-bell.

Roger did not raise his head until the melodious bells of St. Paul's proclaimed noon, and the apprentices began to wipe their hands and put on their coats. The master was still engaged with a client, but Dicconson invited the 'prentices to join him in a glass of ale at a neighbouring Ordinary. One of the lads recommended "The Flying Swan," a house of good reputation, and the little party walked there in company. As they entered the long, low, sanded room, a man in one of the little wooden cubicles which lined it on either side put down his tankard emphatically. The gesture was obviously intended to attract attention, but Roger made no sign and led his friends to the farther end of the room. He was quite sure he had recognized the "Captain" of ill-repute from whom he escaped by Mrs. Wilson's aid. The rogue had abandoned his military greatcoat and was now dressed in the extreme of the fashion. He evidently felt no ill-will towards his previous victim, for scarcely had the 'prentices taken leave than he presented himself at Roger's elbow, bowing and presenting a snuff-box blazing with gems.

"Sir, you'll honour me! Sir, I beg!" he flicked the little box of Vigo with the utmost elegance and smiled so ingratiatingly that Roger was almost persuaded that he had mistaken the man's identity.

He half rose from his chair, and the newcomer took advantage of the movement to insinuate himself into the next seat, pinning in the other between the table and the wall.

"My dear Mr. Harding!" he exclaimed. "I am charmed to meet you in happier circumstances. Times are changed, Sir. I have turned over a new leaf and parted from those monstrous coarse companions and I feel I owe you amends for an uncomfortable evening."

"You owe me nothing," returned Roger shortly.

He made as though to pass, but the other still barred his progress.

"Now, now, now!" he exclaimed. "Sit down, man. I can put you in a better way of living than you'll get by the plucking of those wretched little cits. Engraving is a poor trade—big risk and little gain—but if you're a smart lad and can write a good hand, I can put you into the way of earning a hundred and fifty guineas!"

Roger had been about to push by indignantly, but the last words put him on his mettle. His blue eyes became perfectly expressionless as he sat down again deliberately.

"Oh, aye," he said. "That's easy spoke."

"I took to you the moment I saw you," continued the other. "There's something devilish genteel about you and you have a good accent—a touch of French is not amiss for this job—'twill go down well enough."

"Oh ho! What's astir, then?"

"A glass of hollands, waiter. Why, lad, a popish plot—what say you to that? Safe, bound to please all, and no danger in it! How like you the smack of it, lad?"

"Why, well enough, save that it was tried before—and if I remember rightly a good few folk were sent to Newgate," rejoined Roger. "There was one small man who wore his own hair, the same as yourself, Sir, who was laid by the heels."

His companion put a finger to his nose in a very knowing manner and appeared by no means abashed.

"Stab me, but you have the very face for a Crown witness," he murmured enthusiastically. "Look at me—two years agone I had not a dollar to my name and now I keep a houseful o' servants and live to the tune o' two thousand a year."

.   .   .   .   .

The address on the lid of Martin Buckland's snuff-box was that of a discreet house, facing a narrow court in the crowded dwelling-houses behind the Temple. It contained sets of

chambers, inhabited by gentlemen, most of whom were con-
nected with the Law.

The first floor was occupied by a certain Mr. Green who was
known in Lancashire as Squire Standish of Standish Hall. The
low-ceiled room was dim tonight: it was oak-walled and oak-
floored and the lamp was discreetly shaded. The voices of the
company gathered about the table scarcely rose above whispers.
Each newcomer had announced himself with a peculiar knock—
three soft taps, one loud—until Martin Buckland thumped on
the panel.

"That's Buckland, I know his step," said the host, and his
companions heaved a sigh of relief.

Here was a man who feared nought and knew his own mind.
He laughed loudly as he crossed the threshold.

"Conspiratorial dimness, I vow! How goes it, Standish?
What news, man?"

In a trice he had raised the flame of the lamp, glanced keenly
at the faces of the men at the table and kicked the fire into a
blaze.

"Folk are confoundedly chicken-hearted," answered his host
testily. "Worcester will join in, once there's a proved success, but
at present he's trying to compound for his estates."

"Setting apart the Earl of Worcester," put in another, in a dry,
precise tone, "there are scores of men in the North, Jacobites at
heart, who won't rise until they are assured the King will stand
by them if he does come to his own again."

"I do not blame them," rejoined Buckland coolly. "But if
they have a good following, they can all be captains and colonels—faith! Mr. Jacob cares not how many commissions he
signs."

"Not so loud, Sir!" exclaimed Standish hurriedly.

"I can't stomach men who fight for gain," grumbled another.
"They're over apt to flee at a pinch."

Buckland stood on the hearth with his feet apart; he held his snuff-box in his left hand and inhaled a pinch slowly, flicking the dust off his ruffles with his large white fingers.

"Every man is for ends of his own, it seems," observed the attorney. "Scotland and Ireland would rise only if they are allowed to be separate kingdoms should we prove successful—and how would our stiff-necked city merchants stomach that notion, think you?"

"In my opinion 'tis all too soon. Melfort said as much last time he was over," murmured another. "Mr. James will never take here and the boy is too young as yet—'tis a mere pawn and there are folk still who will cast a stigma on his birth to mar matters."

"If the Duke of Gloucester lives, which is now thought probable, Protestants will rally in a solid block round the Oranges," demurred Standish. "We have been too forbearing in my opinion. Now there is trouble brewing again, and our enemies will not be easily satisfied even by stripping us of horses and arms and mulcting us by fines—they want blood now."

"True enough," agreed Buckland. "But if Catholics and Jacobites all through the country would but rise and show their mettle, we get support enough abroad. Why should we scruple to bring in foreign troops—cannot we pit Frenchmen against the rascally Dutch?"

"Aye, but folk can't rise without arms and horses," objected the timid man. "Mr. Standish hath but a few cases of small arms, and who is to horse us?"

"The Protestant Jacobites must take a hand there," cried Buckland. "The Quakers have money—why shouldn't they buy horses?"

"Tush, man, their religion don't allow them to own aught better than a pacing nag. But Ireland—what can Ireland do?" asked Standish. "I have met one Taafe who tells me he has interests in Ireland."

"Aye, but are you sure of him?" queried Martin sharply. "A complacent, supple devil—he might be useful, but I should have him watched first. The fellow hath kept queer company."

"If you buy arms outside the law it does not do to be nice about the party who provides them," rejoined Standish in a nettled tone.

"There is plenty of the right stuff in the country if they can be got together," resumed Buckland. "And if folk don't care much for Mr. Jacob, there's the boy! A glorious boy as ever was born to wear a crown."

"A general rising might succeed," said the precise man, who was an attorney-at-law. "But no more plots, Sir! We've had too many plots. The plot to kidnap the Stadholder at the Hague and Preston's plot and a host of others invented by their discoverers to push them with the Queen."

"As for treason—so-called"—Buckland interrupted himself to laugh—"there's scarce a man of note in England who hasn't passed letters to St. Germains. Gad! The poor Dutchman has a precious crew of friends—I could find it in my heart to pity him."

"You think it would be safe to rise, then? You think the country will support us?" It was one Blackney who spoke timidly.

"Safe!" roared Buckland. "Nay, is revolution ever safe? It is to those who are willing to die for their faith that I appeal. Are we to lie idle, with rusting swords, while family after family is stamped out, their lands passed to Protestants, their infant heirs perverted? It's now or never, my men! And let him who loves his faith better than his life follow me!"

He strode forward, and ripping out his sword, made it sing in the air and laid the bare blade across the table: his eyes were blazing, his lips parted.

The six gentlemen sprang to their feet.

"You are too dramatic, Mr. Buckland," cried Standish testily. "Of course we are all with you, though I—a married man with children—think it more prudent to consider before we leap."

Buckland, no whit disconcerted, slid his weapon back into the scabbard.

"'Tis not by counting the cost that kingdoms are won—or lost," he remarked, with intention. "But a truce to controversy! I expect a friend—'tis close on nine of the clock and I doubt he'll not fail me. 'Tis a sprig of an old Lancashire family and, if I mistake not, will prove the very fellow to set the sober, stout County Palatine in a blaze."

"What! Hath Derby decided for James after all?" cried Standish eagerly.

Martin's answer was an anti-climax.

"Not Derby, but Dicconson," he said. "And here he is!"

He set the door wide and stood looking down the twisting staircase, up which his old school-fellow mounted, lit by a candle from below. His mind was seething with prospects which an untoward check might spoil for ever. Roger's advent might tip the balance on the right side and his face was eagerly welcome as he grasped him by the hand.

"Gentlemen," he cried, "here is my dear friend and school-fellow, Mr. Roger Dicconson, and, Roger lad, these are—"

"Wait! I seek to know no man's name nor seek his face either." Dicconson spoke low but urgently and a hand, with a fine lace ruffle drooping over it, shot out and turned down the lamp. "I don't know what you are concerned about here, gentlemen, but I'll give you my news for what 'tis worth. There are men going about this city and country who are determined to stage a popish plot as they term it, to ruin Catholic gentlemen and seize on their estates. A suitable witness—that is to say, a perjurer who can make out a reasonably credible tale, may earn a fee of one hundred and fifty guineas. And anyone who likes to take a sporting chance and put up two or three hundred guineas, will be assigned the reversion of an estate worth as many thousands."

"These are fairy-tales!" exclaimed Buckland contemptuously. "Would you frighten us with boggarts?"

"I show you the net," returned Dicconson. "Creep under it if you will."

Standing just within the door he proceeded to recount his experiences on the journey up from Rye and what had befallen him that very day.

There was a rustle as the gentlemen at the table turned their powdered heads simultaneously towards him: Buckland moved impatiently from foot to foot.

"What the devil does it matter?" he burst out. "Haven't there always been perjurers in the country? The very fact that the public condones their venal evidence against Catholics proves what a dangerous position is ours. If you won't rise for your faith, nor your King, nor your conscience, maybe you'll draw swords to secure your own lives!"

"Not I, for one," retorted the prim gentleman. "So I'll e'en wish you all good night."

"Is the door watched?" whispered another in Roger's ear.

"How can he tell?" interrupted Buckland. "Why, Roger, how you have broke up our meeting! What! Have you no desire to strike a blow for liberty?"

"I've no fancy for plots," answered Dicconson bluntly. "If King James raised his standard in the open field, 'twere another thing."

"Alas, my lord—alas, gentlemen, the King is a broken man. He never lifted his head again after the Princess Anne's desertion. But the Prince of Wales is a sacred trust—God bless him!"

"God bless him," repeated the others, but even as they spoke, each man found his cloak and hat and bowed themselves from the room.

"There goes another pricked bubble!" commented Buckland lightly.

"Where do we stand now?" asked Standish, hesitating on the threshold, with a dubious glance at Dicconson.

"No whit the worse," returned Buckland. "You, Tom, continue buying arms, I shall continue to raise money, and you"—he turned to his old school-fellow with a sudden fierceness—"you, Sir, will continue to keep your mouth shut."

"Perfectly, Sir," rejoined Roger. Then, infuriated with the French trick of language he had unintentionally let slip: "I'll take no man's orders," he added, and walked out of the room.

CHAPTER EIGHT

ISTRESS TOWNELEY's notion that Bridget should has-
ten home and hide her diminished head found scant
approval with her sister. She declared that she had
done nothing wrong, and surely there was nothing scandalous
in imitating the conduct of the Queen—that prodigy of beauty
and nice behaviour! In any case—and here her sparkling blue
eyes were apt to roll towards her brother-in-law—'twas fashionable to cut a dash.

"You surprise me, Bridget! La, what are the young folk coming to!" exclaimed Madam Towneley. But the reproof was merely superficial as she was obviously in sympathy with the delin-
quent. Susan liked nothing better than a little gaiety and here
was an excellent opportunity. So after shaking her head and
turning up her eyes and uttering a few moral axioms, she turned
her attention to new clothes and the dispatch of notes, while
Mr. Towneley was ordered to find out at which theatre there was
like to be a decent civil performance to which one might safely
escort a young girl.

One solitary ambition filled Bridget's mind at the moment,
and this no very worthy one. She wished to be acclaimed as a
belle of the first water that Mr. Dicconson might realize the
prize he had missed by his precipitate proposal. To this end she
bent all her powers at the reshaping of Susan's violet tabinet,
which she was to wear with her new sky-blue apron. The blue
ribbons in her curls stood up triumphantly as she set forth determined on conquest. The play was "The Old Bachelor" by Mr.

Congreve: Susan was a little disturbed at Towneley's choice, but Bridget found a greater interest in the admiring glances of the gentlemen seated at the sides of the stage than in the play itself. One, in particular, was monstrous handsome and seemed to have a gay word of encouragement for each of the actors as they stepped past him from the wings. He whispered to his companions on either side, glancing up at the box with raised eyebrows—Bridget was positive that he was inquiring who she was.

In the pause between the acts, when the voices and jests of the orange-sellers filled the air, Towneley went out to talk with his friends and came back with the interesting stranger behind him.

"Sister Bridget," he said, "Mr. Martin Buckland desires to be presented to you. Mr. Buckland—Mistress Bridget Thornleigh."

Though she had promised herself to be a thorough woman of the world, Bridget's eyes sank beneath the stranger's glance. There was something in it at once pleading and compelling.

Commonplace remarks were exchanged for a moment or two, then Buckland threw himself into a chair next Bridget, interposing his person between her and the other occupants of the box.

"You are young enough to London to carry a generous heart —susceptible of compassion," he began persuasively. "Behold in me a man under the influence of a ruling passion! Miss Thornleigh, the weal or eternal woe of this Kingdom rests with the youth of the nation."

Bridget tossed her head.

"La, Sir, I'm not one for politics," she cried, vastly disappointed at his choice of a subject.

"Nor I, Ma'am. But I am a Catholic and I love my country. There's no place like England, and this is the hour of her peril. We can save her, you and I—you and I and our like—if we will."

Her wide, startled eyes were fixed on his face, and Martin

paused in artistic enjoyment of the effect he had produced.

"Your elder brother, Joseph, was a school-fellow of mine," he went on in a more sober tone. "We often conferred together about the future of England—when penal laws should be swept away, and—but we must not talk of it here."

"No, we'll look at the play, if you please, and listen to the actors." Bridget twitched away her fingers on which Mr. Buckland had laid his hand as though by accident. The said actors made jests which brought the bright colour flaming into her cheeks presently, and the young gentlemen lounging inside the footlights made audible comments on the fact. Bridget pushed back her seat with a petulant exclamation, and her companion glanced at her with amusement.

"Ah, Ma'am, you are not hardened to town ways yet! Let me tell you something of the King I serve and his son and Princess— indeed they are the handsomest pair you e'er set eyes on, and as gracious sweet and good as folk in a fairy-tale."

"Why, are you from St. Germains then?" Bridget whispered the imprudent query.

"Yes, Ma'am. 'Tis a fairy-tale Court living in a palace embowered in a forest. Instead of a fat woman intent on food and cotton fringes, the Queen is a little saint of surpassing beauty. What are the Court functions, think you? Well, just before my departure I was bidden to one."

He paused, resuming his tale when he had made sure that it could not be overheard. Bridget listened spell-bound in the shadowy corner into which she had withdrawn.

"I must tell you then that we walked out into the greenwood, and the banquet we carried with us in little baskets. At noon we sat down among the ferns and moss and ate wild strawberries, and shared the cakes and curds we had brought with us. The Princess touched the guitar and sang to us and we were very merry. 'Tis a touching simple life they lead there."

"If you talk of it so freely you will be indicted for treason, though," declared the young lady.

"There's no means of telling friend from foe unless you ask," answered Buckland. "I think you would fain be a friend."

"I am sorry for King James, but 'twas a pity he left England," observed she. "Maybe if he had died fighting at the head of his army here the folk would have rallied to the baby Prince."

"We are too well hated for that, I doubt. The Protestant party would open their arms to a Jew sooner than to a Catholic. And sure the King scarcely practised what he preached and so estranged all parties—he doth not understand the English love of liberty. It has been 'hands off our charters' from time immemorial."

"I think this poor lady on the stage will think us monstrous ungenteel not to listen to her song," protested Bridget. "I'd like to hear it too, and I think, Mr. Buckland, you are in danger of being lodged at Newgate before aught's long."

He shot an appreciative glance at her—a glance that lingered on her flushed face till Bridget began to feel uncomfortable. Susan thought the *tête-à-tête* had lasted long enough and ordered the girl to change places with her. Buckland made no pretence of being satisfied with the exchange. He rose in a few minutes, bowed and withdrew. Bridget thought he shot a fiery glance towards her, but perhaps the semi-darkness misled her. She listened eagerly while Susan questioned her husband.

"'Twas Lady Gerard who made him known to me," said Towneley. "He particularly desired an introduction, she said. He's a good example of our fashionable blades, Bridget, and 'tis said he's a great success with the ladies."

He glanced at her quizzically, but the girl was apparently quite absorbed in the progress of the play. Her fingers still tingled from Buckland's light pressure at parting.

"I'll not be such a fool as to fall in love," she told herself. "But if I ever do, 'twill be with a dark-eyed man."

The Net

How comically different that poor Roger Dicconson had looked, rising up from the muddy fair-ground with his bruised face and swollen eye! Buckland was a finished fine gentleman, but the Lancashire lad had good stuff in him too, and doubtless it was not his fault that he had not romantic and thrilling dark eyes.

"What did the young man talk to you about, Bridget dear?" queried her sister, when they reached home and were sipping the posset heated up on the little silver lamp in Madam Towneley's bed-chamber.

"Oh, la, I forget—politics and such-like," said Bridget, who was already learning to dissemble.

"He is a Catholic, and folk say a Jacobite," continued Susan. "But they are always liable to speak so of folk of our religion to bring us into disrepute."

"I suppose the country *is* full of Jacobites," murmured Bridget. "Why don't they rise and put King James on the throne again?"

"Well, my dear, there's not so many as you think. The country has accepted the present sovereigns, and no one wants civil war again. No one liked King James, poor man, though he did make things better for us recusants, and the little Prince is so young—it's all too chancy."

"So William wouldn't take arms if there *was* a rising?" insisted Bridget.

"You're enough to get us all hanged!" cried Susan irritably, but she did not answer the question.

A few days later Susan rushed into her sister's room with her hair a bristling mass of curl-papers, waving an open letter in her hand.

"La, child! Here's a piece of luck!" she exclaimed in high good humour. "Here's my lady Gerard inviting us to a private ball at her house tonight. They are to stand up about thirty couple, she says! You'll be monstrous discreet, won't you, child? I must send to the mantua-maker, and if I die for it, you must have a silver girdle. I declare my lady marked your looks at the play."

Bridget flushed with delight, but before she could speak, her sister rushed on:

"William says all this talk about you and the Fair will make you an acknowledged belle, but I can't think it's what my dear mother would approve."

"But it's done now, Sue, so we might as well get what enjoyment we can out of it!" exclaimed Bridget unrepentantly.

"There'll be a many Lancashire folk there," observed Susan, eyeing her curiously.

"Are the Bucklands Lancashire?" queried the girl, trying to speak carelessly. "The man we met the other night spoke with a slight French accent—that's usual among Catholics, though he is not fresh from school."

"Buckland—nay, I've a notion they're South-country folk. Come to think on't, I can't call to mind that I have met any of that name before. I'll ask Lady Gerard. And, Bridget, we must get our heads dressed at once, for 'tis the only hour at which Monsieur Pierre is free—and he's the man most *à la mode*."

"But, sister—'tis not yet nine o'clock!" protested Bridget.

Mistress Towneley was inflexible.

"We must have Pierre," she asserted.

. . . . .

Bridget's heart swelled with triumph as she stepped into the ballroom behind her sister. She knew that she was looking her best and noted that the eyes of every man in the room kindled as they lit upon her. She recognized her whilom suitor directly, and thought it would have been only civil of him to inquire how she did. But when after a discreet interval the young gentleman was presented by his sister-in-law, Bridget decided pettishly that he should have stayed away.

She turned her shoulder on him but Roger was not disconcerted. He gave her news of her brother in Rome and conversed agreeably for a few moments until Bridget stood up to dance. Her bright eyes searched every corner of the room, at first meeting only with disappointment, but presently as she paced through a square dance, she saw Buckland come in. She watched him glance appreciatively towards her—but every man did that tonight!—and then seek out young Dicconson. Her partner spoke but she lost the sense of his discourse, while she noted Roger's air of coldness. At length the dance was over and her partner led her back to Susan's side. He had evidently no notion of leaving his inattentive lady, but she pleaded fatigue, and besought him so prettily to conduct her sister to partake of some refreshment that he was beguiled. Directly Susan's back was turned, the débutante shot a challenging glance in Buckland's direction; he responded to it promptly. The musicians had struck up one of the quick Polish dances in fashion on the Continent though little known in London. Bridget felt as though treading on air as Buckland took her hand. Last time she had practised these steps Mère Angélique had been at the harpsichord and her partner had been dumpy little Miss Jane Brown. Hand-in-hand they passed down the room with flying feet.

"Oh, that this were for life!" murmured Buckland.

She heard him well enough, and sent another soft glance at him under lowered lashes.

"The veiling lids are almost as beautiful as the blue eyes," he went on. "What whiteness, what long lashes! Indeed, Ma'am, I can't contain myself—you must forgive me!"

Now they were changing hands and the few couples taking part were separated from each other by gleaming spaces of polished floor. The girls' silk dresses rustled and grated lightly on the floor as they swung about.

"'Tis like dancing with a bird," whispered Buckland. "But let us pause at the orangery door—there, they are applauding you."

There was a light clapping of hands as the pair passed into a glass enclosure filled with shining branches and the heavy scent of orange blossom. Buckland had not relinquished her hand; he pulled it through his arm, and so insensibly drew her form close to his side.

"Ah, Mistress Bridget, if we were but alone on a tropic isle! Would I not teach you to lift those lovely eyes to mine—"

He broke off—was it unconscious innocence, or was the young lady more up in the wiles of the world than he had guessed? Those blue eyes were raised—not soft and languorous, but flashing a challenge.

"I'm afraid to look no man in the face!" quoth Mistress Bridget. She released her arm with a vigour which betrayed the whilom schoolgirl, tucked up a stray curl and dropped him the pertest of curtsies.

She was, however, in no hurry to return to Susan's guardianship, though she prudently chose a chair in full view of the ballroom. Buckland hung over her; her fan could scarce cool her cheek which flamed ever and again as she listened to him. For the young man appeared to forget that he had a mission tonight; he was only conscious of the girl's fresh beauty, and of his power to absorb her attention.

When presently Mr. Dicconson approached she was petulant at the interruption.

"I have been unfortunate, Ma'am, in my first meetings with you," he declared. "It would be charitable of you indeed could you be induced to consider me as a complete stranger. Forget all that has passed up to date and allow Mr. Buckland, our mutual friend, to present me to you. Could you not allow me a fresh start? Martin, I pray—"

"Nay, Sir." A sense of power made Bridget cruel. "We can do even better." She smiled with a mirthless twist of the lip. "Let us remain strangers!"

Roger's eager face grew so blank that she was sorry, yet knew not how to take back her words. He stepped away so quickly that his hat fell from under his arm, and then, without a protest, he left them and went straight out of the room.

"Heaven preserve me from your displeasure!" cried Buckland. But there was a note of triumph in his tone which jarred upon her, and a drop of bitterness remained in her heart under all the sweetness of satisfied vanity.

CHAPTER NINE

ROGER AND HIS BROTHER were seated at the dinner-table, a tankard of ale at the elbow of each and a clean new pipe in hand or mouth. Mistress Dicconson and her daughter had left them, and the tinkling of the spinet could be heard intermittently from the little parlour across the stair-head. Roger had once more pressed that the interest due on his portion should be paid to him, and the Squire had endeavoured to demonstrate the impossibility of acceding to his demand.

"You must e'en make shift to table with us awhile, brother," he concluded. "Here or at home—'tis all one. Ready money is not to be had and as for what I have set out at interest—well, when 'tis paid you shall have your share."

"But that's of no use to me," returned the younger man impatiently. "I desire to enter a profession—to study law. And being too old for an apprentice I must needs pay fees—in any case there's fees, I suppose. Then I shall need books, and a London lodging."

"And how do you imagine I can provide such things?" exclaimed William angrily. "Here am I—a married man with a family, and three young brothers' pensions to pay, and Mary's portion not off my hands yet though she has been married these five years! My father left me head of the family and it is lacking respect, I think, Roger, for you to press me so unmannerly! You, who might have been so well provided abroad too, by all accounts!"

Roger grew crimson.

"I do but ask a share of what is my own!" he retorted hotly, "and sure, I've waited long enough for it. But you could not have given me a cooler welcome had I been a veritable prodigal."

"Nay, but, brother, you have little sympathy for me," declared William.

Roger knew that if he did not persist now it would be even more difficult to raise the subject again.

"It's a question of prudence," he cried. "If you assist me now I can make myself independent—if not I shall become a mere hanger-on as useless to others as to myself."

"I cannot do it," repeated the Squire obstinately, and an embarrassed silence fell between them.

Roger waited, choking down his impatience, but Hugh fiddled with his pipe and tobacco and several times dropped the decorative glass stopper with which he was ramming the bowl on to the table.

"I'm for Lancashire, then," said Roger at last.

William looked up. "You'll make your home with us, brother?"

"Yes, I'll stay a while at Wrightington, though there seems little employment for a Catholic in the country in these days. What can a man do besides horse-matching and playing at bowls?"

"There's aplenty County business if it were not for all the plaguey restrictions to recusants," William rejoined with animation. "There's such a scramble as never was for places, and you've no notion what a passion there is against Catholics! When Braddyl was assessor we poor papists got a little breathing space, for all he took the oaths for the Government."

"Did he not collect the full tax, then?" asked Roger, interested.

"Nay, but the poll is payable on everyone over sixteen, and he winked a bit at the ages of the children of his poor recusant neighbours. But there was never such a to-do about it, and petitions to Parliament and I know not what-all—the poor man got into great trouble. Now they say it must be farmed."

"Do you mean that they will put the King's taxes up to auction?" exclaimed Roger. "That would be a shabby trick! Is there no honest man can be chosen as assessor?"

"If he seems honest to us he is not like to please the bishops—they're monstrous hard on all dissenters. Lord Willoughby had a great set-to with Nicholas Stratfield, that is the Bishop of Chester, a year or two ago—the whole county was in an uproar over it!"

Roger eventually went North by coach and was met by horses at Chester. After the beautiful Roman thoroughbreds to which he had been accustomed of late, his brother's steeds appeared extremely contemptible. He informed Peter Gray, the old groom, that he intended to buy himself a beast worth riding, and was somewhat dashed by the old fellow's dolorous account of all the horses seized of late up and down the country.

"Even a permit will not protect a Catholic gentleman nowadays," he protested. "There was poor old Madam Ashurst o' the Lee as was out in her coach only last back-end. She were on her way to carry a sugar-loaf to the Squire of Ince's lady, as was brought to bed of her first boy, and dash me, if an assessor and his men didn't meet th' owd lass i' the road, and whip the horses out of the traces and leave the poor lady sitting high and dry in her coach."

"'Tis a disgrace and gives encouragement to the worst class of rogues," exclaimed Roger. "Tell me, Peter, is there aught stirring in the country? Where do the young sprigs look for entertainment?"

"Why faith, Sir, they do little else but fuddle themselves i' the ale-houses! Ah, 'tis a sad thing to see so many promising young gentlemen ruined by drink! Not that I've anything to say against a quart o' beer now and again—riding these dusty roads be main droughty work!"

He drew the back of his hand suggestively across his lips, but his young master was not hearkening.

"I forget how the land lies," he murmured. "Whose park is it I see over yonder?"

"Why, that is Squire Thornleigh's place, and a better man never stepped," began Peter enthusiastically.

But Roger drew his hat down over his brow, and touching his horse went forward at a hard trot.

It was nearly dark when he reached Wrightington, and he felt sad enough as they passed the gate-house and went forward up the weedy, neglected avenue. At his last home-coming his father had been waiting to greet him, and his little brothers had run panting on each side of his cob.

Nevertheless the house seemed to distil an atmosphere of peace and family affection. Old servants hurried out to grasp Master Roger by the hand, a little niece escaped from the nursery and came trotting downstairs in her long night-rail, while elder brothers contented themselves with peering over the banisters. He supped alone, but old Dame Tabitha Patten, the superannuated housekeeper, was pushed in in her wheeled chair while he was at his nuts and wine. "Tabby," he had been wont to call her in his childhood. She addressed him at first with a frosty decorum, which broke down after the young man's bold kiss.

"I'm glad the race is not like to die out," he said presently, laughing, but the old lady shook her head.

"Aye, the Squire has fine children, God bless them, but will any of them be able to stand in their father's shoes, my dear? The Squire, poor lad, is pulled every way for money. I wish we don't see the whole family fined out of existence like the Southworths. A great old family, they were, and gave a martyr to the Faith, but their last acres have been sold up, and there are strangers in their place."

"The injustice is enough to force people into rebellion," muttered Roger angrily.

"Nay, God's will be done, my dear! Didn't He tell His apostles that the world would hate them? And we're noan better than St. Peter and St. John, I reckon."

"But it is bitter hard, Tabby! It tempts one to turn Jacobite."

The housekeeper glanced at him sharply. "Hush! That's a dangerous word to speak even in jest," she murmured. "Why, lad, the country is full of Irish soldiers, disbanded by the King, or fled from the troubles in Ireland—and the Protestants multiply every man there is by ten—they'll have it as there are thousands lurking in hiding! But indeed, Master Roger, I doubt the master isn't as careful as he should be."

"How's that, Dame?"

"Well, you know, he were close-fisted as a lad, and he does hate to part. He is heart-sick at these double taxes and the poll-tax and all. Aye, Will would give you sixpence if you asked him, but he would give it a long, loving look first."

"Then he'll not waste his fortune on spendthrift ways," declared Roger.

"Nay, lad, but he'll risk his neck to save it," she whispered, and with that the foot-boy came in to wheel her back to her own quarters.

Roger had food for thought as he sauntered up and down the terrace in the warm dusk, listening to the owls hooting and calling amorously from elm to elm. But somehow his own recent discomfiture weighed on his mind more than his country's grievances, and instead of an exiled King, his thoughts were haunted by an ungrateful and wayward girl. What had turned her so violently against him, he wondered? Then he remembered that Buckland had smiled at his friend's rebuff, and he made an angry movement which sent a little dart of pain along his new scar.

The country in early summer was gay enough: young neighbours rallied round, and Roger was asked out so often that he found himself riding the green leafy lanes every day. Now he was on his way to a cocking match, now to play bowls, now to see coursing along the Formby road. At this last entertainment he was introduced to old Squire Thornleigh, athirst for news of his grandson Joseph at Rome. He looked rather quizzically at Roger as he announced that his grand-daughter was making a prodigious delay in town. The young man reddened, to his own annoyance.

"I wish to tell you, Mr. Dicconson, that I consider your conduct to my young lady was most becoming—most becoming," repeated the old man warmly. "And I trust that you do not take the girl's refusal unkindly?"

"That's a question I'd as lief not answer," cried Roger, striving to hide his mortification with a laugh. "For 'yes' or 'no' would sound equally ungallant."

He moved away at the first opportunity and Thornleigh followed him with his eyes musingly. There were other ladies present at the match who seemed to find young Dicconson's attentions agreeable, though they had not appealed to the "thing called Bridget."

"'Twould have been a nice match too," reflected the old man with a sigh. "And we'd have kept the little lass within a long ride of us. But doubtless God willed otherwise."

It was not until his first Sunday at home that Roger realized that he was living under penal laws. For the first time in his life he was out of reach of Mass! The Dicconsons usually rode to Chorley for their devotions, for since the Squire's imprisonment three years back, he had not ventured to keep a chaplain, though he entertained priests for long periods as visitors. Just now the good Father at Standish lay sick and the whole countryside was deprived of his ministrations. Many people, like Roger, had ridden into Chorley, or tramped down from the moors, early on the summer morning. They dared not wait about the streets of the town, but were received into the houses of co-religionists, and watched, through the diamond-paned windows, their Protestant neighbours stepping along to service in the parish church which their own Catholic forbears had built. It was just possible that Squire Brockholes at Claughton might have a second priest in the house and a messenger had been dispatched with a spare horse in this hope. But after a long delay, the man returned alone—Mass had been said at an early hour and the priest had gone abroad to visit sick and aged members of his flock. The disappointed congregation set forth on their return journey; most of them were afoot, for gentry of the better sort were forbidden to travel more than five miles from home, without a special licence. The horses of even well-to-do farmers had been seized, in the dual excitement of the Prince of Orange's elevation to the throne and the outburst of real and imaginary plots and intrigues which followed it. Dicconson came upon a group outside the town; a stout old country woman was sitting on the bank, surrounded by her son and his wife and a whole pack of children. The ancient dame was quite overcome by heat, exertion and disappointment, and further suffered from "a bad leg," as Roger was informed when he drew near to inquire.

"'Tis your own fault, Mother," her son assured her. "You didn't ought to ha' coom."

"Eh, lad, if I could but ha' got Mass 'twould be worth it an' all," she gasped.

"'Tis four mile, if 'tis a step!" commented the daughter-in-law. "Leather," she added, addressing her husband, "you'd best be off home and put saddle on th' owd mare. We'll wait here wi' Granny till yo' coom back."

"My horse is quiet enough," announced Roger. "It would be better for your man to ride back into the town and borrow a pillion if the goodwife can make shift to ride."

In a district where every Catholic was known to his neighbours, a stranger in the fold naturally provoked suspicion. The No Popery riots and executions inspired by Titus Oates and his colleagues were fresh in the memory of the elders of the party; even the children had been taught to keep a still tongue with any unfamiliar person. The flushed old lady cast a shrewd eye on the young man and then broke the constraint.

"Yon young chap be t' very spit and image of old Hugh o' Wrightington," she remarked to her son. "They had it in the town that he were own brother to Will."

"And so I am, Dame," responded Roger. "So do you take the horse, man, and rest him tonight and send him home to Wrightington tomorrow. Is there not a way across the moor yonder? I mind we used to go tickling for trout there, when we were child-little."

"I'll show you—I'll show you!" cried a little tow-headed urchin of the company.

Lancashire folk are taciturn and there were no fulsome expressions of gratitude. Leather helped his mother to mount, and his wife told him sharply to be off and not keep the old woman all day in the sun. They both glanced at Roger then nodded sideways and muttered: "Thank ye and all," in a tone which might have sounded grudging had it not fallen on Lancashire ears.

Granny added complacently that Roger was a saucy lad, for he had saluted the old dame's hot cheek gallantly at parting. Little Harry ran with him up the hill and pointed out the green track almost hidden beneath encroaching heather bushes, and then Roger strode on alone. The sun was hot, a solitary lark was singing, but when it ceased a great stillness spread on every side. The gentle ripple of the stream was audible a long way off, and the snapping of gorse pods in the heat sounded like the discharge of fairy musketry. Presently the stream was left behind and Roger took to the stony pack-road which led across a rolling expanse of dark heather. He bought cheese and oat-cake at a solitary farm-house and walked on with it in his hand. Riding-boots are exceedingly uncomfortable for rough walking, and after tramping a mile or two farther in a vain quest for trees, Roger was fain to throw himself down in the narrow shade of some tall gorse-bushes.

Large, shining white clouds rode along a sky of burning blue, the air was heavy with the almond fragrance of gorse blossom, through which pierced the delicate pungency of budding heather and the flowering wood-rush—that tiny plant which embalms all the upland pastures. The young man glanced contentedly about him as he munched, rejoicing in the free solitude. But the moor was not after all desert ground: he was startled to meet the gaze of a pair of very bright, dark eyes, peering out from behind a screen of green prickles.

Chapter Ten

A N INVOLUNTARY start betrayed Roger's surprise, but he made no remark and presently took another bite.

There was a slight rustling in the fern as though the hidden form were trying to withdraw itself.

"I see you," remarked Roger, aloud, "so you had better come out and show yourself. I carry no money and I am armed," he added urbanely.

He was answered by a laugh, which might have been either that of a woman or a child. The bright eyes vanished and presently a girl came swaggering from behind the flowering furze, bowed affectedly and examined the young man with a gaze in which boldness, curiosity and anxiety were mingled.

"Scutcher's Peg, at your service, Sir!"

It would have been difficult to guess the age of the curious little figure. Her head was crowned with a tangled mop of hair, originally yellow, but bleached almost white by exposure to the sun. Her dark eyes constantly roved about, and were as bright as those of a bird. Her stature was stunted by premature hard work, but strong and muscular. She wore a short garment of ragged yellow chintz, which displayed sinewy bare legs and sunburnt forearms.

Roger put her down for a tinker's wench and was feeling in his pocket for a sixpence when he noted that her bold glance flickered down pathetically from his face to the great sandwich of oat-cake still clasped in his hand.

"Thou'rt hungry! Come, we'll share," he cried companionably, and broke the cheese and oat-cake in half.

"I am hungry!" She emphasized the statement with an oath, yet took the food from his hand with a mincing gesture. It was dispatched in two or three enormous bites which showed her strong white teeth. Dicconson laconically tendered his own portion, which was accepted and eaten with silent expedition.

"And have you no brandy to wash it down?" she enquired, glancing at him slyly as she squatted before him in the full blaze of the sun.

He shook his head.

The girl looked at him narrowly.

"At first I thought you was a gentleman," she announced. "But now I know different. You might be a jockey out o' trade— but that you speak over nice."

"If you can tell me my trade you know more than I do myself," he rejoined lightly.

Scutcher's Peg cocked her head with a knowing air and winked.

"Oh, all trades is honest," she observed meaningly. "All trade is good trade, but this county is over-throng with millers just now, and I warn you, except for the Governor's specials, there's no comfort in clink."

"So I'm told," returned Roger, who understood by this cryptic remark that the gaoler at the local lock-up was venal, and allowed certain of his inmates special privileges. "'Tis said some of the coiners and clippers continue their job in gaol."

"True enough," she said, and paused a moment as though in uncertainty, her eyes screwed up in the effort to study his face under the glare of the sun. "My father now—they've mewed him up and whatever he done he never had nought to do with clippers."

"There's little work for scutchers, I reckon, now Flemish cloth is all the rage," suggested Roger.

The girl nodded.

"My poor old dad," she said in a choked voice. "They abuse him yonder. Aye, they've put chains on him and tied him up and all sorts. He's nought worse nor a wastrel," she added, with an oath, "and they've no call to mishandle him."

"He's not been convicted then?"

"Devil a trial at all! You have to pay folk to have your case brought nowadays. An' who's to fee the clerk for us, or bring up the witnesses either? He'll just lie there till he rots."

"And how do you live meanwhile?" Roger was beginning, when the girl jumped up, with a flaming face.

"What's that to you?" she cried, and catching up a stone, balanced it threateningly in her hand.

"Don't peg that at me, child!" cried Roger with a laugh. "I asked because you seemed hungry and I'm sorry. Tell me your father's name—maybe I have a friend who could help him."

"He's a good Protestant, mind you," she urged. "It was he led the folks as burnt the papists' chapel at Hornington. Aye, he's strong for King William and the Protestant succession and all that's right."

"That should be in his favour," agreed Roger.

"His true name is George Morley, if you must know. And what's yours?" she asked.

"They call me Howard but I won't swear to it," returned Roger, who began to think he had been rather imprudent. "And I'm for home. But before we part, we'll share pockets as we shared dinner. You shall have my purse—which is devilish light —and I'll keep snuff-box and handkerchief."

Peg caught the little silk bag he tossed in the air, and flung it up again with a mocking look.

"You're a civil lad," she declared, dropping the stone, "and maybe not so simple as you look."

With that she gave him a hearty kiss and bounded off without a backward glance.

Dicconson went on his way feeling pleasantly stimulated. Brother William would vastly disapprove of his squandering his scarce shillings and conversing familiarly with such a ragged gipsy wench, and this knowledge added to his satisfaction. He was free of all tutelage—deciding for himself and choosing his own road! Yet ever and again his thoughts harked back to that disastrous ballroom—to Bridget's angry face and Buckland's covert smile.

"I'll show her who is the better man," he muttered between his teeth.

Strange that Roger Dicconson should esteem himself a better man than his whilom hero.

"Politics," he observed on the bowling-green a few days later, "politics are a disease—'tis a dry rot will spoil the best of men. Do you not agree, Mr. Towneley?"

"Aye, but they're mighty interesting too," agreed the other.

"'Tis all a dirty intrigue to me," declared Roger. "A foul pitch which sticks to the hands of great and small."

"Aye, but a lot of hard cash will stick to a pitched hand, as our magistrates tell us. And no one will notice dirty fingers if they're thrust into a fine glove! But what set your mind running on politics, lad?"

"I scarcely know," said Roger, reddening. He did not intend to confess his belief that the Squire's long sojourn in London was being spent in the hope of obtaining a "place." Countless presents would have to be bestowed, countless strings pulled, and countless noble lords flattered before such a piece of business could be brought to fruition.

While visiting the country neighbours Roger made some cautious inquiries on the subject of the House of Correction and persons awaiting trial. The woes of these unfortunates were generally accepted as a necessary evil, impossible of remedy. Mr. Clifton, a local Justice of the Peace, was easily induced to take him on a tour of inspection by way of gratifying a young man's natural curiosity. Dicconson was appalled at what he saw. In the prison men and women were confined together in close, filthy, airless rooms. Some wretches were shivering with ague, one lay raving on a wretched straw pallet. The reek of the place, the evil faces, the screams and curses, pursued him through his dreams for many a night after. Then there were the Messengers' houses to be visited. Some of these men had bought their unenviable posts, and proceeded to recoup themselves by a course of brutal tyranny over their inmates. A suspected person committed by a magistrate often lingered for months or even years without being brought to trial. If he could not pay his gaoler the sum required, he might be loaded with fetters. Fancy prices had to be paid for food, bed and coverings, and the prisoner who did not indulge continually in drink was soon out of the gaoler's good graces, as it was here that he obtained his best profits.

"This is the house of one Bayley," announced Mr. Clifton. "An honest enough fellow as these rogues go. There is a Morley on his list—maybe it is the man you seek for."

There was a small grated window in the wall and as there was no immediate reply to their knock, Roger stood on tiptoe and looked in. He could see into a small room immediately below, in which five or six men lay huddled together in irons. The door was ajar and he had a momentary glimpse through it to a narrow corridor at the far end of which was an animated group of people. A curious-looking machine, like a large coffee-mill, stood on a table, and two men were busied with it while a third was rapidly sweeping some glittering fragments off the table. A woman stood by, and presently, glancing over her shoulder, met Roger's interested gaze. She instantly ran along the passage and closed the door—Dicconson could hear the clatter of the bolt. He was about to impart his discovery to his companion when the main gate was opened and the turnkey presented himself, wreathed in smiles.

They were ushered into the house and Roger noted that the table and all the paraphernalia had vanished from the passage. He felt himself boiling with indignation which he could hardly repress.

"I should be glad, Sir, if you would inquire why all these unfortunate men should be kept in fetters," he exclaimed. "Surely a turnkey has no right to inflict such a punishment on men who have not yet been tried?"

"The young gentleman is ignorant of our customs, I reckon," returned Bayley with a grin. "I'm responsible for producing the bodies of these men at the Assizes, young Sir. And if they want to, they can always buy their ease—or get their friends to pay the charges for them."

Clifton laid his hand repressively on Roger's arm.

"They would be glad of the wherewithal to drink your honour's health," continued the turnkey insinuatingly.

Dicconson looked him squarely in the face. "I'm told some of these unfortunate wretches still continue their trades while in confinement," he announced, but the gaoler did not blench.

"Oh, aye, we have a cobbler here, but folk don't wear out their shoes when they're tethered to the wall, I warrant ye," he returned with a brutal laugh.

"Ye have a houseful of coiners and clippers, I suppose?" said Clifton, stepping in front of his companion.

While he and the turnkey conversed, Roger walked into the cell which had been opened for their inspection and spoke to its inmates. He had a friendly way with him and soon discovered Morley, the scutcher. The poor fellow was sitting on the ground, his thin hands, scarred and disfigured by years of toil, were clasped round his knees, his head was bowed upon them. Dicconson touched him on the shoulder.

"Have you no one to speak for you at the Assizes, my poor fellow?" he asked.

The scutcher shook his head. He looked up dumbly for a moment and then suddenly broke into vehement speech.

"Nay, I've no one to speak for me—and what's that to you? Why don't you hang us right off—innocent and guilty, instead o' leaving us here to rot? I've allus lived in the oppen—"

He glanced up at the dirty closed window overhead with the frantic, helpless passion of a trapped animal. "They've tied me down here like a rat!" he screamed, and broke into pitiful tears.

"Oh, God!" exclaimed Roger in horrified pity. He rushed out of the cell, and made his way to the door, by which Mrs. Bayley stood on guard. She was the woman he had seen through the window.

She unfastened the bars and let him out into the street, where he stood drawing in great gasps of fresh air, and fighting the impulse to fly from the place in panic. Roger had stocked his purse to the best of his ability before leaving home, and he presently turned back, forced himself to speak civilly to Mrs. Bayley and bargained with her for Morley's better treatment.

"He'll not live long, I reckon," she said carelessly. "If your honour cared to pay the indemnity and bind yourself to produce him back to my husband before the Assizes, we could let him out on bail. Only there's a risk and it must be paid for accordingly."

"I'll consult my friend," replied Roger coldly.

"I'm sure we would gladly pleasure your honour," whined the woman, leering up at him. "A matter o' twenty pounds and your honour's bond."

"Five pounds," answered Roger. The words seemed to come without his own volition, compassion was stronger than judgement. He strode past her back into the cell and interrogated Morley again.

"Have you no neighbours who'll go bail for you, man? I mean who would go bond for your appearance at the Assizes? I don't even know where you live."

The scutcher gazed at him dully.

"Live? I used to live upon t' moor—up i' the wind and the sun," he muttered.

"Maybe the parson would be answerable?" suggested Dicconson.

"Aye, but he's no brass! Bonds and bail mean brass, dunnot they? Who's to pay twenty pounds or twenty shillings for such a carcase as mine?"

"There's not much against the rogue, your honour, and small profit if he dies on our hands," said Bayley, coming up behind him. "Pay the five pounds, Sir, and I'll engage to get him back when he's for trial."

He winked boldly at Dicconson as he spoke, and added hardily: "I always likes to keep on good terms wi' the gentry."

"I'll call again tonight," said Roger.

Hope had suddenly irradiated Morley's face; it was cruel to see the light die away, and Roger went out in deep trouble.

Good Mr. Clifton took the case philosophically enough as he and his friend refreshed themselves at the tavern.

"It is shameful, devilish to traffic thus in human souls and bodies," declared Roger vehemently. "In God's name can nothing be done to remedy it? Why, there was a mill in action and clippers at work in the very prison itself! The gaoler is a corrupt, vile fellow—"

"Gently, gently! My good Dicconson, Bayley was put in his place by Mr. Kenyon—a great man—a very great man indeed! He is a member of Parliament and lawyer for my lord Derby! Nay, nay, you'll find no one hereabout who'll see aught amiss with Kenyon's choice."

He lit a long pipe and sipped his glass of ale while Roger railed on. At last the young man took leave of his friend without having the satisfaction of feeling that he had moved him one iota from his attitude of benevolent indifference.

There was only one way in which Roger could possess himself of five guineas, and that was by selling his newly purchased horse. This would be absurdly quixotic, he thought, and would render him incapable of getting about to see his friends, save on brother William's sorry nag.

It was a warm evening: the air as he rode slowly home was impregnated with the fragrance of the wild honeysuckle which wreathed the wayside hedges.

"I don't hold with sentiment," Roger told himself, trying to harden his heart.

As he crossed a grassy upland a lark sprang up almost at his feet and soared into the warm air, showering down its silvery notes as it went upward in a series of darting flights.

Roger whirled his horse round and galloped back to the town. He was angry with himself and cursed his own weakness, but before dark, five golden guineas were flung on Bayley's greasy counter, and a haggard prisoner slipped furtively out into the street.

Bayley had been strictly warned to keep the affair quiet and not to name the scutcher's benefactor, but he considered it a good joke and made merry over it with his boon companions.

Hence when Roger visited the Cliftons some days later he was hailed with derisive applause by the company. Lancashire has ever had a fondness for nicknames, and Dicconson found the sobriquet "Weaver's 'Prentice" even harder to bear than the loss of his horse. He had been in hopes that this would have been taken as a result of misfortunes at play, and would have greatly preferred to be reproached as a gambler than to be praised as a Don Quixote. There were some merry suggestions that the scutcher must have a lovely wife, and Roger had retorted that if that were the case Morley would certainly have been left to languish in prison.

But when Roger walked abroad during the ensuing weeks and breathed the fresh moorland air, he felt that it was well worth personal inconvenience to have set at least one poor prisoner free.

CHAPTER ELEVEN

THE GARDEN at Wrightington Hall had been somewhat neglected owing to the rigour of the times, but it was nevertheless a very pleasant place; indeed Roger found its very wildness refreshing after the primness of the so-called "English gardens" in vogue on the Continent. Madam Dicconson had in no way conformed to the rage for clipped yews and coloured pebbles which had come into the country with the Prince of Orange. Nothing had been changed when the new hall was built—nothing indeed since the borders had been laid out in the reign of Queen Elizabeth: there was the pleached alley of limes, haunted by bees and perfuming the house now that pale green flowers dangled from the leaf couplets; the roses were untrimmed but marvellously sweet, for the red damask had been planted in great quantities to supply the still-room. The herb bed was inside the sunny wall which encircled the orchard and vegetable plots, and there was a long, smooth bowling-green adjacent to the house with a pollarded wych-elm at its farther end, and a bench where spectators might enjoy their long pipes in the shade. Cherries were already reddening and apricots and plums promised a good crop. Clumps of perennials grew at random, and great masses of irises had increased unchecked and now showed a mass of knotted corms in their centres. Lilies, too, had overflowed their allotted spaces and pushed forward their honeyed bells over the weedy paths; but these were fading now, roses and honeysuckle held the day. It seemed a sin to soil such

85

sweetness with tobacco, and Roger strolled about, his church-warden in his hand, now inhaling the garden fragrance and now a puff of virginia. He felt at peace with himself and with the world, and well satisfied with life in general. No doubt in course of time William would obtain a lucrative post and would then be able to pay his brother at least a part of the portion due to him. Thus furnished, Roger would repair to London, pass all his Law examinations in brilliant style and begin immediately a profitable practice. People would begin to talk of Roger Dicconson, and Mistress Bridget Thornleigh would realize the value of the man she had thrown away! So ran his day-dream, while the light deepened on the tree-tops and turned the stable roof to molten gold and the vane to a glittering jewel.

The peace was suddenly, unexpectedly shattered by the arrival of a horseman: not dashing on mettlesome and romantic steed, but crawling along on ancient shaggy pony—a dusty figure in a shabby coat which Roger identified as the black-and-white of the Thornleigh livery. He turned his back and strolled away towards the hedge of sweet-peas, humming an air, and choosing a flower with meticulous care to stick in his button-hole. Even when old John rushed out ringing the dinner-bell to attract his attention, and the children came shrieking in search of him, he would not hurry the pace at which he returned to the house. He was annoyed to find his heart beating faster in spite of his nonchalant demeanour as he took the sealed note from the messenger.

"What is it, Uncle? What is it?" clamoured the boys. "Squire Thornleigh's Tom said he was bid to find you and to give it into your hands without losing a minute!"

"Indeed, Mester Roger, I never stayed for as much as a pint of ale," put in the man, who stood in the open doorway holding his sweating pony by the rein.

"Well, we can make that good at all events. Go to the kitchen, my lad, and, Peter, pray serve him a good tankard and put the nag in the stable with a feed."

He turned away, breaking the seal with studied calm. After all, there was not one word of Mistress Bridget in the letter, though the pretty, delicate writing might indeed be hers.

"My very dear Sir," wrote the old Squire, "I am a prey to my old enemy the quartan ague and must dictate these lines to be writ by a younger and steadier hand than mine. My son, just returned from London, brings heavy news with which I feel it my duty to acquaint you without delay. It appears that your brother hath been arrested while walking in the street, and taken first to a Messenger's house, and subsequently lodged at Newgate. My good neighbour, your sister, could by no means obtain leave to speak with him nor could she find out on what cause he is to be indicted. Feeling runneth very high against the folk of our nation, and my son considered it his wisest course to return post-haste to Lancashire and has but reached Thornleigh this hour. I trust that you will honour my poor house and come instantly to confer with my son if you consider that anything further can be devised to help your brother. My son believes the arrest to have been made on question of the *old trouble*: there is no question of debt.
"Your ever truly loving friend,
"William Thornleigh."

The old trouble! Roger stared at the paper. This must allude to the time when William was arrested four or five years ago when first the Prince of Orange seized the throne—hundreds of Catholics had then been thrown into prison and afterwards released. But now— The country was quiet enough today. Through the open window bird song poured in, the blackbirds were vyeing with each other, and the chaffinch struck through their golden measure with his loud, gay reiteration. Two pictures flitted before Roger's inner view: first the cell at Wigan lock-up with its wretched inmates chained to the filthy wall, then an inconsequent image of the Roman bird-catcher with his helpless prey beating their wings vainly against the cruel meshes of the net.

It was annoying that on young Dicconson's first visit to Thornleigh he should be compelled to ride a tired plough-horse, instead of "Noble," his spirited grey pad, but he was not the man to waste time in self-pity. He wore his new bag-wig and a waistcoat striped brown and canary, and a big sword-knot of white ribbon on his shoulder.

It was nine o'clock of a warm summer night when he clattered up to the stone porch at Thornleigh, and there were already lights in the hall and parlours. The old Squire, pinched and trembling with his illness, himself received him and brought him in. Mr. Nicholas was sitting over the polished table with a glass of wine before him, and the ladies of the family had brought in their tambour frames and sat grouped about him.

Roger bent as gracefully as he could over many hands, kissing old Madam Thornleigh's fingers gallantly but contenting himself with a distant *congé* to her grand-daughter. Bridget looked very dazzling in her new clothes, which shone in brilliant contradistinction to the well-worn tabinets and tiffanies of her family. Her hair glowed without a touch of powder, and she wore white with a narrow silver ribbon round her waist and little shoes with scarlet heels.

"Red at both ends, Bridget," muttered a scoffing cousin, but the girl tossed her curls unabashed.

After a few moments the ladies withdrew and a supper tray was brought in and set before Roger. Thornleigh waited until the servant had gone and then turned a serious face to his guest.

"Have you destroyed anything compromising among your brother's papers?" he inquired, and the urgency in his face startled the young man.

"No," he rejoined. "I know nothing of Will's affairs, and he would not thank me to pry into them."

"My dear young friend!" The Squire laid his thin, shaking hand on Roger's shoulder. "This is no time to be over nice. I dared not name it in writing, but the thing brooks no delay."

"But surely, Mr. Thornleigh, there can be no danger. A man of my brother's known integrity—"

"Pooh, lad, you've lived over long abroad," interrupted Nicholas Thornleigh. "Danger—why of course there is danger. Ain't every Catholic surrounded by sharks ready to swallow him alive? I know, Sir, we've got some honest neighbours," he added as his father made an inarticulate protest. "But none the less if you value brother William's neck, you'd best break open his cabinet."

"Do you indeed believe this?" stammered Roger, fixing his eyes anxiously on the old man's troubled face.

Thornleigh bowed his head, and his son burst out vehemently:

"I tell you I've rode and posted all the way from London without pausing so much as a night on the road. The pursuivants are at my heels no doubt, and we've nought to hide from them here." He stopped and then added somewhat lamely: "I think it but right to warn our neighbours."

"I've been over slow at the uptake, I doubt," rejoined Dicconson. "And with your leave, Sir, I'll return as soon as my horse is baited—poor old lad, he has a day's work in the field behind him as well as the journey here."

"'Tis a moony night," announced Nicholas, going to the open window and lifting a corner of the curtain. "I think, Sir," he went on, turning to his father, "that inhospitable as it seems, we had best mount the young man on daughter Bridget's horse and speed him away tonight."

"The little lass is but fresh home from school," remarked the Squire, "and we had a mount of our own breeding broken for her to ride. It's the best in our sorry stable, and I trust you'll ride him back tomorrow and taste our rough country hospitality."

Roger had reddened violently and looked the picture of misery.

"You are too kind, Sir," he muttered, and then added something indistinct about "painful events—somewhat recent."

The Thornleighs exchanged a glance and the Squire nodded gravely.

"Well, at some later date you will honour us, I trust," he said. "And for the nag you will have no scruple. Do you intend to go to town?"

"If you think there is occasion, Sir, I will go tomorrow."

"I think these are ill times," said Thornleigh. "God's will be done, we'll be ready to lay down our lives if need be for the old cause—our faith."

"But there's no general move against Catholics, Sir—we may be safe enough," protested Nicholas, and he filled Roger's glass and thought himself very tactful in not suggesting a move to the Oak Parlour where the ladies were still eagerly discussing the news.

Bridget Thornleigh peered out behind the heavy curtain as a horse clattered on the flags below. Her father's voice was raised, and the young gentleman with the white shoulder-knot was standing beside her own pretty chestnut cob. He mounted with vigorous ease, and flattered the creature's satin neck while he listened to Nicholas's parting words.

"Poor young gentleman!" remarked Bridget patronizingly as she returned to her embroidery, making a détour and passing behind the harp and the flower-stand in order that Grandmamma might not suspect that she had been so monstrous uncivil as to look out of the window. Buckland would have known the right thing to do at once, she felt sure, and would not have wasted time jogging over on a plough-horse and then going straight home again—on a borrowed steed!

Her father came in presently and stood, yawning portentously between phrases.

"I saw Buckland before I left town," he announced, as though answering his daughter's unspoken thought. "He was much put about to hear of neighbour Dicconson's arrest."

Bridget looked up with a bright, interested face.

"Mr. Buckland has such a kind heart," she declared. "I warrant he flew to offer his services to poor Madam Dicconson?"

"Faith, not he!" exclaimed Nicholas, and paused to gape, exasperatingly. "He has a feeling heart for himself and for a straight neck and keeps himself close in his lodging. Well, I'm for bed," he went on. "My legs are as stiff as a pair of stilts, I declare! I don't envy young Roger his two hundred miles tomorrow after riding thirty tonight."

"Nay, but he is going in the Flying Coach from Chester," observed Grandfather.

"It's a plaguey rough road as how 'tis," returned his son.

The family parted after a gentle reminder from Grandfather to remember neighbour Dicconson and all the other poor folk in danger in their prayers.

Bridget peeped out again at the quiet moonlight before she went to bed, but it was of Buckland that she was thinking, not of the lonely traveller trotting away between the level fields of springing corn—Buckland with his head so nobly set upon that strong throat! How could her father jest thus horribly! It was shameful that men should be so cruel as to threaten anyone so brave and gay.

Roger reached home at last—roused the wondering house, and laboured till the small hours emptying drawers and escritoires behind locked doors. He felt it dishonourable to examine his brother's papers, but dared take no risks: everything was flung pell-mell on the floor and then, by the light of a lamp, Roger hastily sorted: bills and unimportant notes and indentures he tossed back into the drawers, but tied up all letters from home or abroad in hastily assembled bundles. At last, lamp in hand, he approached the wide, smoke-stained hearth. There was a hiding-place on one side if only he could remember how to open it! As a child he had seen his father laying in a ciborium and the little pewter chalice, which on a later occasion of yet more pressing danger had been beaten flat and unrecognizable between two bricks. His fingers explored the panelling and memory acted mechanically; the spring was touched, the panel slipped aside. Roger noted that the wheel had been well oiled and that there was no dust on the packets of papers already occupying the shelves within.

Mrs. Tabby was in great consternation next morning when news was brought that her young master had passed the night in one of the library chairs and had gone off to London at dawn. She was yet more alarmed and indignant when a few hours later a King's Messenger, accompanied by a magistrate and a posse of constables, came knocking on the door.

"The gentlefolk are all away!" exclaimed the old lady, vainly trying to prevent their entrance. Her wheel-chair and its gaping attendants were pushed aside, and the house was searched, while the magistrate stood by, unmoved by her protests.

The Squire's locked desk was broken, and beds pulled to pieces, but the Messenger's men returned empty-handed, save for a couple of ancient fowling pieces found in the gun-room and the blunderbuss which had hung over the hall mantelpiece from time immemorial. Seals were set and vague threats uttered, but no reply was given to old Tabby's anxious queries. Instead the most extraordinary questions were propounded:

How many Irishmen did her master keep hid about the precincts, and where was his store of arms? Was it not a fact that he often received visitors o' nights at an hour when all honest folk were asleep?

"I wonder at you, Sir John!" declared the old woman, turning indignantly to the Justice of the Peace. "How can you stand by and hear the poor Squire miscalled this way! Didn't you and his father sit on the Bench together year after year! I wonder at you, I do! There's no men in this place—nobbut the honest lads from the village."

"As for visitors," put in the old groom, "it's rare we have a visitor here, unless 'tis the owd lady from Standish as rides over with sugar sticks for the children."

"If you claim the best fowling-piece, I'll have nought to keep down vermin wi'," struck in the ploughman who acted as a kind of honorary keeper. "And then you'll have small sport next winter when you come to shoot Squire's pheasants."

"Well, woman, 'tis your master's own fault. If he went to church as he should, he'd not lie open to suspicion," exclaimed the Messenger impatiently.

"Humph!" snorted Tabby, undisconcerted. "I heard some talk o' Lord Willoughby calling sodgers out to shut up one o' your churches the other day—what was that for?"

"She means the Presbyterian chapel at Kelsey," murmured Sir John Rowton.

"Very likely," chimed in Tabby. "Presbyterians was all the rage, as t' saying is, when I was a girl. But we Lancashire folk follow our fathers and we don't change the same as politicians. William is maybe not the man his father was, but he's jannock for all that."

"You admit they are all Jacobites here then?" asked the Messenger sharply.

"La, no, man! 'Tis the Crown they stand by," retorted Tabby, who was shrewd enough. "We're noan Jacobites this side o' the country. They're more like to be that up in your part, Sir John, nearer the border. We're right Lancashire here."

The Messenger and his party rode away without further comment, and Tabby returned in triumph to her still-room.

Chapter Twelve

Lizzie Dicconson came down to the parlour with her eyes red and swollen from crying. Her young uncle did not inspire much confidence, as he sat stifling his yawns, his great muddy riding-boots stuck out before him and his face haggard with fatigue.

"My mother is out," she said. "Aye, my poor mother spends her whole time driving from one place to another in a hired coach. But the great folk won't see her, and the big lawyers won't accept the fees we can give, and it seems as if—"

"But what was your father arrested for, child? Surely you can tell me that!" interrupted Roger.

Lizzie opened her eyes very wide.

"For politics, I suppose, Uncle! But they never say till a man is brought to trial for fear he'd get witnesses to prove he didn't do it."

"Didn't do what, Lizzie?" How incoherent the girl was!

Lizzie thought her uncle very stupid.

"Why, didn't do anything for the priests or King James, of course! That was why they arrested all the Catholics before— on the plea that they were conveying estates to Jesuits or Friars—'twas three or four years ago, just after the Revolution. Surely you must remember for all you were in France then?" she asserted.

"I never heard the rights of it. Your father and his friends were not brought to trial, I believe, though they were detained awhile in prison—was that it?"

"Yes—it came to nought in the end. But everyone says 'twill be worse this time." She began to cry again, adding through her sobs, "My mother went to Mr. Atherton herself—he's considered the best Counsellor-at-Law in London—my Aunt Mary went with her—and they said they'd raise five hundred pounds if he'd defend my father, but no—he would not."

Roger consoled the girl to the best of his power. He was glad to hear that his sister, Madam Culceth, was in town, though rather afraid of being overpowered by feminine lamentations when he desired rather to take counsel of some keen masculine intelligence. Having lived almost entirely among men and boys for the last eight years, he was disposed to a patronizing view of female judgement.

When the two ladies returned he found that he had underestimated their powers. There were no tears: Sophia Dicconson looked so wan and aged that Roger could scarcely recognize the buxom, voluble matron of a few weeks since. Mary Culceth, after a brief, affectionate greeting to her brother, returned immediately to the matter in hand.

"Have you thought to go through the papers at Wrightington?" she inquired. "That's well—in a case like this even proved familiarity with a suspected family might destroy innocent lives."

"And I would not that any should suffer from their friendship with us," added Madam Dicconson.

Her voice was hoarse with the fatigue of useless, reiterated pleading, and Roger was touched to the quick that her thought should be of others at such a pass.

"I cannot believe it to be as serious as you fear," he urged.

"You don't know," returned Mary. "It is what is ever done here. If the folk aren't over loyal, there's talk of a plot against the life of the sovereign. It rallies all his supporters for they fear to fall with him if he dies. It makes the King popular and there are always some pickings for those who bring information to help the King's Evidence."

Roger looked round to assure himself that the door was fast closed and that there was no danger of being overheard. Then he gazed steadily at his sister-in-law and asked bluntly:

"Did my brother take part in any plot? Is there any iota of truth in what might be urged against him?"

"None," she rejoined.

Mary was more explicit.

"Why, of course you know, brother, we were all a deal happier under King James!" she exclaimed. "Catholics could lift up their heads and breathe again, and if he came back 'tisn't likely we would draw swords against him. But to plot against the Government is another thing and William never did that, nor would he hear it spoken of."

"Then we have nothing to hide and must get a good counsel forthwith. If we only knew what witnesses there are to be against us! We must have money, that's a sure thing."

"'Tis hard to come by with the estate settled and the boys not of age," returned his sister-in-law.

Roger was convinced that it would be easy to raise a sum from friends, and tired as he was, he set forth directly he had changed his clothes, to return exhausted and heart-sick late that night.

One of King William's first acts on taking possession of the throne had been to forbid Catholics to live in London or Westminster. Many Catholic houses had been burnt by the mob, but in the ensuing years of comparative toleration, adherents of the old Faith had crept back to their homes. Now once again danger had suddenly loomed up, and Roger was refused admittance by some, and treated with the greatest constraint by others. At last in desperation he pledged his watch and ring in return for a loan. He had never before realized how difficult it was for a Catholic to raise money at a pinch.

In the next few days rumours reached London of the arrest of other neighbours. Lord Molyneux lay ill under guard in his own house, where fifteen Dutch troopers and their followers were quartered upon him. Mr. Legh of Lyme, Mr. Philip Langton, and Sir Roland Stanley were in custody at Chester Castle. Mr. Walmsley had been taken at his lodgings in town and was confined in the house of a Messenger: his friends were not allowed to visit him, nor could Roger get leave to speak with his brother.

He was determined not to allow himself to be discouraged, and returned so often to Colonel Leveson's door that he at length gained admittance, though he had been told repeatedly that the gentleman was out of town. His whilom comrade greeted him very coolly, but Roger schooled himself to show no resentment.

"It is unfashionable, I know, to stand by a friend in adversity," he declared. "But this will not weigh with you."

"Faith, but it does weigh, and confounded heavy too!" rejoined the other. "But converts are all the rage—converted rakes are best—the ladies like them! You must contrive to gull a bishop. Burnet, 'tis said, is easy flattered—or there's Hooper—the Queen is monstrous devoted to Hooper!"

Roger stared at Colonel Leveson in blank amazement, quite unable to follow this line of reasoning.

"But, my good Sir, I doubt bishops are of no avail here," he interrupted at last. "I want you to get the ear of the Queen or at least of Lord Nottingham, and obtain for me an order to the Governor of Newgate, giving me leave to see my brother and take steps for his defence."

"But you're not a *persona grata*, my dear friend!" exclaimed the Colonel. "You have kissed the Pope's toe, or belong to his party at all events! Her Majesty would positively shudder at you! Faith, she'd smell brimstone if you entered the precincts of the

Palace! You might as well be a follower of the Princess Anne as a Catholic—I can't put it more strongly than that!"

Roger laughed in spite of himself. "Am I to abjure my religion then?" he cried. "No—a thousand times, no! If the shadow of the scaffold must fall upon us, doth it not behove every man to stand yet more loyally for the Faith?"

"But it is so plaguey inconvenient!" complained Leveson. "And you could easily make it right with the Jesuits afterwards. Indeed, I suppose you could buy an indulgence in advance. 'Tis only a question of policy."

"I must commend you as totally free from the vice of curiosity," cried Roger. "You are ready to accept such ridiculous misrepresentations of what Catholics believe and yet you never inquire what's the truth of them! But we've no time to spare—enough that I hold my faith dearer than my life and so does my brother, and we would far rather be unjustly branded as traitors than behave as false Catholics. But as to that, why must religion be involved? Several Protestant gentlemen are to be indicted—young Mr. Legh, for instance, and Sir Roland Stanley."

"'Twill be given a papist flavour though—you'll see! Jacobite and papist—'tis all the same thing just now. And the country is always pleased to be told there's a papist plot. However, if you'll not take my advice, I'll"—he hesitated—"I think—I'll—yes, I'll give you a letter of introduction—"

"No, no," said Roger very seriously. He jumped up and took his friend by the hand. "You will wait upon Lord Nottingham yourself—"

"The Lord Shrewsbury is the proper man," interposed the other.

"Or the Lord Shrewsbury then. And you will come away with my permit in your hand."

"Bless the man! It's not done like that. Why, the Queen must be consulted—she looks into everything while the King is abroad."

"Nevertheless you will obtain it for me," insisted Roger. He saw that he had made an impression, for in spite of his foibles the fop had a heart.

Next morning early, Dicconson waited upon Mr. Legh Bankes, the Counsellor-at-Law who had occasionally transacted business for the family.

The gentleman was in, but his countenance fell when the name of his visitor was announced.

"It's a devilish difficult case, my dear Sir," he interrupted pettishly, almost as soon as Roger had begun to speak. "The Government wants scapegoats and it wants money, and their witnesses are as thick as blackberries—and as cheap!"

"But there is the Jury to be reckoned with—let alone the Judges!" exclaimed Dicconson. "There are still Englishmen with a spark of justice in them who won't see their innocent countrymen done to death!"

"You are young and innocent!" returned Bankes, leaning back in his chair and pushing up his wig on his flushed forehead. "Yet you must know yourself that scores of these honest North-country squires have drunk a cup or two in honour of King James, thinking no harm; folk that never meant to strike a stroke—folk that wouldn't hurt a fly! And think you, when all the rascals in the country went about after the King's Messengers, and whipped my lady's horses out of the coach—think you there were not those who wished the old King back on the throne? Aye, and with an oath to it?"

"Well, but surely a man can't be hanged for that?" protested Roger. "'Tis but five years since James was our lawful anointed King, and the whole country swore fealty to him."

"Best forget that now," said Bankes. "Oates, whom the Law still regards as a perjurer deprived of civil rights, is in receipt of a handsome pension from our present noble lady, the Queen. What think you of that? Perhaps the Crown would not be so pinched for funds, were there not such a heavy leakage on the Secret Service list."

"But now as to my brother—" Dicconson began again.

"Why, as to your brother, I have other clients in the same case. Old Madam Legh of Lyme went on her knees to me yesterday—faith, Sir, these be ill times."

The attorney spoke with a certain zest nevertheless, and Roger divined that the man's fighting spirit was already roused.

"If a gentleman of spirit set the example of fighting a case such as this and vindicating the innocent, it would be a triumph indeed," he declared. "Here is my brother without a shadow of guilt upon him and sure Mr. Legh is the same—a worthier good gentleman never stepped shoe-leather, as we say in the North, and—"

"Yes, yes, granted, Sir, granted!" exclaimed Bankes testily. "But it is by no means easy to prove that an accused person did *not* do a thing! How are we to discover what the indictment is, I should like to know? Or what witnesses that scoundrel Aaron Smith has up his sleeve? If they choose to call a game of bowls a 'treasonable gathering,' bringing the bowls into Court will not prove the contrary!"

"Nay, but the Counsel-at-Law will prove the contrary!" insisted Dicconson.

"How? He might impugn the witnesses of the Crown, if he knew anything to their discredit. But if he sees them and hears their names for the first time when they confront his client in the dock? My advice to you is to go back to Lancashire; be busy, find out any who have a spite against your brother and search into their past history. If they can be proved clippers or coiners or footpads, it is a slight weapon in my hand."

A thoughtful expression flitted over Roger's face: it occurred to him that Peg-the-Scutcher and her father might be helpful here. He nodded curtly.

"Aye, but I'd fain speak to my brother first. If I can get the requisite permission, will you accompany me?"

"Yes," returned Legh Bankes gravely. "I assure you I will do all in my power to assist these unfortunate men."

Roger experienced an unpleasant and most unfamiliar sensation of dread at the man's gloomy tone.

"They are not condemned yet!" he cried sharply, but Bankes made no reply other than a valedictory bow. In his estimation these lives were already forfeit to political expediency and private greed.

Roger found his heart thumping as he slowly descended the stairs; he was too deeply preoccupied to depress the hilt of his sword and the point of the scabbard trailed after him, tapping on every step. He had a bewildered feeling that every moment was of infinite value and yet he scarce knew where to turn or what to do first. He felt shame that such a system of injustice should be tolerated by a great nation, and reflected that we scarce notice abuses until they touch our own lives.

CHAPTER THIRTEEN

RIDGET THORNLEIGH was sleeping, wrapped in romantic dreams, when a loud, insistent knocking at the outer gate roused the dogs. The girl opened drowsy eyes: rain was beating heavily on the window and it was still dark; she turned over and was about to close her eyes again, when the dogs' clamour broke out afresh and she heard doors opening and closing on the floor below. Could one of the children be ill, she wondered? But no, the dogs would not bark just for folk stirring about inside the house. Maybe one of the new stacks was afire.

Bridget got up and looked out of the door. The passage was dark but a little flickering light illumined the end of the stairs. Now the noise began again: she heard loud, angry voices and blows on the great gate.

Wrapping herself in her coverlet, Bridget pattered down the stairs. In the big gallery, or landing, outside her parents' room a candle was flaring in an iron holder. Her father himself was standing at the head of the staircase in his night-clothes, his old darned nightcap pushed up over his anxious face.

"What is it, Sir?" she asked, disturbed and yet exhilarated at the emergency.

"I doubt they've come to arrest us," he answered. "Hark, Walter is parleying with them at the gate."

Bridget was quick-witted.

"Then do you go from the house," she cried. "Swiftly, before you are seen! They'll never arrest Grandfather, as old and ill as

103

he is! If you are not here they will but go through the house and away again and you can come back. Quick, Sir!"

But Thornleigh did not heed her agitation.

"I'll dress," he said calmly. "And do you hold them in talk till I come. I would not have them disturb my father, for such folk can be monstrous unmannerly. Your mother has gone to quieten the maids who were frightened. Put this round thee, and say I'll be with them presently."

Bridget obediently slipped her arms into her father's old frieze coat, which covered her to her little bare feet. She took up the rushlight and paused for an instant to contemplate her reflection in the mirror which hung at the angle of the stairs. Her appearance was undignified but not ungraceful, and fortified by this conviction, she hurried on and confronted the group of armed men, who stood shaking their dripping cloaks in the hall. One glance assured her that they were folk of the common sort—not a gentleman among them.

"How now, Walter, what does this mean?" she inquired sharply of the serving man. "What is the disturbance, and how came you to admit folks to the house in the night-time?"

"They have a warrant, Mistress Bridget," quavered the old man. "Three of 'em are King's Messengers and they've come to arrest our old gentleman, by all I can make out."

"My father will be down in a moment," announced the girl. She was still standing on the stairs, and as she looked down at the hard, cruel faces lifted towards her, a pang of fear shot through her being.

Instinct warned her that the six men who stared at her so boldly were utterly pitiless, and her girlish coquetry fell from her as she realized the imminence of danger to those she held most dear. Had Buckland but been here how safe she would have felt! But, as the woman Buckland loved, she was ready to do her part—to be worthy of him.

"Rouse the servants," responded the leader. "Look alive now, men, and search the house."

"There's no need to search," declared Bridget, standing her ground and even stretching out a slender arm to bar progress up the stairs. "My grandfather is asleep in bed—an old man, crippled these forty years, and just now shaken with ague—what should you arrest him for?"

"Treason," answered the fellow, and pushing rudely past her, he marched up the stairs, only pausing to fling his cloak, dripping with mud, upon the delicately stitched cushions of the long-legged couch in the gallery.

The girl flew after him, pursued by the jeering laughter of the posse as they scattered to their work. The door of the "Blew Chamber" where her parents slept was ajar, and her father came slowly out to meet them.

A small man, who wore his own hair, accompanied the Messengers and now twitched one of them by the coat.

"'Tis the old papist we want," he declared.

The officer had a loaded pistol in his hand, and Bridget's breath fluttered as she saw it pointed at her father.

"Show us the Squire's room!" shouted the fellow with an oath.

"No need to use violence," remarked Thornleigh. "His chamber is here, but he is ill—far too ill to accompany you."

He went before them and tapped at his father's door: Bridget heard the bewildered tones of the old gentleman suddenly roused from sleep, and presently he unlocked the door and showed his attenuated frame and haggard, fever-stricken face.

From the ground floor came sounds of heavy furniture being dragged about, and presently the crash of splintered wood as the Squire's beautiful rosewood desk was split by the blow of an axe.

Bridget suddenly turned and rushed back to her own room. These coarse, common men were masters of the house—no one dared say them nay! She had heard her mother's piteous tones:

"Stay but a moment! I will bring all the keys!"

A frenzy of indignation possessed her. Why should they be treated so? Why should a good, upright Englishman like Grandfather, lamed for life in fighting for the Crown, be subjected to such contumely in his own house?

Treason!

Bridget remembered the gibbet in Hyde Park which she had come on unawares one day while strolling with Buckland. She remembered the sudden stench poisoning the air, the blackened, twisted, dangling horror which had once been a man, and remembering, she fell upon her knees, and raised her terror-stricken eyes to the crucifix which hung beside her bed. But she remembered that even this was proscribed and sprang up to hide it away.

In a short time William Thornleigh came out of his chamber leaning on his stick. Bridget heard him ask to see the warrant, and the Messenger pulled a paper from his pocket and flapped it rudely in the old man's face. Her father was pleading that he should not be taken out in the raw night air.

"We will obtain a coach if you wait till daylight," he protested, but without avail.

Bridget's heart sickened as she watched the old man pushed and hustled down the stairs. He was limping more grievously than usual, and when they presently heaved him on to a horse, he could not stifle a groan of pain. She ran down to get a draught of wine for him: the Messengers were being detained meanwhile in a dispute with the house-steward, and her father was not to be seen.

"What is the matter, Walter?" demanded Bridget, as she came back with the empty goblet in her hand.

Thelwall related that his private desk had been rifled and the money it contained had been stolen.

"And that's the man who did it!" he ended, pointing an accusing finger at one of the Messengers who was called Womball. "'Twas one pound, eight shillings and sixpence."

"Well, Sir, how much money of your own have you upon you?" queried Bridget briskly.

"I have twelve shillings," retorted the fellow.

The young lady turned to the other Messengers.

"It is easy to prove who is in the right then," she observed. "Have the fellow searched."

"It is all my own money—it's a plot to rob me," declared the man.

The chief Messenger, however, gave the order and, in spite of his indignation, Womball was searched. Bridget stood by, and after the money in the man's pockets had been counted, suggested that his waistcoat and boots should also be investigated.

Coins were found tucked away in various parts of the rogue's clothes, and the search continued until the whole of Walter's store had been discovered and returned to him.

The old Squire was dragged off to Liverpool and his son, who had hidden himself for a few hours, presently surrendered to the nearest magistrate. His hope that this act would obtain his father's freedom was not realized, for the anxious household at home soon got news that both men had been sent prisoners to London. In this crisis Bridget became the mainstay of the household. She rode about the country, collecting news and rallying the spirits of friends and neighbours, a gallant figure in her mannish riding-coat with great cuffs turned back at the elbows. Her red curls were arranged for all the world like a gentleman's bob-wig—as the country damsels noted between horror and admiration—and the black hat perched atop was, in truth, an old one of her father's.

Day after day the Thornleighs waited for tidings, learning at last that their men had been committed to a Messenger's house in Warwick Street and later to Newgate. When Madam Thornleigh heard that Lord Molyneux of Croxteth had been arrested, she broke down completely.

"Bridget, Bridget child! If they are flying as high as Lord Molyneux, what chance is there for us?" she wept.

Old Mrs. Massey, who had come to visit her cousins in their trouble, answered sturdily.

"Nay, but the poor Lord is imprudent in his speech. 'Tis known where his sympathies lie, and you remember he was vastly troubled before—in '89."

"We'll have to get money for them," said Mrs. Thornleigh. "They'll be fast till the Assizes, I warrant, unless they have a special Court."

Bridget stood listening and swinging her hat in her hand to shake off the raindrops. As long as she could ride about and make believe that she was being useful, she felt fairly happy. But inaction was terrible: it was terrible to think that dear Grandfather might die for want of comforts—that Father would have to stand his trial. If only she could do something! She longed to go to London, but the older folk seemed to think such an expense out of the question. Susan was on the spot—but Bridget had not a very high opinion of sister Susan's brains or powers of contrivance! She had written that she had consulted Mr. Legh Bankes of Grey's Inn—a most insufferable, conceited, dry, tedious gentleman, in Bridget's judgement. Surely these affairs needed a bold, dashing, handsome man to carry them by storm! There only seemed to be one suitable man in the town to the girl's romantic fancy, and trembling at her own boldness she wrote to Martin Buckland and begged him to use his best endeavours on her father's behalf. Never in her life before had she sent a letter without the sanction of parent or Reverend Mother;

but until Martin or some of his kin-folk approached her father with an offer of marriage, it was difficult for her to explain how matters stood between them.

"Will you not trust me, sweetheart?" he had murmured at their parting. And he had pressed into her hand a tiny signet, with a hidden jewel, which she had since worn secretly about her neck!

But he had not written and sometimes she was shaken with gusts of sudden anger at his neglect. Yet had he addressed any letter to her Mr. Thornleigh might have considered it un-gentlemanly. 'Twas pity indeed, reflected the young lady, that people could not go simply about such a business—that folk could not speak frankly about matters which they had so much at heart.

A month had passed since the Squire's arrest and Bridget was riding back alone one afternoon from a visit to some kins-folk at Lydiate. It was early August, the hedges were wreathed with pink wild roses and the air was heavy with the smell of elder-blossom. The deep ditches which divided the fields from the road were full of meadow-sweet, forget-me-nots and flow-ering sedges. Bridget cantered along the grass which bordered the highway, and her spirits rose unconsciously. She could see the long, jutting wing of her home between the trees, and was about to put her horse at the fence and take a short cut across the meadows, when a man stepped out from behind a shrub and stood in the road as though to arrest her passage. Bridget reined in her horse so sharply that it plunged and her hat flew off into the ditch.

The fellow was a stranger and did not look like a footpad. He seemed to bear no arms, and after a moment's hesitation the girl advanced at a foot's pace, grasping her riding-whip in her right hand with the doughty intention of using it to defend herself, should it prove necessary.

To her surprise the stranger bowed low.

"Madam, I implore your forgiveness," he called as she drew near. "I have matters of the utmost importance which I must disclose to the Thornleigh ladies. Matters of life and death, and of mortal secrecy, Madam!"

He dropped his voice to a husky whisper at the last words, for the girl had pulled up a few yards from where he stood.

Bridget's first impulse was to wheel her horse and gallop away with all speed, but second thoughts followed speedily. She favoured her interlocutor with a very earnest scrutiny, which he bore without a change of countenance. The man was not so young as he had at first appeared; there were lines about eyes and mouth which might have been written there by dissipation. He wore a fair peruke and carried himself with the utmost boldness and assurance.

"If you want money you must apply elsewhere," said Bridget bluntly at last. "We know not where to find sufficient for our own needs."

"You have got your home still," he remarked. "And the old Squire and his son are living, breathing beings—not tarred, dismembered fragments dangling from poles and—"

"Oh, hush! Be silent!" she implored, horror-stricken at his tone. "They are innocent!"

"You'll find they'll be brought to the Bar on an indictment of treason, nevertheless—and the Crown is never short of witnesses. However, 'tis unsafe to speak here on the highway, and if you are not greatly interested, I'll say good day to you."

"If you were honest," faltered the girl, "and had evidence of importance to disclose, you would not seek to sell it."

"You are but a child, young Miss," said the fellow pertly. "But tell your mother that I shall lie at the 'Three Tuns' tonight since—plague on it—there's no inn at Thornleigh village. If she needs me, let her send for Mr. Taafe, at your service!"

"I think you had better wait upon my mother at once," remarked the young lady with a dignity of manner which might have impressed a more suitable subject. "I will ride ahead."

The two senior ladies of Thornleigh were of opinion that Bridget had been taken in by an impostor, but that it would be wise to receive the fellow none the less.

Old Walter, the house-steward, did not at all approve of the visitor's appearance: he crept several times to the door of the Little Parlour, and even applied his ear to the keyhole, but he could distinguish nothing but a low, continuous murmur of voices.

After Mr. Taafe's departure, a sense of subdued excitement spread through the house, and presently it leaked out that Mistress William and her daughter were off to London on the Flying Coach the very next day. There was little sleep for the inhabitants of the old house that night. The menservants were abroad with fowling-pieces and snares, the kitchen chimney smoked valiantly while the housekeeper and the drowsy maids prepared substantial pies and pasties to be carried to the prisoners. Bridget was ordered to bed when she had packed her valise, but she could not close her eyes. Now she lay shaken with terror—for Taafe's revelations had made manifest a danger before remote and shapeless—now tingling with excitement at the thought that she was about to take a share in the drama.

In her young self-confidence, Bridget felt sure that she was to act a victorious part, and by her intervention save the lives of father and grandfather. Was it not her determined accusation which had forced the Messenger to refund the money, stolen from the steward's room on the day the house was searched and the old gentleman arrested? Taafe's communication necessitated their instant departure for London, and once there, Bridget had her own plan for dealing with the emergency.

CHAPTER FOURTEEN

M R. BUCKLAND was not in the best of humours; he was a person who loved stir and company and he had now been forced to lie close at his rooms for nigh four weeks. He had considered it prudent to change his lodgings several times since May, when the two Jacobite agents, Colonel Parker and Colonel Crosby, had been committed to Newgate. More gentlemen had been arrested of late, and Buckland felt his own safety insecure. He was fully aware that the time was not ripe for a Jacobite rising. Though there were plenty of good country squires who were prepared to dine together, talk politics and quaff the health of the King over the Water, there were few arms to be had, and such volunteers as were likely to present themselves were quite untrained to military service. There was no system whatever for co-ordinating the groups of health-drinking gentlemen, and no proper census of available horses and arms had been made. Martin's own father had sent him word that it would be more prudent if he kept away from home for a time, as he was like to be a marked man, and the sudden return of a traveller such as he might bring trouble on the family. This intimation carried with it a very small draft for current expenses, which did not improve the young man's humour. When he called at the coffee-house where his letters were addressed and perceived, among miscellaneous accounts and bills, a missive in a lady's hand, he looked upon it merely as another complication. A glance within the folded paper made his pulses quicken—it was from Bridget Thornleigh. Though she had signed herself simply

"Bridget," he was instantly sure of her identity, and reflected somewhat cynically on the pressure he had himself put upon her to exert herself for the Jacobite cause. It would be mighty inconvenient if the charming creature intended to take him at his word! She had writ him imperatively to meet her at the chambers of Mr. Legh Bankes in Grey's Inn that very day.

He sat, weighing his cup in his hand and reflecting deeply. The coffee-house was cheap and unfashionable and its provisions correspondingly ill-prepared. Buckland had not dared show his face at Dick's or "The Rainbow" for an age. What did this letter mean? The wise thing would be to destroy it and think no more of the pretty wench. This whisper of treason made a man deuced uncomfortable, especially since the good Princess of Orange had had the happy thought of offering money rewards to informers. On the other hand, he would not willingly appear ungallant to any woman or at least to any fair woman.

"I'll go," he decided. Just once again he would allow himself to gaze into the eyes and touch the hand of charming Bridget. Gad, 'twas worth a little danger to see her face light up and her colour change! But he admonished himself that the thing must go no further. Unless, indeed, the musty old inn would provide a nook upon its worm-eaten stairway, where one might slip an arm round a trim waist and taste those honey-sweet, childish lips in a valedictory kiss. It must certainly be valedictory, for Mr. Buckland had no intention of marrying until a suitable heiress should present herself. A portionless country maid was quite out of the question.

"Doubtless she'll cry her pretty eyes out!" he muttered to himself, not without satisfaction, as he arranged his wig and studied the exact slope at which to set his hat before the dim square of mirror on the wall. The chamberlains watched him, laughing behind their hands and exchanging comments on the contents of the gentleman's letter. Martin always enjoyed being an object of attention, even though it was only that of a couple of pot-boys; he prolonged his posturing before the glass and flung the lads a fivepenny bit to drink his health as he finally strode out into the street. There he paused a moment, struck by the reflection that a lawyer's office was a strange place to choose for a lovers' tryst— then convinced that he was still being watched with admiration, he walked hastily on: it would never do to appear a laggard.

.　　　.　　　.　　　.　　　.

"I have undertaken the defence of these unfortunate gentlemen against my better judgement," announced Mr. Legh Bankes, repeating to Madam Thornleigh what he was careful to state to the anxious relatives of all the other defendants. "You are sensible, I presume, that I cannot appear for them in Court?"

"Is that the law?" faltered Madam Thornleigh.

Bridget leant forward, her eyes blazing with excitement.

"But, Mr. Bankes, we have very strange and startling information for you. 'Tis all a plot to steal the estates of the gentlemen accused."

Mr. Bankes, a dried-up, fairish man, who might have been any age between thirty and sixty, listened intently whilst Bridget poured forth the story of Taafe's revelation.

"The rogues have quarrelled already about the spoils, no doubt," he commented as Bridget paused. "I don't know Taafe but he mentioned Lunt, you say, John Lunt? There's a rogue of that name who was concerned against your father in '92 when he was accused of conveying estates to Jesuits and friars." He flicked over the pages of a ledger. "Aye, here it is, '*John Lunt*, also known as Captain Johnson or Jackson.' H'm, yes, he might be useful, but I have little trust in venal witnesses. 'Twill be said we've paid him."

"Yes, but that is not all, Mr. Bankes. He swears if we can find a gentleman of courage among our own friends, he will introduce him to Lunt as a necessitous person, anxious to obtain money, and not squeamish about perjury. He will then be able to discover all the wretches who propose to bear false witness and will disclose their villainy at the trial."

"Possibly—if he lives so long," commented the lawyer dryly. "Lunt has a habit of getting rid of his associates pretty smartly. At his last endeavour, both his confederates died violent deaths, I remember."

"I have no son in England," declared Madam Thornleigh, "else I doubt not one of them would willingly have taken the risk for father and grandfather. But as 'tis—to whom could we appeal? The double danger is desperate indeed—danger of murder on the one hand and danger of a cruel execution on t'other."

"Nevertheless I will guarantee to find the man!" exclaimed Bridget; her face was glowing, her blue eyes starry—even Mr. Bankes felt his heart stirred by her beauty.

As though in answer to Bridget's thought, there came a discreet knock at the door, and a clerk poked in his head to announce that a gentleman had come to wait on the young lady.

Madam Thornleigh, completely bewildered, gazed from one face to the other inquiringly, but Bridget was quick to act.

"You will allow me to see him alone, dearest Mother!" she exclaimed, and hurrying away, she closed the door behind her.

"Bridget! Gentlewoman!" gasped Mrs. Thornleigh as soon as she could draw breath. "What's the child thinking of?" She jumped up in such haste that her stiff hoop overturned her chair. "Pray, Mr. Bankes—"

"Nay, Ma'am," he interrupted, stretching out a snuff-stained hand to restrain her. "Let me advise you—leave the young lady to conduct the business. Rot me, if she'd turned those heavenly orbs on me, I'd have been weak enough to do her bidding myself."

"Ah, if you would, Sir! You with a shrewd, clever head and a man of the world withal. But that chit and her beau! Nay, Sir, here's a lot more mischief will be done. Let me to her!"

But Mr. Bankes laid his hand firmly on her arm.

"It is the best chance we have," he said urgently. "If the girl has chosen a gallant who has his wits about him."

They waited, both listening eagerly, and poor Madam Thornleigh praying aloud in little disjointed phrases.

"O good God, good God!—Have mercy, sweet Saviour—Mother of God, tender Mother—O plead for us! Nay, but my husband will be vexed if he hear of this!"

The time seemed long indeed, but in reality scarce a quarter of an hour passed. At length the watchers heard the clatter of manly boots on the uncarpeted stairs, and looking up found the door open and Bridget standing on the threshold, such an altered Bridget that Bankes could scarcely believe his eyes. Her beauty seemed all washed out, even her figure looked diminished as she stood drooping in the extremity of grief and shame. Her young face, ravaged with passionate revulsion of feeling, looked quite drawn and aged.

"I've failed," she whispered.

"My girl, my little poppet!" exclaimed her mother, holding out her arms, while Bankes stepped forward eagerly.

Bridget closed the door and leant against it, too stunned to notice her mother's agitation.

She forced herself to speak though her lips felt stiff and dead.

"What must we do now?" she said. Her whole world seemed to have fallen in ruins about her—life was done, but those dear ones in peril must still be saved. Martin Buckland had failed her: he had been quite cynical about it, evidently thinking her proposition ridiculous.

"Faith, I'll fight for you any day of the week, but even your pretty looks wouldn't lure a man into such a snare!" he had said. "A duel is one thing, but to court a dishonourable death—"

"To save the innocent," she had pleaded.

"Dear heart, you are indeed innocent to propose it."

He had been hardy enough to try and take her hand, but she had struck aside his fingers and bidden him go.

Buckland had protested, but in a light tone that pierced her heart. He had been glad, she thought, to be dismissed. No doubt acquaintance with such as she was more dangerous than sweet.

"I'll not grieve," she told herself fiercely. "He is not worth it. He never was the man I thought him."

Yet now while Madam Thornleigh and the lawyer tormented her with questions she felt as though her heart had really broken—it seemed so difficult to breathe or speak.

"It was Mr. Buckland, I suppose?" exclaimed her mother, swaying from anxiety to anger. "I wonder at you, Bridget, that I do, to make little of us all to that stranger."

(Yes, thought Bridget, he was only a stranger—she had not known the real man until today.)

"I hope he don't warn Lunt! The fat would be in the fire then!" commented the lawyer in some alarm. "Buckland—there are Bucklands down in Hampshire—but they are papists and keep themselves quiet. My dear young lady, 'twas a bad plan to call in anyone like that—I had thought you meant another young gentleman—one whose family is already involved."

And with an odious chuckle the tactless lawyer quoted:

"'Fair Bridget claims the life she saved,' you know! I jumped to the conclusion that your beau was Mr. Roger Dicconson."

"There were a chance!" exclaimed her mother eagerly.

Bridget had thought herself beyond the reach of all further feeling, but now the blood leaped into her pale face: there were then greater depths of degradation still.

"Oh, no, I couldn't! I couldn't!" she cried imploringly.

"The danger to your father and grandfather is very great," said Bankes.

117

Her mother said nothing, but Bridget, glancing from one face to the other, saw on both the same inexorable look.

"There must be some other way!" she panted.

"Oh, Bridget," whispered Madam Thornleigh, "what is a little humiliation compared to their lives? I'll ask the young man myself—nay," she added with a sudden agonized sob, "I'll go on my knees to him!"

"Not you, dearest Mother," answered Bridget. "But I will."

CHAPTER FIFTEEN

OTHER AND daughter conversed little on their homeward way, but once safely in their lodging, they turned to each other with full hearts.

"I doubt I ought to chide you," began Madam Thornleigh. "For my mind misgives me as to your conduct. But, Bridget, Bridget, I can think of nought but your father, and I needs must trust you to act as his daughter should. Yet—oh, child, to write to a strange gentleman without e'en a word to me!"

The girl looked at her mother mutely.

"I think thou's suffered too much to scold," said Mary tenderly. "Poor bird—poor lamb! I should have fetched you myself from the Convent. You were all too young and innocent to trust to Susan."

Many a parent would have shut up her child on bread-and-water or even have whipped her instead of folding her in her arms. Mrs. Thornleigh's conscience misgave her a little, and she endeavoured to introduce a few severe phrases among her endearments, uttered in that Lancashire idiom which the Thornleighs were wont to use familiarly in moments of emotion.

"Thou's done very wrong and I wonder at thee, but don't cry so, my sweet lamb! There, kiss Mother, and do not ever dare to behave so again."

After a few moments Bridget controlled her convulsive sobbing.

"We must think of my father now—only of my father and grandfather," she urged. "Remember it is tonight Mr. Taafe is to come to us—or rather to Mr. Bankes' chambers."

Madam Thornleigh thoughtfully regarded her daughter's tear-stained face.

"I will send a note to Madam Dicconson and suggest that we wait upon her tomorrow," she said. "And now tell me, child, about the young man. Is he of mettle to run this risk for—his brother, think you?"

"Oh, for his brother!" The coquette was not yet dead in Bridget, and a wan gleam lit up her drowned blue eyes. "That were hard to tell. He might have been more inclined six weeks since—had I asked him, but I fear I treated him monstrous unkind."

"Oh, child, not so as to make him an enemy? He'll not seek to be revenged, think ye, for the mortification you put on him?"

"Lord, no, Ma'am, 'tis a good honest youth I dare swear. Only—only—if we must ask such a favour I would 'twere of anyone else in the world."

"We'll put our own feelings on one side, daughter, in this strait."

"Yes, Ma'am, but what about his feelings? And is he clever enough for such a task, I wonder? For 'twill take shrewd wits and a steady head to compass it."

"There's no one else that I can think of," returned the elder woman after a pause. "Being newly come from abroad he'll not be known by sight as all our kith and kin would be. Go to thy room, child, and say the rosary for our guidance while I write to neighbour Dicconson, but see thou, Bridget—kneel not near the casement or where you might be seen."

Before Bridget left her convent school she had been reminded that in her native land the old Faith could only be practised in secret. Mother Abbess had pointed out that, although no doubt all the young ladies were aware of this fact, life in a Catholic country had engendered a happy freedom—rosaries and prayer-books were left lying about; crucifixes worn outside the dress—in England all this must be hidden away. As Bridget went slowly upstairs she reflected how much easier it had been in the Convent to keep up all the observances of religious life. They were roused in the morning by the Angelus bell and began the day with the thought of the Incarnation of Our Blessed Lord. The first spoken words were the beautiful words of the gospel: "The Angel of the Lord declared unto Mary... The Word was made Flesh and dwelt amongst us."

The first thing young eyes fell upon was the image of that spotless Mother with her divine Son in her arms. Then came Mass in the Chapel, the bell again at noon and dusk, grace before meat, holy pictures in every room! Instead of thanks for even the slightest service rendered to a nun, a gentle murmur of "God reward you," and even when one walked out of doors there were the crosses surmounting all the churches to remind one of God's love. Bridget sighed: her little crucifix hung round her neck inside her gown, her rosary was hidden away in her box. She went to the window and looked out at the people hurrying by. Had this been France there would have been a shrine with a lighted lamp at the street corner, as there had been here in old days, before the cry of "Idolatry" had torn away all that could bring the comforting thought of the Divine Humanity into constant remembrance amid daily toil and woe. She knelt down but with a heart still seething with anger and pain.

"I'll never trust any man again—I'll never love again," she murmured.

Perhaps Buckland had laughed with his fellows at such an easy conquest! Perhaps it had even embarrassed him! Her cheeks burnt with mortification at the torturing thought.

"I'm in no mood to pray," she cried aloud, jumping up from her knees. Then she forced herself down again. "At least I can offer up this pain! I *will* do so, I will!"

No words would come, not even the familiar ones of the Paternoster. It seemed as though she could only creep in spirit to the foot of the Cross, and offer her tiny sacrifice with that great Sacrifice, unite her humiliation with the love of that sinner whom the Saviour had chosen to stand beside His blessed Mother, purest of all created beings, at the hour of His death.

Bridget was still on her knees when her mother called her urgently:

"Get your mask and hood, child. Here's Madam Dicconson begs us to wait on her this very moment. She has sent a hired coach for us."

Bridget sprang up and then stood for a moment irresolute, wondering what this hurried summons could well mean. Madam Thornleigh called again, and the girl snatched up hood and mantle and ran down the stairs.

Sophia Dicconson awaited them in a state of suppressed excitement. She met them at the door and in a hurried whisper imparted the information that she had a visitor.

"Mr. Taafe, I'll go warrant!" exclaimed Bridget irrepressibly.

Madam Dicconson assented in surprise.

"Aye, my mother had a letter half wrote to you when your messenger came," went on the girl.

"Then you know the business, neighbour," said their hostess, with a repressive glance at Bridget. "We must not speak on the stairs. He is above in the withdrawing-room, so come you into the dining-parlour."

She led the way and carefully shut the door behind her visitors.

"Now how to find the man who will have courage to mingle with these fearful villains?" she asked.

"We had thought of your brother-in-law, Roger," answered Madam Thornleigh bluntly.

Sophia's tired face paled.

"Roger—he is so young and inexperienced—and then 'tis such a slender chance he be not detected. Oh, I dare not ask Roger!"

Even as she pronounced the words, the door opened and the young man himself came hastily in. He stopped short at the sight of the visitors, and Bridget thought a shade of annoyance passed over his face as he recognized them and bowed.

"I have got the permit, sister," he cried then, turning to Madam Dicconson. "You can see William today." He was holding the precious paper in his hand, and now glanced inquiringly from one grave face to the other: "Why, is there news? What is it? Did I hear you say there was something you dared not ask me?"

The elder ladies questioned each other with troubled glances, when Bridget suddenly took the lead.

"There is something which I want to ask you," she said. "But we must speak alone."

"You do me too much honour," responded the young man, and he promptly opened the door and stood aside for the two matrons to pass out. When their rustling hoops had brushed by, one after the other, he closed the door and turned expectantly to Bridget. What could she have to say to him, and why should her mere proximity have the power to raise such trouble within him?

"Won't you sit, Mistress Bridget?"

"Nay, Sir."

She stood before him, clasping and unclasping her hands.

"Would it help you if we pretend that we meet now for the first time?" he suggested kindly.

Bridget raised her heavy eyes, fixing them on his face.

"I am looking for a very brave man," she said. "And I'll not deceive you—my first thought was of Martin Buckland—"

Roger stepped back as though he had received a blow.

"But he refused me," concluded Bridget in the same level tone.

"And what commands have you for me, which Mr. Buckland was too nice to accept?" inquired Dicconson sarcastically.

"Not commands," corrected Bridget; she added bitterly: "'Tis a request I made to Buckland on my knees."

"You won't kneel to me, however," said Roger, with a short laugh. He marched forward and taking her hand stiffly, led her to a chair. "Now, have done with heroics, Miss Thornleigh, and tell me plainly what is the matter. Come, what business is the brave man to undertake?"

"Do not say anything till I have quite finished," pleaded the girl. "I have begun badly and perhaps offended you, and indeed you have no cause to love me—to wish me well, I mean," she added hastily, for Roger had jumped up at the unlucky phrase and had marched over to the window, where he stood with his back to her in the most impolite way in the world.

"I cannot keep to forms and weigh every word!" cried Bridget petulantly. "If I were a man, I'd do this myself to save my poor father, and all the rest of the gentlemen, or if I had a brother I'd ask him—"

"I'm not your brother," interrupted a sulky voice from the window.

"This is the affair," continued the girl rapidly. "A person called Taafe—one of the conspirators who are plotting against our relatives—is prepared to betray his comrades, and promises to introduce a man among them to find out all their designs, if we can discover anyone willing and able—to—to—"

"To personate a villain, a perjurer and a would-be murderer?" commented Roger smoothly. "I am flattered that you chose Buckland in preference to me."

"Don't mock me!" cried Bridget. "Do you think I don't understand the danger? If a woman could do it, do you think I would ask another to dare in my place?"

He looked at her more kindly.

"I wish you had thought of me first! Is this fellow Taafe here? Shall we go to him?"

"Yes, but first I will tell you all I know," said Bridget.

Dicconson sat down near her, listening attentively but not looking at her as she spoke.

At the end he was silent for a few moments and Bridget, stealing a timid glance at him, met his eyes.

"I want you to promise me something," he said abruptly. "I want you to promise me very solemnly that whatever happens you will not personally do anything more in this matter. You must not see Taafe or any of his crew again. May I have your promise?"

"I don't know," answered Bridget doubtfully. "Circumstances might arise—"

"Believe me, I know what I am asking," urged Roger. "I will do my very utmost to save our people, but it is safest for us all that I act alone. You are too innocent to know what devils these creatures are—I could not have an easy moment if you—"

He stopped suddenly in the midst of his vehement appeal, fearful that she might resent his tone or imagine that he spoke from selfish motives.

Bridget understood and was touched. "I'm not afraid of danger," she declared. "And I beg of you to let me share it if I can be of any help. But I promise, since you desire it."

"Thank you!"

He made as though to take her hand, but checked himself and stood up rather awkwardly.

"Well, Bridget?" whispered her mother eagerly as her daughter led Roger Dicconson into the room where Mr. Taafe and Madam Dicconson were seated in close talk.

"He undertook the business very readily," answered Bridget.

Her eyes followed Roger and her heart sank. He had such a fresh, free country look about him, and he was so young: handsome too—any maid might have loved him! And she, who had no love to give, had required him to walk into a trap from which he might never emerge alive.

Chapter Sixteen

HERE WAS NOTHING heroic or inspiriting in the part which Roger was now called upon to play. He entered into it with a dogged determination, and after arranging a rendezvous with Taafe at which he was to be introduced to Lunt and the other plot-mongers, he called his sister-in-law aside.

"Here is the permit, my dear. I think you could get Mr. Legh Bankes to go with you to Newgate, and be sure you have a bribe for the gaoler ready in your hand. Say nought to my brother about me, for there is sure to be someone present, or hearkening at the door."

"William will think it strange," she objected.

"Never mind. Keep to the business of his defence. And do not fret yourself if you neither see nor hear from me for awhile. I'll have to go North, very likely. Keep your heart up, sister! And now tell me—where in London may I find a priest?"

She shook her head doubtfully.

"I scarcely know, for all the poor holy men have changed their lodgings since the whisper of fresh trouble. 'Tis a sad loss when Queen Catherine left England for one was always sure of a priest at Somerset House."

"Bishop Leyburn is at liberty now, is he not? I heard in Rome that he had been released from Newgate."

"Aye, but it is scarce safe to approach him, poor old man; he is for ever being harried by spies and pursuivants. Bishop Ellis has fled the country and Doctor Giffard is in France, too. There is the convent at Hammersmith, of course—they are always in touch with a priest there."

"What—is there actually a house of nuns in England?" exclaimed Roger in amazement.

"Oh, yes, brother, and schools for young ladies as well—one at Hammersmith and one at York. 'Tis the congregation of nuns founded by the Yorkshire woman Margaret Ward—those they used to nickname 'The Jesuitesses.' I only wish there had been a foundation in Lancashire so that I could have sent Lizzie, but 'twas too far."

"'Tis a strange Order," observed Dicconson. "They are not enclosed, I think, but go about among the poor like the Sisters founded by that holy priest in France—Monsieur Vincent they call him—I don't know his real name?"

"Yes, but France is Catholic, thanks be to God! Here the poor ladies have to wear lay dress. They teach catechism and instruct folk, and prepare lapsed Catholics to be reconciled— 'tis a great work."

She gave Roger full instructions how to find the house, yet when he got off the coach that afternoon and strolled to the place Madam Dicconson had described, he paused irresolutely.

There was a large country mansion standing in its garden, but just ahead of him a very gaily dressed lady had alighted from a post-chaise and had entered the door with the lack of ceremony which proclaimed the return of the mistress of the house. Yet the garden within the high wall rang with the sound of children's laughter and he could hear the pattering of many running feet—too many surely for a private family. He decided to knock at the door, which was promptly opened to him by an old woman in a plain black dress and cap. He inquired for "Mrs. Gould," which was the Reverend Mother's alias, and was informed that she had just come in and would be disengaged in a moment.

"I am a Catholic," said Roger frankly. "I want to see a priest. Here is a letter from my sister who is known to Reverend Mother—it will prove to her that I am no impostor."

The old lady smiled and went away in silence. She returned very shortly and asked him to follow her to the Oratory where Mr. Petre was hearing confessions. Roger noted that all the furniture in the chapel was easily movable, even the altar and the small tabernacle. The tiny lamp, which stood on one side of it, proclaimed the presence of the Blessed Sacrament. The only windows were high in the wall and the light was dim. The priest sat in a corner and the penitents went in turn to kneel at his feet. Two or three persons were waiting, one a poor orange-woman with her basket, the next a lady dressed in the height of the fashion. Dicconson knelt down and began to prepare himself without observing them more particularly. But though he told himself that this might be his last Confession and that it behoved him to get himself ready for death, his thoughts wandered. Our Lord was here, blasphemed and proscribed even as in the days of His life on earth. His true presence in the Blessed Sacrament was loudly denounced as idolatry in all the pulpits in the land. Yet how patiently He bore all, coming down upon the altar at the word of the priest for the comfort of the faithful few!

Roger prayed:

"I do believe—Lord, increase my faith! I hope in Thee—I love Thee."

There were no benches or kneeling chairs in the chapel; the floor was waxed and polished and spread with rugs like any ordinary parlour. A girl came in presently and knelt down a little way from Roger. She wore a hood pulled over her brow but he knew her at once as Bridget Thornleigh. He seized the first opportunity to move away nearer to the priest, and after Confession, when he had finished his prayers, he went out and was taken to the street by a side door through the garden. He thought himself unrecognized, and the idea irritated him and kept forcing its way into a mind which he strove to fix on serious matters. He was glad he had not saluted her—in church people should only think of their prayers—but perhaps it would have been friendly to wait for her at the door. No, on second thoughts he was sure he had decided rightly and must now cut himself adrift from all his respectable acquaintance. It was not as though the young lady had any kind feeling for himself: Buckland was the man on whom she had fixed her choice!

When Roger Dicconson emerged from the Convent, he told himself that he had doffed his own personality. He was now a cunning rogue called Dick Howard, with no scruples about any undertaking which would yield a profit even at the risk of the gallows. He visited various shops on his walk back to London. They were booths for the sale or purchase of second-hand clothes, and by degrees he succeeded in changing each article of dress: here buying a waistcoat, there selling his hat, until he was possessed of a completely different outfit. He obtained a lift on a wagon for the last few miles and finally sauntered towards Temple Bar. The tavern where he had agreed to meet Taafe was in a little alley called Butchers' Row just outside the gate, but the man himself was lounging against the wall on the city side and came eagerly to meet him.

"How goes it, friend?" cried Roger, taking him familiarly by the elbow. He was surprised to find that the man was trembling, though he tried to pass off his agitation with a nervous laugh.

"Rot me, I thought you was going to fail me," he declared. "Legh Bankes won't come, the cur, and if Lunt smells a rat 'tis all up with us."

"He will certainly do so unless you compose yourself," retorted Roger. "Come, let us take a turn to and fro in the court yonder, before we go to the 'Ship.' I have a notion I may have met this rogue before—a small, wizened rascal?"

"Now don't you be deceived with John Lunt, young man," murmured Taafe as he swaggered along at his new comrade's side. "He is a little fellow you could knock down with a tap, but he's a devil! He's as cold and as bold as brass so don't be took in by looks. He'd skin his own mother and he's four wives if he has one."

"That must be somewhat awkward," commented Roger.

"He'll ask you if you can write a good hand," continued the other rapidly, "for I know he wants someone to write out the commissions—"

"Commissions—what commissions?" interrupted Roger.

"Why, man, don't play the simpleton or all's lost! The whole plot is concerned with the commission which King James has entrusted to Lunt, you and me to distribute among his adherents in England. That's the game—I thought you were fly?"

"So we begin by writing out the commissions—I suppose there's a model?"

"There's the copy of one—quite enough to go by. Lunt was employed to bring some over from Ireland long ago in '89, but I think 'twas merely as a messenger not an agent. He was go-between for two accredited agents, you understand, but they found him out and he's been scheming to make a honest profit of it."

"Was Lunt concerned in the affair two years ago—indicting gentlemen who were supposed to have conveyed estates to Jesuits?" asked Dicconson.

"Yes, with Dodsworth and Threlfall. They are dead." Taafe stopped short and glanced hastily over his shoulder.

"There was a man called Ellis too," prompted Dicconson. "He was one of the Crown Evidence, I believe—is he concerned in this?"

"No—Ellis disappeared." Taafe stealthily passed his tongue over his dry lips, and looked away as Roger glanced keenly down at him.

They had wandered into a secluded spot in the Temple garden, and after a moment's pause Taafe hurried on with his instructions. "Lunt will accept you gladly enough, for he told me he needed some gentleman-like person and that he could hear of none but glimmers, clippers, and such, who as like as not would give themselves away when they were examined."

"And what's a glimmer?" inquired Roger.

"Why 'twas a trade invented a score years ago, after the Great Fire: they are folk who have lost their all in a fire—they have to be decent-looking men, not too young, for they have always seven small children and a sickly wife dependent on them. 'Tis not a bad trade, but it can only be worked in town, of course."

"Well, I'm not a glimmer," assented Dicconson gravely. "You can tell Mr. Lunt that I have no trade but that I am anxious to make some money. I'm not a stickler for a special share in the properties to be obtained—I suppose they are to be shared?—so long as I am handsomely paid."

"That will do very well," agreed the other. "Mr. Smith was wrath, I know, because we had not provided better witnesses. Lunt was a highwayman once, and then a pot-boy, for all his grand airs, and Womball has been a pursuivant's man and has been branded for stealing—he's the broken carrier that's to depose of carrying arms."

"You had better propose me as a person who knows Lancashire well," suggested Roger. "I know all the landowners by sight and can point out anyone with whom he is not acquainted."

His heart was thumping uncomfortably against his ribs as he made the suggestion, but a daring idea had occurred to him which might perhaps turn the scale, unjustly weighted by these perjurers, in the prisoners' favour.

Taafe nodded.

"That's a good notion—aye, stick to that. And hold out for a stout fee, or he'll suspect you. Come, he'll be there now—let's to the 'Ship.'"

"What other witnesses are there, besides Wilson and Womball?" inquired Roger, trying to speak in a casual tone. Taafe reminded him of a rat, for all his smart clothes. His little eyes continually roved about and never seemed to fix themselves on any object. Now, as he glanced up, his gaze seemed to flicker over his interlocutor's face.

"How should I know? Lunt is as close as wax," he answered. "Maybe some of the wives?"

As there was no answer Roger tried a further query. "Are any other gentlemen to be indicted besides those in custody?"

"Why, I suppose two or three folk who may be at St. Germains now. We'll need have some more named—six aren't enough for a plot, though we've mixed in Protestant and Catholic this time to make it more natural."

As he spoke they passed into the crowded street which led through Temple Bar and went through the gateway into the medley of narrow alleys outside. Only freemen of the City of London were allowed to trade within the walls, but beyond the boundary were alleys crowded with wooden booths and "bulkheads" where country produce was exposed for sale, and brazen-throated apprentices bawled their masters' wares. As he made his way slowly along Butchers' Row, keeping well to the middle of the street, Roger's thoughts wandered to the gallant layman martyr Richard Langhorne who had laid down his life in the "Popish Terror" of 1679. He was a barrister and must often have walked this way from his house in Sheer Lane to his chambers in the Inner Temple. Roger had now deliberately placed himself outside the Law, and he was very conscious of this, as he followed Taafe into the ale-house with its sanded floor, slopped with spilt liquor, and its rough company of drovers and butchers.

The place smelt foul and it was all Roger could do to hide his disgust. Mr. John Lunt was leaning against the dirty counter engaged in a whispered conversation with the wench who filled the tankards.

Roger recognized him at once as his sinister acquaintance of the London Road and the City tavern. Fate seemed determined to bring them together, and though he had half expected it, he experienced an unpleasant little shock as he met the cold, bold stare of the plot-monger.

"We have met before, Sir," he remarked, assuming a dignified air.

"My friend I spoke on—Mr. Howard," put in Taafe.

CHAPTER SEVENTEEN

OR A LONG MOMENT the two men faced each other, Roger assuming an air of careless haughtiness, and Lunt a penetrating look as though striving to put the other out of countenance. At length he nodded and made a sign to the woman, who invited them to step upstairs into a private room. She went before them and ushered them into the apartment and asked what they would be pleased to drink.

Dicconson elevated his eyebrows. "Can one get anything drinkable here?" he inquired. "Have you any French wine? Or claret? Bring me a beaker of mulled claret."

"Best stick to ale or spirits," advised Taafe.

"Brandy?" queried Dicconson. "Let's try your brandy. Here!" —he flung some money on the table. "Gentlemen, allow me! A stoup of brandy, my girl."

Lunt had been frowning heavily, he now leaned towards Taafe and muttered behind his hand:

"I told you I wanted a gentleman. I have too many beggarly mechanics in the business already."

"Who says I'm not a gentleman?" countered Roger, with a little swing of the hip which brought the hilt of his small sword prominently into view. "Isn't Howard a good enough name for you? I tell you my family have borne arms for hundreds of years."

"When I met you before you said you had been abroad for your health," said Lunt with a sneer. "And your name was Harding."

"And when I met you the first time you were in company with as damned a lot of cut-throats as ever I saw!" declared Roger. "But here's the brandy—drink with me, gentlemen, it shall never be said that Dick Howard was niggardly. If you don't like my looks we'll go no further in the matter."

"You could not say fairer!" cried Taafe enthusiastically. "And indeed, Captain, my friend knows the North well—there's not a landowner in Lancashire or Cheshire he does not know by sight, and he can drink and game with gentlemen as you see for yourself."

"I suit myself to my company," said Roger with a grin, tossing off his brandy in a few gulps and wondering what the result would be. It made his head sing and he reflected ruefully that he would have to swallow quantities of bad liquor before he came to the end of this business.

Taafe went on whispering:

"He's been in nothing before—no, he's had no misfortunes of any kind."

"Well, Mr. Howard, before we go further with this business you must take an oath of secrecy," declared Lunt. "We are engaged on very great matters, such as will be the ruin of many, and I'll not open them to you further unless you take the oath."

Roger had not expected this, and he felt himself redden, but he passed it off by a pretended explosion of anger.

"Damn it all, Captain, you mistake your man!" he exclaimed. "I'm not the sort of person that is in present want for a crown or ten shillings. I must have a notion of what terms you offer before I decide about joining you."

"There's money to be gained," said Lunt cautiously.

"Oh, if it is but a question of a crown here and a shilling there, no doubt you'll find plenty to serve your purpose," returned Roger, filling up Lunt's glass. "But if I saw a chance of making my fortune—"

He broke off.

"We've gold for a hundred thousand pounds!" boasted Lunt. "And the informants are to have a third part of all estates that are forfeited to the Crown after the prosecution."

"Say you so?" Roger appeared unconvinced. "But then there are other witnesses besides you and myself. This Womball now seems to me a very dull, silly fellow. He will spoil all to my thinking. I cannot entertain the notion of coming in with you if Womball is to be a party to it."

"You are right, Mr. Howard. Both Womball and Wilson are blockheads and say nought but what I myself have taught them word by word. I would not have taken them in at all only that the Attorney pressed me so hard for more witnesses. He declared—"

He stopped, gazing doubtfully at Taafe for a moment, and then said bluntly:

"We'll not detain you, Taafe. 'Tis best Howard and I should settle terms between us. You can come to me tonight at my lodging—but not till after dark."

Taafe glanced vengefully from one to the other but dared not rebel. There was rather an awkward pause after he had left the room. They listened to his footsteps slowly descending the stairs.

"Do you know that gentleman well?" inquired Lunt.

"Well enough," returned Roger evasively. "But I agree with you—we'll come to a better understanding alone."

Lunt's face cleared. He understood this to be an admission that Howard would not allow his professed friendship with Taafe to stand in the way of a profitable deal, and came to the conclusion that he had found a confederate after his own heart.

Dicconson went on speaking, cautiously feeling his way.

"I believe I am as prompt to be able to make out a creditable account as another," he began. "But I've been abroad of late. I don't know all the prisoners by sight even."

"That's to the good then," cried Lunt, who was becoming mellowed with his potations. "They won't know you in that case and so they can't bring any objections to you as a witness, which they would be like to do otherwise."

"I had not thought of that," answered Roger truthfully. "But have you no fear that the prisoners may lodge an objection to you?"

Lunt laughed triumphantly.

"Nay, they have tried that already," he declared, "for Mr. Aaron Smith, the Solicitor to the Lords of the Treasury, told me so himself. He gave them short shrift, I warrant you! Nay, he protested he would not allow the Crown Evidence to be interfered with."

Roger's heart sank at this news, but he forced himself to laugh.

"Why indeed, you appear to have managed everything to admiration!" he exclaimed. "And of course *you* know the prisoners well and can point them out to me, and anyone else you mean to include?"

"Of course," returned Lunt. "Or if I do not 'tis easy to find a way. I can get Sir John Trenchard to make out a warrant for a person and then go with the Messengers to arrest him. In this way I can have a good look at him and swear to him afterward when need arises."

"Faith, that's a clever idea!" cried Roger. "The Dicconsons now—do you know them?"

He looked Lunt squarely in the face and brought out his question boldly.

"Do I know the Dicconsons?" repeated Lunt, with a sharp sidelong glance. "Certainly I know the Dicconsons. Hugh, William and Roger. I brought them all their commissions and handed them to them with my own hands."

Roger felt a little breathless as he stood considering the villain who uttered this lie with such a bold countenance. Was it possible that he was detected? His mouth felt dry but to pause overlong was dangerous.

"I'll swear against Roger Dicconson in particular," he said in a low voice. "I know him at least—but I'll not swear without a good reward."

"And so you shall swear," returned Lunt genially. "We'll hang all the Dicconsons, and as to reward, have no fear—the Attorney-General, and Sir John Trenchard and Lord Bellamont are all generous, free-handed gentlemen."

"But there have been so many plots that have come to nought," objected the supposed Howard. "There was the plot of '89 about money being set to superstitious uses and lands conveyed to Jesuits—no one was a penny the better for that, they say."

"Nay, 'twas mismanaged," agreed Lunt. "I was in that very thing but it miscarried, for there were fools and knaves in the company. I believe you will suit me very well, Mr. Howard, and I am glad to be concerned with a gentleman—hitherto I've had to deal with a parcel of mechanics, but now I'll put them off, if you'll join with us—I'll get rid of them."

"I must know something of the business first," said Roger. "I'm willing enough to get money, but I doubt this is an affair of some consequence?"

"Well but here's the whole thing planned forth in writing," said Lunt proudly. "Captain Baker, our clerk, wrote it out for us in good form, and Mr. Smith finds no flaw in it. And who should know but he, since he managed a plot or two of his own before he became Treasury Solicitor!" he added with a mocking laugh.

Roger took the paper, which was headed: "The Information of Mr. John Lunt, Gentleman, given the 15th day of June 1694," and as he ran his eyes rapidly down the closely written pages, he endeavoured to plan what his next move should be.

"This informant upon his oath saith" were the first words. The paper was long but gave few substantial statements as to places and dates. It set forth that "this informant" had followed King James to France in 1688 and had made ardent protestations of being his loyal follower. That my lord Thomas Howard (without any evidence of long acquaintance with Lunt) had told King James that he would "engage Life for Life for him this Informant that he would not betray him in the Service and that if he were taken would rather die upon the spot."

"These are strong words," protested Roger, pointing to the paragraph.

"Aye," agreed Lunt with the satisfaction of an author convinced of successful accomplishment. "But I had to pretend to be within their secret counsels else they would never have trusted me with the affair of taking off the Prince of Orange."

"For murdering the King!" exclaimed Roger, genuinely startled.

"Oh aye, you'll find it all there," said Lunt. "Aaron Smith and Captain Baker have been carefully over it, and have amended it in several particulars, I think now it can stand. I would have had a written order from King James for the taking off of King William, but Baker decided 'twas too hazardous."

"But murder! That is surely going too far," protested Dicconson.

"No, not at all. Smith said we must have something new: the public are used to Declarations and Commissions and so forth. But an attempt on the King's life is always a good draw."

He had risen and now, leaning over Roger's shoulder, turned over the pages and ran his dirty thumb-nail along the lines.

"'Tis somewhere here. I think we made it a promise of five hundred per annum to the three men concerned. 'Twas to be done at a convenient time when the King was a-hunting. Now read swiftly for you must swear all this is true."

Roger noted that the informer made no pretence of having been in any way shocked at the suggestion that he should make one of a gang for the "taking off" of King William, though he went into details of the reward to be earned by the successful accomplishment of the murder. He represented himself as the trusted go-between of the Jacobites, and Roger noted that only two of the prisoners—Sir Roland Stanley and Peter Legh of Lyme—were included in the list of names and places at which Lunt swore he had delivered commissions.

"You see I have left a lot of blanks," remarked the informer with satisfaction. "We can fill 'em up at our leisure."

"Excellent! But I see here that you have delivered commissions to some gentlemen already," Roger said.

"Yes—and that's sworn to before Sir John Trenchard, but 'tis a fact we have not the commissions wrote out yet. If you write a good hand you can assist us there, friend."

"What! Counterfeit King James's hand?" exclaimed Roger. "How can that be done?"

"Easy enough! I have an old commission here; issued before the Revolution. And I have a signature of my lord Melford's too. But there's no time to lose! We must get these commissions copied, and we'll have 'em all signed by King James and we'll drop them in such gentlemen's houses as Mr. Smith thinks well to have searched."

"My hand is not good enough for this," declared Roger.

"Well, we can easily take them to the Savoy or across the water and get them done. But I'd sooner not take in more folk than we need," grumbled Lunt. "I could have been in Dodsworth's plot—I was asked—but I'd rather have one of my own. We'd be snug enough, us three, you, me and Taafe—we'll have a third part of the gentlemen's estates between us, and a pension as well if it's managed right. You, Mr. Howard, must have your commission from Mr. Legh of Lyme and you must swear you had it from his own hands."

"Poor old gentleman," said Roger with a grin. "He's a passing good estate, I believe. A monstrous tall man, ain't he, very black?"

"That's the party," asserted Lunt unsuspectingly.

Roger knew that Legh was extremely young, of small stature and fair. He was confirmed in his belief that these villains did not even know the pretended conspirators by sight.

"I see here the name of Dicconson twice mentioned," he remarked.

"Aye, and if there is any other person of good estate against whom you have any little private spite, I'll put his name in," promised Lunt obligingly. "Say the word—you're a lad of the right metal and I'm willing to oblige you."

"Yes, but I must have a good reward as well," insisted Roger for the third time. "'Tis not sufficient satisfaction to get an arrogant puppy set down or hanged, I must have money!"

He endeavoured to assume a brazen, swaggering air. "I'd as lief have something to go on with too, for you know, Captain, one can't go into gentlemen's houses to drop commissions without a guinea or two, and a good coat."

Lunt shook his head.

"We'll meet again tomorrow," he said. "Let's see—come to me at the little coffee-house in Fetter Lane, next the Globe tavern—that's a good place. And hark'ee—I have witnesses for Legh and Stanley already, but you can swear to Thornleigh—that's a pretty estate."

"Aye, but too heavy encumbered," demurred Roger. "I will have none of that, for the sequestrators aren't paid off yet by all accounts."

Lunt darted an angry glance at him but answered smoothly:

"There's gold and to spare—if so be you'll be guided by me."

"That claps neatly with my humour. I have no desire to have a great rambling old country house thrust upon me. No, I'll be plain with you, and I'll not hold out for a percentage neither. Come, I'll swear to bring that dog Roger Dicconson into Court for you. I'll stake my life on't."

"I see, friend, that we shall hit it off to a nicety," observed Lunt. "I'll wait upon Mr. Smith at once and propose your name. But, hark'ee, Mr. Howard—there's no call to be over frank with Mr. Smith if he desires an interview. Bear in mind that you are King's Evidence and have received a commission—"

"From old Mr. Legh of Lyme," concluded Roger boldly.

"Aye, you'll do," said Lunt. "Shake hands on it—nay, I must embrace you."

He staggered towards Roger with outspread arms, but the young man contrived to keep the table between them.

"I swear I'll serve you as you deserve, Mr. Lunt," he exclaimed vehemently.

There was a sincerity in his tone which pierced to Lunt's fuddled brain, and completely satisfied him: he did not guess that the words might bear a double meaning.

CHAPTER EIGHTEEN

MR. LEGH BANKES had dismissed his clerk and sat alone in his office, smoking his pipe meditatively. His friend Mr. Beresford, who had rooms on the same staircase, had looked in to see him a short time ago, but Bankes had given him a hint to depart. He was awaiting a caller whom he would fain keep private.

The evening darkened, and little squalls of rain struck sharply against the windows, but the expected visitor—Roger Dicconson—would not arrive until it was night. Bankes flung another log on the fire and then stood listening. There were sounds of someone stealthily mounting the narrow staircase: a cautious foot-fall, the friction of a heavy cloak against the panels. Legh Bankes whipped round, took a pistol from the mantelpiece and hastily cocked it: one never knew but some thief or footpad might creep up to attack a solitary watcher.

"Come in!" he called, his apprehension lending a certain testy tone to his voice.

The door opened, revealing such a very unexpected guest that Bankes swore aloud before he could check himself.

"Why, Miss Thornleigh! And at this hour!" he exclaimed. "A thousand apologies, my dear lady, for my rude greeting."

Bridget looked round.

"You told me Mr. Dicconson was coming to see you tonight," she said breathlessly. "I'm not alone, Mr. Bankes. Peggy, my maid, is waiting at the stairfoot. I want you to give something to him."

Bankes always considered himself as a dry, unemotional lawyer, but as he gazed appreciatively at the girl's charming, eager face he felt a pang of envy for the rôle which Roger had chosen. Perhaps this lent additional vigour to his next speech.

"Mistress Thornleigh, you ladies must keep out of this dark business. Apart from the danger to yourselves, it is no moment at which to distract the attention of a man such as Dicconson, who has already but a slender chance of coming through this ordeal unscathed."

Bridget flushed.

"I perceive, Mr. Bankes, that you rank me as a vulgar coquette!" she exclaimed indignantly. "But I dare swear you have not thought of a material point—"

She paused with a hand at her breast for they both heard Roger's tread coming lightly up the stairs. Bridget's first impression when he entered was that he had grown years older in the two weeks which had elapsed since their last interview. She was furious at her own heightened colour and spoke abruptly to hide her confusion.

"Mr. Dicconson, I am here only to propose what may be useful to you. Does it not strike you that if any Jacobite gentlemen in Lancashire are discovered with arms or dangerous papers that it will ruin our cause? My father, Grandfather, your brother—"

Roger nodded.

"I had thought of that," he said. "Indeed I have made up my mind that I must get down to Lancashire without delay."

He looked rather doubtfully at Bridget and then glanced inquiringly at Legh Bankes.

"I see you do not want me at your counsels," remarked the young lady, tossing her head, "but answer me this: if you go to Lancashire openly as Mr. Dicconson, think you such Jacobites as there be will open their hearts and houses to the brother of a prisoner? And if you go as Captain Howard, what credentials have you to show to enable you to get into their houses?"

"That's a good point," interjected Bankes approvingly. "But surely the mere fact of all these house-searchings of late will have put everyone on their guard?"

Roger stood by the chimney-piece, deep in thought. His profile was dimly outlined against the dark hangings on the wall. Bridget was piqued to notice that he was not looking at her nor seeming to be occupied with her at all, or even to be aware of her daring in coming thus courageously to meet him.

"Lunt is a very dangerous villain," murmured Roger at last. "I have seen the Information he made on oath before Sir John Trenchard in June last. I believe we can throw discredit on his witnesses and some of the prisoners may be able to plead an alibi. But if a discovery of hidden arms should be made on the very eve of the trial, it might influence the Jury, and if—"

He stopped.

"Go on," said Bridget in a low voice. "What is the worst you fear? I will not tell my poor mother unless 'tis needful."

"Why, you frighten Mistress Bridget unnecessarily," exclaimed Legh Bankes, with the obvious intention of deluding her. "Even if the trial goes badly, we could always appeal."

"He does not think so," declared Bridget. "Come, Sir, tell me the worst."

"I believe we must look upon the trial as decisive," said Roger hurriedly. "I have a great deal to communicate to Mr. Bankes which he must note down, but we need not detain you, Mistress Bridget. Mr. Bankes can repeat everything to you later. Let us hear your suggestion now. Have you thought of any special means by which I could introduce myself to Standish Hall and the Shirbournes, for instance? I had thought to apply to the resident priest—but in my assumed character, of course."

"Surely you'd be recognized by the Standishes," exclaimed

Bridget. "Isn't it the very next estate to Wrightington?"

"Yes, but they had an illness in the family this summer, and though I waited upon them, I saw none of them. 'Tis true the servants might recognize me, but a different name and a different style of peruke should prove sufficient shield."

"There are others who are not Catholics," breathed Bridget, speaking softly as though she wished to be heard by Roger alone. She glanced deprecatingly at Mr. Bankes, whose eye kindled responsively—too responsively for Bridget's present mood. She frowned involuntarily and he began to laugh to hide the fact that he was disconcerted.

"Now, my good clients, if you have, as I suppose, arranged a tender rendezvous here, there's no sense in my being a party to it," he cried. "I'll withdraw for a few moments, but I must warn you to be brief."

"You are pleased to be facetious, Sir," said Roger quickly. "Do not heed him at all, Mistress Thornleigh—these old married men give themselves plaguey insolent airs! Mistress Thornleigh has come to make an important suggestion and your levity is most ill-timed, Sir."

"Please do not leave us, Mr. Bankes," besought Bridget, with great dignity. "My business is short. 'Twould be well for you to warn the Girlingtons, who are Protestants, as well as the Standishes and Shirbournes, and here is that which will admit you to any Jacobite house and give you credit there."

She had been holding her hand at her breast. Now she extended it to Roger with a little object on the palm. It was a small seal with a pretty device of doves and rose wreaths such as a lady might use.

Bankes would have seized the pretty hand, but Roger merely waited.

Bridget moved so as to place herself with her back turned to the lawyer. Then she pressed a tiny spring with her thumb-nail.

The seal opened and revealed a rose in diamonds on a background of dark blue enamel.

"You try," said Bridget, closing the lid and putting the signet frankly into Roger's hand. "'Tis a secret, Mr. Bankes. I doubt I have no right to reveal it except in such a case as this—a case of life and death."

"And whichever way fate decides, will you think kindly of me, Bridget?" asked Roger suddenly.

Nothing had been farther from his thoughts five minutes ago than such a speech, but the mere transient touch of the girl's hand seemed to have thrown him off his balance.

She was startled, and watched silently while with awkward, trembling fingers he opened and closed the token.

"A white rose," he said, so low that only she could hear. "That is what you are to me—the secret rose in the midst of my heart—nay, my very soul!"

He held himself quite stiff and straight, but the ardent words came from white lips. He was suffering and Bridget was full of compassion, but she drew back involuntarily.

"Of course I think kindly of you," she stammered. "I owe you eternal gratitude."

"There's no question of debt between me and you," said Roger. "Tell me the truth, my dear."

"I wish you hadn't asked me," murmured Bridget, speaking pettishly in an effort to hide her distress. "But if you must have the truth I can only say this: I'm not to be easy won."

A tremor shot through him, for the disappointment was sharp, coming thus on the heels of hope. His hand closed on the token, and he wondered with a renewal of the old jealousy from whom she had obtained it.

"The signet is not really mine," said Bridget hurriedly, as she began to muffle herself in her cloak.

Bankes came forward.

"Let me see you to your carriage," he proposed.

"Pray accompany her home, Mr. Bankes," suggested Roger formally. "I'll await you here. You must send someone immediately to St. Germains to fetch witnesses to swear to Walmsley's presence in France on the dates when he is supposed to have given my brother and others commissions."

"I have obtained a permit from the King and Queen for such witnesses to enter England," answered Bankes, "but whom can we send over?"

Roger did not answer, though there was a name in his mind.

"Why, Mr. Buckland might serve," went on Bankes, "for by all accounts he is anxious to quit the country."

Bridget motioned imperiously to the lawyer to open the door. She noted that Buckland's name had fallen on Roger's ears with a most unpleasing sound and tried to carry off the situation lightly.

"He will not very easily be able to return to England himself," she remarked, "for the authorities will be aware of him."

"No, but he could remain in perfect safety abroad," rejoined Roger.

"It's wonderful what an amount of bitterness these quiet men can put into their voices," remarked Bankes, as he led the way downstairs.

"They speak from their hearts, I suppose," she answered; and she sighed.

Bankes found his client in a very brisk and businesslike mood on his return. He was sitting at the desk, completing a written account of his discoveries; chapter and verse were not lacking; he had set down the exact places, dates and hours at which Lunt had tutored the witnesses Taafe, Womball and Wilson to swear they had seen the prisoners; the dates at which treasonable meetings were supposed to have taken place in Lancashire, and the persons whom Lunt claimed to have been present.

"You must get another witness before whom I can sign this," said Roger, glancing up as the other approached his chair and stood looking down at the paper. "Or think you I could make an affidavit before one of the secretaries?"

"No use at all," replied Bankes. "I tried already after my first meeting with Taafe. I went to the Lord Chief Justice and he declared it would not be proper for him to receive our affidavits—'twas 'discursing the King's Evidence,' he said, though it might be useful to the gentlemen if they were brought to trial."

"Well then, you must call in some trustworthy person and I'll sign this statement here and leave it with you," remarked Roger.

"It is near midnight," demurred Bankes. "And 'tis rumoured that there are warrants out against certain persons for suborning Crown witnesses. Nevertheless Beresford will oblige us, I dare say."

Bankes accordingly went out and up to the set of chambers immediately overhead which were inhabited by his friend. Roger waited just within the half-open door, listening to see if his errand would prove successful. Suddenly he changed his position stealthily and looked keenly down. The well of the stairs was dimly lit by a lantern suspended from a hook at the bottom; the place was thronged with shadows, but Roger was certain he had seen something move, though when he glanced down he could distinguish nothing. What more easy than for a couple of men to lurk about the doorway and trepan him? He remained motionless, his eyes fixed on the angle of the staircase, his heart beating a little faster than usual. Then as Bankes and his friend emerged on the landing above and made a noisy business of closing and locking the door, he slipped off his shoes and crossing the narrow space which lay between the light of the hanging-lamp below and Bankes' lantern, he flattened himself into the shadow and ran lightly down the stairs, exploring the wall with cautiously outstretched hand. He paused when within a few yards of the street. There was no sound, no sign of any human being: a section of the road was faintly illuminated and he saw a marauding cat prowl half-way across, then stop, flatten itself down, and turning, leap back over the gutter. Had it seen him, was it disturbed by the noise of the two gentlemen coming down the stairs, or had it marked some other form, invisible from within? As though in answer to his thought a dark shadow suddenly encroached on the lighted doorway, and was immediately withdrawn; it was like the huge black wing of some malignant bird. A tall figure must have intervened for an instant between the street lamp and the door-way, but there was not the slightest sound.

Roger retreated as carefully as he had come, and shut both doors of the chambers noiselessly behind him.

"There's a spy in the street," he announced. "Your servant, Mr. Beresford, you are most obliging and I owe you a thousand pardons."

He sat down immediately and signed his document, muttering between his teeth the while.

"'Twould be plaguey inconvenient if any of Lunt's friends marked me down here."

"Aye, exceedingly unwholesome indeed," returned Beresford, elevating his eyebrows at his colleague.

"You had better spend the night here," suggested Bankes.

"That would make it worse," asseverated Dicconson. "For they could not fail to recognize me by daylight, and would certainly manage to take me up on some trumpery excuse, for I fancy 'tis folk in government pay. But would *you* be willing to stay here overnight instead of returning home? Would Madam Bankes be greatly alarmed?"

"Not at all," answered the lawyer. "It is my custom to sleep here if I be detained late."

"Very well then. Pray lend me your peruke in exchange for my bob. Your greatcoat too, your little habitual cough and your blue bag. Come—shall I not pass for Mr. Lawyer Bankes tonight?"

He mimicked the other's speech so neatly that Beresford was staggered.

"It may pass," he said. "I'll go with you to the street and bawl for a chairman. You must make play as though locking the door as you go out."

"Shall I quench the lamp?" inquired Bankes.

"Nay, but turn it low that they may think their prey is still within," suggested Roger. "And Mr. Beresford must close the outer door on his return, that you may not be subject to attack."

"Roger, this is mighty dangerous," exclaimed Bankes breathlessly. "Don't go."

Dicconson answered only by a slight smile, as he forced Bankes' wig over his close-cropped head and swathed himself in the cloak cunningly, so as to leave his right arm free.

Bankes listened anxiously as the two men descended the stairs conversing together in lawyer's jargon about a case then before the Courts. They must have reached the outer door by now! He was stooping, his ear applied to the crack in his outer door which he held ajar, when suddenly there was an outcry in the street below—a volley of oaths and sounds of stamping feet.

"What, would you steal my purse, you villain!" shouted a voice—a strange travesty of his own. "Watch! Watch!"

"Stop, thief! Stop, thief!" bawled Mr. Beresford, and there came the sound of running feet.

"Watch! Ho, the Watch!" screamed a shrill female voice from an upper window.

But there was no reply; the casement was closed with a bang and Beresford laughed down below.

A little later the two legal gentlemen sat together over the fire, sipping the brandy which Beresford had demanded on his return.

"That's a cool hand, Bankes!" he ejaculated. "Egad, the street seemed empty when we looked out, but a man came out of a doorway and brushed against us, and your friend acted as quick as lightning. Egad, he shouted so manfully anybody would know he was an honest householder!"

"And the rogue fled?"

"Aye, did he! But none the less, Legh Bankes, I wouldn't be in Dicconson's shoes for a fortune—nay, not for all the world can give."

Mr. Bankes had tied a handkerchief round his head to replace his wig. His face looked pinched and grey below the gay folds of his bandanna, and he made no reply.

The cats had the street to themselves now and rent the air with melancholy cries.

Chapter Nineteen

IME HUNG HEAVY on the hands of the pretence informer. The pleasures and occupations that would have filled the time of a real Dick Howard made no appeal to Roger. He drank only when with Taafe or Lunt, and found the company of the vulgar wenches, with whom Lunt was ever ready to philander, extremely unattractive. He was too wary to take part in the games of cards which engrossed the other frequenters of the pot-house; to be seen reading would have been quite out of character, and he found himself tramping the streets with Taafe for hours at a time for lack of anything better to do. To an observant, quiet fellow such as Roger this proved an amazing education—there was no form of crime or rascality which was not practised in the great city. Apprentices sold their master's goods, merchants adulterated their wares, thieves were divided into innumerable classes and specialized in particular lines. Roger's new companions credited him with being a forger of false notes, and after having mingled with them for some days and finding that he could pass undetected he resolved to advance a step further in his plan. There was nothing more to be gained by remaining in town, and, after his last interview with Bankes, Roger decided that the sooner he could get away without arousing suspicion, the better. There was no time to be lost as Lunt had heard it mooted that the trial of the Lancashire gentlemen was to take place next month at Manchester. The names of the witnesses and of the men who were to serve on the Jury were to be kept a dead secret. The prisoners were not even allowed to know the terms of the indictment until the day of trial.

"There's no fear of a slip between cup and lip this time," declared Lunt gleefully.

He, Taafe and Dicconson had met by appointment at one of the shady little coffee-houses frequented by the conspirators. Roger had brought the conversation back to the subject of the witnesses time and again, but had not been able to tempt or surprise Lunt into a mention of their names. Taafe knew only of two—Womball, a carrier, and Wilson, who was occasionally employed by him.

Roger busied himself with his long clay, and with his eyes fixed on the small white bowl, proposed between puffs at the newly kindled tobacco, to accompany Womball on his next trip to Lancashire.

"What for?" inquired Lunt suspiciously.

"Why, if I'm to swear I know the houses, I'd best have a glance at them before we go into Court," returned Roger. "You know all these gentlemen by sight, no doubt, and their habits and all?"

"Blast 'em, I know nought of them except that they're a beggarly lot of papists and High Churchmen. I've found out which have good estates and that's all that need concern us," said Lunt cheerfully. "However, maybe you're right—you can take half a dozen commissions with you and hide 'em in the houses I tell you of."

"If Mr. Smith sees fit to include any others we can always bring a few more up later," put in Taafe. "But how is it to be fixed, Captain? Haven't these folks' houses been searched already? How can you get the commissions found now? Can you have another search?"

"Easily enough," quoth Lunt. "But it would be better for you to break fresh ground, Mr. Howard. You must get in conversation with any likely Jacobite-inclined sort of gentleman. Choose them of the simpler sort—country squires whose fathers were Cavaliers and fought for Charles—and persuade 'em they'll all be sent to the gallows unless they band together and strike a blow for King James."

"What, am I to provoke 'em to conspiracy?" exclaimed Roger.

"Certainly you may. But act cautious! If you could get a loyal letter addressed to King James, with a signature or two, 'twould be worth a heavy purse."

"Heavy? How heavy?" queried Roger promptly. "Would it be worth fifty guineas?"

"Yes, I'll engage for that. Make the folk think that now's the time to strike—if they wait longer 'twill be too late to do us any good, and timid folk will be frightened off by the sight of the smoking quarters of your friend Roger Dicconson and the like."

"But they aren't tried yet, still less convicted," declared the supposed Howard, feeling a most unpleasant inner qualm.

"No matter, Smith and the Attorney-General are agreed on their death. Aye, they've written out the warrants and signed 'em already and that's a great comfort to me," Lunt remarked contentedly. "But before you depart, Dick—I'd— What's that noise?"

"'Tis only a brawling woman: she has just descended from a coach and seems to have a couple of constables with her," said Roger, who was nearest the window.

Lunt turned pale and glanced quickly about him.

"A woman?" he repeated. "Here, let me look at her."

He leaned over Roger's shoulder and burst into a volley of oaths.

"I'll be the death of you, Taafe, if you have brought this hussy down upon me," he cried, looking hastily round for some means of escape. But there was only one door to the inner room, and the large, gaudily-dressed female who had entered the outer precincts of the coffee-house was now approaching it.

"There he is! There he is!" she screamed, pointing through the aperture. "There's my cruel husband as has deserted me!"

"Away!" whispered Taafe.

Roger was longing to witness the end of the drama, but he recognized the prudence of Taafe's hint. Clapping his hat on his head and shaking forward a long curl to mask his face, he strolled to the door, bowed to the irate woman politely, and pushing his way through the gathering crowd, walked rapidly off.

Roger sought out the carrier Womball without losing a moment, and persuaded him to take him with him on his journey to Lancashire which was fixed for the next day but one. As they stood talking in the stable where Womball housed his pack-horses, Taafe came sidling in, full of the story of Lunt's arrest by order of his wife.

"Egad, the wretch claimed him, and would have made good her claim too, but Lunt sent post-haste to the Lord Mayor and demanded bail. Faith, he'll get it, I believe. He had the effrontery to ask for a post-chaise, and off he went with the officers to the Lord Mayor of London himself."

"If the woman brings a suit for bigamy it will greatly discredit the chief witness and I dare say the Crown will let the whole thing drop," said Roger. "'Tis all in our favour."

They were standing in the doorway of the stable in the flickering illumination of a horn lantern, hooked on to the lintel. Taafe's face clouded over at this speech.

"It will ruin us," he protested. "Why, we'll get no reward if that happens! 'Tis that pestilent old Madam Legh, I'll go warrant, who has hunted up this woman. And, by the way, you made a sad slip today. Legh is a young man, just married—the widow is his mother."

"Indeed?" observed Roger.

"Yes, and twice you called him 'old Legh'—'tis lucky Lunt don't know him by sight."

"Does he know any of them by sight, except those he arrested himself?" asked Roger quickly.

"How should I know?" parried Taafe, with a suspicious glance. "This is no place to talk in—we had better listen to what is being said behind us."

The carrier and his underling were moving about tending their horses in the semi-darkness of the stalls. Womball came strolling out presently with a straw between his teeth.

"Did that harridan of Lunt's come here seeking him today?" inquired Taafe.

Womball was chewing tobacco; he laughed, spat and shifted his quid to the other side of his mouth.

"Two of 'em," he said. "Ellen Simpson and the stout party— Johnson she calls herself, I believe."

"Aye, he married her. Well, friend, the Captain has been taken up for bigamy and he is in a tearing rage, and vowing vengeance on those who put Madam Johnson on his track. Can't you travel a day earlier and bear this young man along? He has business in Lancashire for the Captain."

"I understand horses," put in Roger laconically.

Womball scowled at him.

"I told Lunt I won't consent to have my share split up—if he takes in any more folks he must pay them himself," he grumbled.

"Aye, so he must," agreed Taafe hastily. "But this lad has a delicate job to perform—one you couldn't undertake."

He leaned heavily on Womball's shoulder and whispered in his ear. Roger caught the word "commissions," and opening his coat, showed the end of the folded papers in an inner pocket. The carrier still looked doubtful.

"Mr. Aaron Smith's orders, I understand," said Roger cheerfully.

"Well, I've nought to do with that," declared Womball. "Carrying arms is my business—and war-saddles—Lunt said it was to be war-saddles because they knew there was still a good many in Lancashire as James sent up before he lit out for France."

"That's a notion," said Dicconson admiringly. "And are we carrying arms tomorrow?"

"Nay, there's no call for it now. 'Tis only ordinary business tomorrow, but if you come with me I can take you to Thornleigh and Standish Hall and Ince, and you can take good note so as to swear to all the places in Court."

"I've been to Thornleigh Hall," answered Roger quickly. "And I know Wrightington too. How many horses have you?"

Womball jerked his thumb over his shoulder, and Dicconson accepted the mute invitation to inspect the occupants of the stalls. There were ten all told, and he imagined that he and Womball would each ride one animal and lead two others. At the far end of the stable were piles of boxes and bundles lying among dusty heaps of hay and bags of corn.

"I suppose you'll sleep here tonight and move off early?" asked Roger, after he had looked with some interest at the carrier's sorry collection of horse-flesh: every animal was blemished in some way, one blind, one spavined, one with a swollen joint, two with broken knees, and the last a very old mare, gone in the wind.

"Yes, you had best sleep here too, for the horses must be fed before three," said Womball, still eyeing him uncertainly. "Wilson travels with us too—can you bring your own nag? No, then you must carry some of the smaller stuff in your saddle-bags."

Roger agreed and went to his lodging to pack up his parcel of spare clothes. He was aware that Womball and Wilson were talking together and looking after him as he went down the street. No doubt his sudden entry into the conspiracy was displeasing to them, and he must set himself to allay their suspicions while on the journey. He went a step further than Taafe in his plans, for it was obvious to him that a mere deposition of the plotters' perjury would carry little weight; he must by some means make them give themselves away in Court, else his intrigue would avail nothing. As he was to be a carrier for the nonce, he sold his sword, and purchased instead a pair of pistols which he endeavoured to conceal in his coat. The recollection of the sudden death of Lunt's first partners and the "disappearance" of Ellis was unpleasantly in his mind as he settled himself for the night upon a heap of Womball's musty fodder. Rats squeaked in the wainscot, the carriers reeled in at midnight, reeking of liquor and stumbled over Roger's legs, uttering maudlin curses.

Wilson made sundry incoherent observations about a "blasted swab as come between an honest man and his profit," but Roger feigned sleep. The horses rattled their halters in the manger-rings, the men snored, and there were occasional cries and sounds of running feet in the mean little alley outside. Roger dozed by fits and starts, and rose when the clock on a neighbouring church struck three, to attend to the horses.

Wilson presently came to help him, red-eyed, yawning and in a surly humour. They slept again while the horses munched their corn, and then roused Womball and began to load the pack-saddles. The taverns were not open as yet, but the carriers had each secreted a bottle behind the sheaves which had served them for pillows, from which they now refreshed themselves with a morning draught. The clocks chimed five before they took to the road, and the country traffic was already streaming into town, and blocking the narrow streets. It was Roger's business to ride ahead and make way for the string of pack-horses, pushing through herds of bullocks and hectoring the men leading heavy hay-wains, until they dragged their teams against the mud-encrusted houses so that the pack-horses could sidle past. Roger proved so unexpectedly energetic and fluent at this business that he earned his companions' respect, and enabled them to advance at a good pace. On the outskirts of the city he refreshed himself with a draught of ale and a hunch of bread and cheese, while Womball and Wilson pledged him in more fiery liquor.

It was a mild October day, and the soft air was pervaded with the smell of dying leaves. The wayside trees were still gay with gold and orange tints, and here and there wild cherry had shed upon the ground its whole burden of rose and crimson foliage. The horses knew their business and ambled along steadily in single file. Presently a coach dashed by them, its four horses all a-lather, for it was one of the "flyers" pledged to average seven miles an hour. All other traffic pulled aside to let the heavy vehicle go lurching past.

The grey road stretched ahead bearing steadily to the North, now empty, now with wains and hurrying horsemen upon it, and the sight of it filled Roger with a sense of adventure. Perhaps British packmen had first traced it, travelling Northward with their families and treading out a narrow way among the grass and fern. Then Romans, marching to Hadrian's Wall, or branching off along their new, stone-made thoroughfares to Wales and the West. Saxons too, forefathers of his own Lancashire folk, blue-eyed and sturdy like their descendants. Adventure haunted the road, winding away among the trees. Here were farm lads whistling as they went to work, here was a milk-maid, balancing herself on a stile, with a foaming bucket at either end of her wooden yoke, and there was a group of gipsies still huddled round the remains of their fire. Roger's spirits rose as he rode along, for youth and a fair morning will always have hope for company.

Chapter Twenty

IN THE COURSE of the long days in the saddle and during the evenings round the tavern fire, Roger learnt many things from his companions. His newly acquired knowledge made him suspect that there was a certain amount of Jacobite activity in Lancashire in which the Standishes—father and son—were probably involved. Neither Womball nor Wilson knew anything definite, except that Lunt had a deep grudge against the family as he considered he had been insufficiently rewarded for some secret service.

The carriers' first consignment was for Manchester, and Roger resolved to part company with them here on pretence of disposing of the forged commissions. By treating them freely on the road he had worked himself into the rascals' good graces, and when he invited them to sup with him on the last night and to bring any friends they might chance to meet in the town, they accepted without suspicion.

"We'll get Brereton and Brown," remarked Wilson. "They are to be used as witnesses too, so 'twill be a good chance to make you acquainted."

Dicconson had never been in Manchester, and his ignorance of town and people forced him to take desperate risks. He was anxious that his companions' habit of railing against the prisoners should be overheard by some respectable persons who might be used as witnesses at the trial. But there was no time to make cautious inquiries: a certain tavern-keeper named Richard Shone was well spoken of as an honest man and good citizen and Roger approached him boldly. Without revealing his own identity, he spoke of the approaching trial, and remarked that innocent gentlemen would be done to death for lack of witnesses to the spite and greed of their accusers.

"If a gentleman of any respectable station could be present in your tavern tonight, he would hear for himself how they rail against these unfortunate men," he declared. "Yet what sort of quarrel should there be between a gentleman of rank and a common carrier? There's a perjury in it, I warrant you."

"If you know so much—" began Shone, then he broke off. The young man spoke authoritatively, but he wore an exceedingly shabby coat and carried a teamsman's whip.

"There's many of the prisoners well respected in Manchester," he observed. "Squire Thornleigh now—he's own cousin to Sir Roger Bradshaigh, and Mr. Legh—he's many connections here and—"

"You're a householder yourself," said Roger. "And mind you, it is no light matter to be the means of saving eight innocent lives. If there was any other person in your house tonight—a physician—a clergyman—anyone who chanced to be eating near the corner table where I shall be supping at nine of the clock—"

"H'm. And whom will you be supping with, young man?"

"Faith, Mr. Shone! A strange crew, I warrant you!"

With that Roger withdrew. He took care to arrive with Wilson at supper-time and avoided any private conversation with the landlord, but in the course of the meal he marked the arrival of a respectable-looking man in a bag-wig, whom Richard Shone escorted to a table near.

Brereton and Brown joined Roger's party. The former was a discharged dragoon, the latter a dishonest servant who entertained a deep grudge against his former master, Squire Standish. He had been drinking already, and it required no effort on Roger's part to make him inveigh in his accustomed manner.

"Damn Standish! I'll have his blood!" was his conclusion to a tirade.

"Aye," chimed in Brereton heartily. "And damn Sir Roland Stanley and his cousin Legh of Lyme—they are two pitiful fellows and would give me nothing. I'll be revenged on 'em, you'll see."

Womball laughed uproariously.

"Captain Howard here is in the like case!" he declared. "He swears he'll bring down the Dicconsons of Wrightington—'tis young Roger he has a special spleen against."

"Aye," chimed in the supposed Howard darkly. "You can leave Roger to me."

.　　　.　　　.　　　.　　　.

Legh Bankes was still in London, but he had fee'd an attorney, one Mr. Pigott, to act for the prisoners in Lancashire. This gentleman was in Manchester, and, before leaving the town, Dicconson was able to call upon him and give him the names of several witnesses for the defence, among which appeared that of Richard Shone. His next act was to warn the Standishes, and this he accomplished by aid of Bridget's token, in the character of a Jacobite agent. The elder Standish was already in hiding, and his son not only agreed to dispose of any objects which might give rise to suspicion should the house be again searched, but also mentioned the names of sundry country neighbours to whom it would be wise to carry a warning. Roger was interested to note that none of these names occurred in Lunt's list of treasonable persons.

Young Standish had married a daughter of the Duke of Norfolk, and Lady Philippa welcomed "Captain Howard" very kindly as an unknown cousin, and thereby caused him acute discomfort. He had arrived at dusk and left almost before daylight the following morning. He had been in dread every moment of being recognized, but the Standishes were completely without suspicion, and when the young man presented himself, muffled in his cloak, they thought it extremely natural that "a gentleman of his persuasion" should wish to "keep himself private," and saw to it that even the servants scarce caught a glimpse of him.

It was a dangerous neighbourhood for the Wrightington estate marched with Standish's, and Roger was eager to be away on his next quest, which was the apparently hopeless one of finding Peg Morley and her father.

The task of hunting for an itinerant scutcher in a sheep-keeping part of Lancashire seemed like searching for a needle in a bundle of hay, yet Roger undauntedly set about it. He rode briskly to warm himself, for it was a raw, drizzling morning.

The cold mist congealed on the leaves of the elms and chestnuts and dripped on him as he passed under them, avoiding alike high road and cultivated fields. As he cantered along the pasture fields bordering the Wrightington deer-park, he reflected grimly on the changed times. His father had been a Protestant in the days when he inherited the large estate from a Protestant uncle, Sir Edward Wrightington. No doubt the inheritor thought himself fabulously rich, for he not only made the great wall round the demesne, but abandoning the old black-and-white timbered hall, built a fine new stone mansion and stocked the park with deer. It was scarcely fifty years ago, but sequestrations and double taxes had wrought so heavily upon the family that William was sorely pinched for money, the new house had already a curious unkempt air of decay, and coping stones had fallen from the wall, leaving gaps over which no doubt the deer leaped out to harry the neighbours' crops.

He drew rein at the top of the rising ground, where he could contemplate the glimmering sheet of water with its island—the Wrightington lake, which had been the scene of many a boyish exploit. The house itself lay half a mile beyond, hidden by the wood which clothed the farther shores of the pool. Roger could not see the pretty River Douglas, but as he presently rode forward, crossing the road and bearing north-eastward, he reflected on his father's plans for canalizing it and making a navigable waterway from Wigan to Preston.

Hugh Dicconson had abandoned worldly prosperity, however, when he became reconciled to the Church. The Bishop of Chester had taken great exception to the attitude of such a considerable landowner when he abandoned the parish church. The Lord-Lieutenant of the county was also highly indignant, and though in King James's time the staunch convert only suffered by double taxes and the like, the arrival of the Duke of Orange brought fresh troubles. These, combined with a passion for building, had reduced the family fortunes to a low ebb when Hugh died, leaving his widow and a large chargeable family for his heir to deal with.

Roger's intention now was to aim for Stonyhurst Park, the seat of Mr. Shirbourne, travelling across country by the moors, where great flocks of sheep were fed. Here he hoped to learn of the whereabouts of Morley the scutcher. It was necessary to find someone of the sort to gather the information he required. It was a disagreeable journey for the mist soon thickened to rain, and he had to try three taverns in succession before he could find anything on which to dine. The meal was even then an extremely simple one, consisting of ale, oat-cake, black cheese and a dish of black puddings.

The landlord was a small farmer, who kept the ale-house for the convenience of the drovers and wool-higglers who travelled through the country on their way to attend the Chorley wool-fairs. Roger represented himself as a lawyer's clerk, sent by a kinsman of a poor weaver's assistant who had been imprisoned for debt and who was now at large but in bad circumstances.

The landlord had stiffened at the mention of the Law, which was looked at askance in country neighbourhoods.

"An old master of his has left him a trifle," continued Roger, "but if I don't succeed in finding the man soon, my charges will eat up the whole estate—for 'tis but a few pounds to start with."

"Weavers and spinners are always agate of quarrelling," observed the landlord. "And 'tis like enough they dispute wi' their underlings too. There's always grumbling—carders and scutchers against spinners and weavers and I don't know what all, except that the farmers gets little for their fleeces."

He spoke with zest now, evidently spurred by a long-standing grievance, and Roger hastily rose from the table.

"I have got an acquaintance in these parts," he said. "About eight miles away I reckon—Tom Leather."

The landlord's face became alive with interest.

"An honest good man is he, and I care not who hears me say so!" he declared. "But if it's his place you're bound for now there's a short way across the moss, but you must look out for peat-bogs. It's easy enough to get bogged—aye and drowned too—if you don't know the moors."

He walked a little way with his guest, giving directions as to the land-marks which must be looked for, and at length bid him a civil good day.

Roger was a little doubtful of the wisdom of visiting the family whom he had obliged with the loan of his horse on that hot June Sunday: they knew him by his real name, and though honest Catholics, they might talk incautiously. However, as he jogged slowly along, debating the point in his mind, fate flung him in with what he sought.

The moor stretched away on every side, intersected here and there with drains of sluggish water half-choked by luxuriant growths of feathery sedge. The turf bore as many blades of the tiny tough meadow rush as of grass, and the whole surface seemed to quiver beneath the horse's hoofs. The wind, though of no great force, had a peculiarly searching quality, and the cries of seagulls feeding in the marshy ground added to the general melancholy. Such stunted trees as there were had already lost their leaves; there were few sheep, and these when not in movement seemed to melt out of sight against the colourless background of faded grass and bleached weed.

Roger kept a careful look-out for areas whence turf had been cut; he was aware how the long open trenches contract until only a treacherous slit is left to trap the unwary.

His horse—an uninteresting beast of poor quality—fell into a walk, but Roger pressed him forward, anxious to regain the road before it was dark. The hanging wood on the farther side of the moor indicated the situation of the farmhouse for which he was bound, and it seemed no nearer than when he had parted with the landlord of "Pause-and-be-thankful." His eyes were fixed upon the distant trees when his horse shied violently, nearly upsetting the negligent rider. Roger pulled up and looked back in surprise: a curious figure was climbing up the bank of the broad ditch which bordered the track he followed. A huge creel appeared first, piled with silvery prickles; it was bound to the shoulders of a girl who crept up the sodden grass on hands and knees.

"Peg, as I live!" exclaimed Dicconson joyfully.

His mount snorted doubtfully, as he turned back, and the girl paused on the brink of the dyke and grinned impudently.

"I knew 'twas you!" she cried. "I spied you awhile back and I thought to skrike out to you, and then I unbethought me."

"And that was very unfriendly of you, Peg," cried Roger, dismounting as he spoke. "For I have pressing need of you. I was prepared to search the Duchy for you."

"I'm no bird to be caught wi' chaff o' that kind," exclaimed the girl in scorn. "Hold on to your pony, for I doubt he'll be frighted."

She slipped her arms out of the thongs which attached the basket to her back and heaved it on to her head, where she balanced it with customed ease. The horse, tired as he was, much resented this manœuvre and Peg had walked smartly away before Roger could rejoin her.

"You'd best ride," she called over her shoulder. "'Twill look more natural."

Roger presently drew level with her, and she glanced up at him with a saucy laugh.

"I doubt you're but jesting, my bonny lad," she cried. "You've never thought of me these three months, I dare swear."

"Peg, I am in a sore strait," answered the young man seriously. "You'll see my head blackening on a spike, unless you stand by me."

Her face changed in a twinkling to an expression of alert anxiety.

"Must we hide you?" she asked quickly. "I know a place."

The horse being now resigned to Peg's abnormal head-gear, Roger rode close beside her and stooping low, poured his story into her ear. He left out all mention of Bridget Thornleigh, but painted his brother's danger in vivid colours.

"Father will be fain to do your bidding," remarked Peg as he paused. "But the old bird has not his wits so bright since he was in the lock-up. I'll be well able to find out what you need, though. Where are you bound now?"

"Why, I was going to inquire at Tom Leather's yonder, if they knew of any carder or scutcher hereabout who might put me in touch with your father."

"We're working there oursen," announced Peg. "I've been gathering teasels for the scutching, see yo'." She pointed upwards to her burden. "The little spiky heads draw out the wool better than anything, and as 'twas a dry summer, there is a good few to be had about the moor."

She stopped, looking about her uncertainly.

"You'd best not go to the farm though," went on Peg earnestly. "You can't trust the folk there; they've treated us well enough but"—she sank her voice to a portentous whisper—"they're papists."

"Well, and so am I a Catholic," returned Roger cheerfully.

"You!" She appeared horror-stricken. "Nay, you'll never persuade me you're that wicked."

He laughed.

"I hope I'm not wicked, Peg, I would be a bad Catholic if I were. I reckon you don't know many papists?"

"Nay, one is enough!" said Peg, glancing up provocatively. She had short curly eyelashes and very bright eyes. "Shall you come into t' barn, where we're carding wool? Or will you go talk to the master?"

"I'd rather keep myself private if possible," he said.

"Well then, you must wait up above among the trees. In half an hour I'll send a lad to take your horse to a safe place where he'll be cared for and fed and maybe changed for a better."

"Nay, no witchcraft," he cried with a laugh.

"There's no telling! The lad will bring you a bundle of wool and you mun bring it to t' barn—the mester will be safe in the house then, and there's a little bothy in the yard where we have a fire and cook our meat."

"Admirably planned," he agreed.

Peg quickened her pace to a rapid jog-trot and bade Roger follow a track which branched out to the right.

"Give the buildings a good wide berth and ride up to the top of the slope," she ordered. "You'll find the wheel-marks where they have been carting fern and you can wait at the bracken stack in the wood."

"Thank you, my lass," said Roger. "I would indeed make shift to thank you more civilly if you had not that hedgehog head-gear."

"Well," returned Peg, with a simper. "We'll meet again, you know. Yet I reckon the proud lady you're courting will chide you for idle kissing."

"What lady?" inquired he, in vexed amazement.

But Peg only laughed and marched away, whistling an air remarkably similar to the catch sung by the vulgar in the streets of London on the morrow of the May-day Fair.

Roger sat still. Had the ridiculous story of the toad and his fight and Bridget's intervention really penetrated to Lancashire? And what had Peg meant by "changing" his mount? Was she in league with horse-thieves?

He rode forward slowly, pondering how to employ the Morleys. He had an inkling that Lunt had acquaintances in the valley of the Hodder—among the secluded villages tucked away between Pendle Hill and Clitheroe. Peg and her father might make cautious enquiries in the neighbourhood, while he visited and warned the Shirbournes.

Roger had not long to wait beside the dark, pungent-smelling stack. A ragged boy soon came whistling up the path, with a bundle of wool under his arm. Roger took the packet and held out the rein not without misgiving, but the lad sprang into the saddle.

"Gently—the beast is weary," cried his master, but there was no answer—horse and rider vanished silently among the trees. After a moment's hesitation Roger stepped briskly towards the farmyard. Sweet whiffs of hay and corn stacks mingled with the woody fragrance of moss and leaf. Presently he crossed a fence and perceived the long, undulating ridge-roof of the old barn outlined before him against the sky. There was still an apricot glow in the west, and circling the building, he approached the great door which stood wide open. A monotonous clacking sound within denoted that the carders were still at work, and the unpleasant, heavy smell of wool soon came to his nostrils.

The interior of the barn was heaped with great piles of wool, some already cleansed by washing and boiling, and ready for carding, some still rolled in the fleece, while a great feathery cloud surrounded the scutcher. Tubs of dirty lather stood in the yard, and Peg leant over one, laboriously pressing and wringing a heavy lump of wool.

"He is a bit in drink," she observed over her shoulder. "'Tis cruel hard work, and we have noan had too much food of late."

Morley did not cease his toil as Roger came in and stood looking at him speculatively.

"You've a right to command me," he said sourly at last, "but I never thought to do aught to aid and abet a Catholic."

At this unexpected remark Dicconson burst out laughing.

"Why, what harm have we done you, man? Sure, trade was a deal more flourishing in the last reign than 'tis now."

"Maybe, but I've no liking for 'em. I don't hold wi' bringing in the Pope o' Rome to rule over Englishmen," growled the scutcher, his thin, scarred hands continuing to ply the carding board with machine-like regularity.

"You'll always have company then," returned Roger. "Our Lord Himself said the world would always hate us, and you'll never be alone if you take part with the world."

"But Our Saviour wasn't talking of papists—'twas Christians He meant!" exclaimed Morley, deeply scandalized.

"All Christians were papists as soon as Simon was chosen head of the Church," returned Roger. "But if you don't choose to help me, you needn't. It is hardly fair to ask you, for there's danger now in my company."

"It's not that he's chicken-hearted," put in Peg quickly. "He's turned stupid, that's what it is. He's been listening to those —— preachers up at t' chapel. What is it you want to learn?" she added, coming in with the great hank of dripping wool in her hands.

"I forbid you to meddle in it, you hussy!" exclaimed the scutcher. "Give the gentleman his own horse back, and let's call all even."

"Shut thy mouth, thou ugly, ungrateful old brock!" retorted Peg, aiming a blow at her parent with the hank.

He parried it, staggering back with an oath.

"Thou'rt fuddled!" continued the girl fiercely. "Else thou'd never be so wicked to the gentleman as got thee out o' quod. Shame on thee—get over to t' bothy and sleep it off—I'll straighten up here."

She hung her wool on a line which was stretched across one corner of the building, and ordered Roger curtly to close the doors after her.

He obeyed and stood dubiously in the yard, holding the carding boards which Peg had thrust into his hands, while she fitted a great key into the lock.

"Now you'll sup wi' us," Peg announced; "and then we'll talk. I reckon you're sorry now you sold your horse for such a cussed old devil?"

"It makes no odds—I'm glad he is free. But, Peg, I doubt you can do no more to help me. Give me a handful of oat-cake if you have it. I'll sleep in the barn, and you must bid the lad have my horse ready at dawn."

"That means you won't trust me any further, I suppose?" said Peg; she lingered a moment and then darted into the little windowless den which was dully illuminated by a covered fire.

There was a short interchange of angry voices, then Peg returned, snatched the carding tools out of his hand and reopened the barn door.

"You can't have any light else the master would notice. Bolt t' door on inside and I'll noan lock it. Here's the oat-cake—I'd fetch you a drain o' gin, but Feyther has drunk it all."

"Good night, Peg. You're not crying, are you, child?"

"Crying? Me? Nay, but I'd like to choke th' owd mon with his own wool! To serve you so ill after all you have done! And you trusted me!"

"I do still, and if you were only a lad—but no matter."

With this cryptic remark Roger stepped into the barn, cried a cheerful good night, and bolted himself in.

Chapter Twenty-One

OGER AWOKE to the sound of heavy rain drumming on the roof. He had chosen to lie on the old hay in the loft rather than on piles of wool. The wooden shutter was ajar and let in fresh smells of oak-leaves and wet pasture to refresh the atmosphere within. The sound of horses' hoofs presently smote on his ears; he was surprised to note that there was more than one animal, and reconnoitred through the shutter before he went down. Dark though it was, he could distinguish the shapes of two horses against the paler background of the cobbled yard—a short figure bestrode the smaller of the two. Roger hurried down.

"Good morning to you," he began.

At the sound of his voice the led horse turned its head and gave a low whinny. Roger started.

"Why, it's Noble!" he exclaimed.

"Come on," said the figure on the other horse. "We'd best be off—before the folk are astir."

Instead of answering, Roger walked round and pulled aside the ragged cloak which the rider wore about her face.

"I cannot see you, but I am pretty sure it's Peg," he exclaimed, peering up at her.

She burst into a cackle of laughter.

"'Tis me, sure enough, though I tried to fool you by speaking gruff," she exclaimed. "Come on—throw your leg o'er the saddle. You wished for a lad and a lad I am."

"Nonsense, child, you can't come with me—"

"Cannot I then!" exclaimed Peg with a jerk at the rein which caused the horse to plunge and nearly unseat his rider. "I'll spirit away the horses, I promise you, if you say me nay. And how will you find your way to Clitheroe without a guide?"

"Do you truly know the way?" he demanded.

"Aye. And you need have no fear, I'll make no claim on ye. You can keep your heart for your carroty mistress!" cried Peg viciously, and flinging the reins of the led horse to Dicconson, she switched her own mount and rode out of the yard at a hard gallop.

Roger was laughing when he rejoined her.

"Now, you mad witch—how come you by Noble? I hope he's not been stole for I sold him fairly."

"Nay, the beast was in Catholic hands and was taken by Captain Baker and his Dutch troopers. They had a parcel of horses and I sent a friend of mine to watch for this one—is it a he or a she?—and he got it off Baker when he was in drink. You'll be too proud to take it back from me, I reckon?"

"I'll gladly buy him back at the price you gave for him, Peg. But no, that won't do—we shall be recognized."

The girl laughed—a queer eldritch screech which jarred on her hearer.

"You'd pass him in the road by day-leet and never know him," she exclaimed, "the same as ye would me, for folk like you believe all your eyes tell you at first glance."

"What! Is Noble dyed a new colour?"

"Wait and see for yourself. And I trust you'll be more civil than to give me 'witch' for a name in future."

She hit her horse again and he bounded ahead, with Peg clinging to the saddle with ungraceful but determined grip.

"I'll call you jannock!" called Roger as he hastened after her. "Come, lass, thou's jannock, I warrant, and I'll trust you with my life itself."

"We'll get away a bit first," cried Peg. "We've a long way to go. Let me lead and do not follow too fast for I'm an ill horsewoman."

She pulled her mount on to the grass bordering the lane and Roger followed obediently. It was raining and the gusty wind whipped the heavy drops into their faces, but there was something invigorating in this brisk ride in the semi-darkness. As the light insensibly increased, feeding sheep became visible, pale shapes with the silvery rays gleaming on their wet backs: black, twisted trees stood out sharply on the horizon and easterly clouds were laced with orange and yellow gleams.

Peg presently drew rein.

"Well, and what do you think of me?" she inquired impudently. "Your sweetheart wouldn't make nought of me, would she? I have not set myself out to please you."

Roger was tempted to laugh at the queer little figure. Peg wore a boy's jerkin and breeches and a pair of riding-boots much too big for her. She had successfully extinguished any symptom of femininity and looked like a vagrant who had once been a post-boy. Consideration for her feelings kept his face quite grave.

"You look your part very well," he said. "And now let us walk our horses while I tell you how I am trying to undo the work of a parcel of wicked informers who are determined to lie away the lives of innocent men."

"You've no call to meddle with it though," Peg declared. "But I declare you're a lad as can't keep out o' trouble. I know all about you, I do. For I know a lad whose brother is courting one o' the maids at Thornleigh Hall. Aye, he made us all merry with the tale."

"What tale?" asked Roger shortly.

"Why, about the toad flung into the fine ladies' carriage, and them all falling into fainting-fits and you having a mill with the chap as threw it."

"True enough, but I see no humour in it," he declared.

"They're saying the young Madam fainted in your arms and then wouldn't marry you," said Peg maliciously. It was now light enough to see his face and she scrutinized it curiously.

"No, the young lady did not faint, not she! She leaped out of the coach and called on the crowd to form a ring and let us fight fair." Roger spoke proudly and then he sighed.

"They say you fought for her twice?" insinuated Peg in a small voice.

"Well, it doesn't signify now," he rejoined impatiently. "We are concerned to see justice done at Manchester Court, and I want to find out anyone who has been subpœnaed for King's Evidence—that means people who have been asked to act as witnesses to Lunt's story."

"I can find out that for you, I dare say," answered Peg. "I have friends here and there about the country and folk won't suspect me. But what do you mean to do?"

Roger had resolved to place complete confidence in this ragged, impish creature who, he felt convinced, would be true to his interests. As they pushed forward he told her his plans in detail and what he had accomplished up to date.

Peg stopped him in the account of his visit to Legh Bankes' chambers and of the spy who had waylaid him.

"Did he know you, lad?"

"I am pretty sure he didn't, nor did I know him."

"You saw his face then?" she queried anxiously.

"No, it was too dark and he was all muffled up, but I noticed his hand—a large, coarse hand, and the backs of the fingers were hairy."

"The devil!" exclaimed Peg violently.

"Why, child, sure you don't know these London rogues," returned the young man soothingly.

"Don't 'child' me!" she cried in scorn. "Sure you must know we poor folk travel up and down the country, and the professionals know each other from one end of the land to t'other. A crown to a farthing that was a chap we know as Dirty Tim. The King's Messengers had him up here in the winter and he got so much a head for every coiner and clipper he laid hands on, blast him."

"Was it he got your father into trouble?" asked Roger after a pause.

Peg's face was scarlet, her expression vengeful.

"Ask me no questions, and I'll tell you no lies!" she exclaimed. "But 'dirty' is too good a word for the likes of him."

She cursed without ceasing for a moment or two, spitting out the foul words venomously between her teeth. Then she glanced up sideways, with a little smile.

"If you don't like my way o' talking, I can't help it. That rogue has no cause to love me for I broke his shins for him with a metal carding comb. He took his revenge on my poor old Dad, and if I can thwart him again it will add a sweetness to helping you."

"Peg, have you ever seen Lunt?" demanded Roger, struck by a sudden thought. "He calls himself Johnson too and Jackson and all manner of names, and he is always running after women."

"Do you mean Lunt and Dirty Tim might be the same chap?" inquired Peg, who was quick at the uptake. "Has Lunt hairy hands?"

"I don't know—I cannot remember ever seeing him save in gloves," answered Roger. "Wait a bit while I think if I have ever eaten with him."

He rode on with knitted brows, trying to visualize all his meetings with the informer.

"Nay, he wore gloves always, but stay—I'll draw his picture."

Hurriedly dismounting, he pulled out paper and pencil and leaning against the saddle jotted down line after line, murmuring half aloud as he drew:

"He wears his own hair—a small man, given to finery. A great talker too, and with a habit of wrinkling his brow—like this."

Peg had been staring before her whistling an air. Now she glanced round and started.

"Lord save us! Show us the picture."

Roger held up his drawing and Peg looked at it keenly for a moment or two. Then she said very softly, but with horrible intensity:

"I wish he were dead! I wish his flesh was withering on his dry bones on the gibbet."

"It is Lunt, then?" asked Roger.

Peg nodded and rode forward, while he tore his drawing into little bits, and stamped them into the soil.

"He was going about the country with a Captain o' Dutch dragoons a few weeks back," Peg observed presently. "At one place where there was a good bay gelding, Tim clapped his own saddle on and rode it away. 'Twas at Walmesleys, I think—no, 'twas some place in Cheshire."

"Find out exactly about that and if your Tim or my Lunt had a lodging at Chipping or anywhere about Clitheroe, and you'll do me a real service, Peg. I hope it will not make great trouble for you with your father?"

"He'd never raise his hand to me as how 'tis, poor old cock, but I'll not leave him longer nor is needful. We're due at Altcar— that's not far from Thornleigh and—"

"We must avoid Chorley," interrupted Dicconson, who was anxious to evade further banter. "I'm known there. And I ought to get out of this neighbourhood, for anyone might recognize me now 'tis broad day."

"Turn to the right then, yonder by the willows. We'll canter if you like."

She struck her horse with the long hazel wand she carried and galloped up a green lane. Roger followed. The clouds had broken, showing a long rift of blue sky, a lark was singing in the pale shafts of sunlight as though it were spring again. Obedient to Peg's command, Roger would not allow his horse to pass her, but kept close in pursuit as she threaded her way along the edges of common fields and through narrow by-ways.

"We folk know all the quiet ways," she announced presently, as they slowed down to ford a stream. "Oh, 'tis we have the best of it, I think. We can marry when we please and to please ourselves, and you must have a house and gear and gold to keep Madam amused with apes and trinkets."

Roger made no reply, but after a pause he asked if she had any acquaintance at Clitheroe.

"Aye—my Aunty—she'll be proper fain to see me," answered Peg.

"Then I believe it would be best for us to part there. I am afraid my company might bring you into danger. If you will gather such news as you can, I'll ride north to Girlington, take Stonyhurst on my return journey, and then come find you at Clitheroe."

"My Aunty lives at Chipping," said the girl. "She's married to a gipsy sort o' chap as sells besoms. He cuts the heather up on t' moors—'tis a lonely place enough."

"The better to our purpose for I can come and go without causing remark. And now, Peg, we'd best divide my purse for partners must share their moneys."

The girl shook her head.

"You can give me a shilling or two—that is all I'll need. You can settle for the horse later. If I need a messenger I'll find one as travels for friendship, not for fee. Tell me, if folk ax what you are what am I to say?"

"I was a carrier on Monday and a gentleman on Tuesday, but the devil knows what I am now!" exclaimed he.

"You must pretend to some business or they'll take you for a highwayman, especially as you are well-mounted," declared Peg. "Do you know enough about wool to be a wool-dealer?"

"Not I!"

"Well then, will you be a fustian-maker looking for weavers to whom you can put weft? Nay, but this is too much of a country district."

"Weft? I don't even know what you are talking about," answered Roger. "Cannot I be a mere young gentleman, visiting my relatives in the North?"

"Of all simple schemes! Why, a gentleman would be followed by his man, and a led horse with saddle-bags full of fine clothes. You can't be a gentleman."

"Very well then, I am not a gentleman. If I had but thought fit to bring my portfolio I could have represented an itinerant print-seller."

"Aye, but you didn't bring it," commented Peg dryly. "Can you play aught? You're no fiddler, I suppose?"

"I used to play a penny whistle when I was at school," confessed Roger modestly.

"Oh, lad, a penny-whistler never rode a good horse."

"I'll be a horse-dealer then," he cried. "I know something about horses."

"H'm, be careful then, how you mix with other dealers," warned Peg. "Eh, lad, they're as full of tricks as a sieve is of holes. And though you're a decent, civil lad, I doubt you're not over clever."

She spoke seriously, shaking her head. The hair hung loose about her face, and she had cut it at the neck like a country boy's. Roger noted—in a purely academic spirit of appreciation—that her lips were as lovely a shade of red as the brilliant berries on the rose briars.

"I wish you had a more happy settled way of life," he said, later in the day, when they had eaten together at a wayside inn and were riding up the rising ground east of Preston. "Is there no trade you could be 'prenticed to? I doubt you would never take service?"

"Do you think I shall not marry then?" she queried indignantly. "There's others think different."

"I'll be bound they do! But married folk too can fall on bad times."

"I'll call on you, never fear, if I'm ever in want," she answered cheerfully.

"But I mightn't be here!" rejoined Roger. He spoke in a low voice and Peg made no reply, but the wind which came soughing down from the fells struck on her ear with a dreary note. She shivered and gazed searchingly at Roger.

"What are you looking at?" she inquired presently in a pettish voice.

"Nothing," said Roger promptly.

But Peg knew that his eyes had been fixed on the little hill behind Preston town rising up above the river: she knew the name of it was in his mind—Gallows Hill.

CHAPTER TWENTY-TWO

DURING ALL the weary weeks which had passed since the Thornleighs' arrest, their friends had made ceaseless application for the old man's release upon bail. This boon was unexpectedly granted almost on the eve of the trial. Sir John Trenchard, the Secretary of State, had consulted with his colleagues and the Governor of Newgate. They came to the conclusion that William Thornleigh's renewed illness might terminate fatally if he tarried longer in prison, and his death under the circumstances might rouse the indignation of the populace and alienate sympathy from the King's cause.

"'Twas most improper to have arrested him at all in my opinion," declared the principal King's Counsel, Sir William Williams, bluntly. "An old man full of infirmities and lame these forty years."

He gazed accusingly at the Solicitor to the Lords of the Treasury, Mr. Aaron Smith, who coloured up furiously as he replied:

"I perceive, Sir, that you have been regaling yourself with the scurrilous stuff that rogue Ferguson has put about. You have seen his open letter to Sir John Trenchard."

"The man is a scandal," interposed Justice Eyre, who was to try the case. "He should be in the pillory—a stirrer-up of mischief, and a damned venomous pamphleteer."

The gentlemen were travelling to Lancashire in a great coach, four Judges and four King's Counsel, as well as Smith. They had been forced to put up with each other's society for the past six days, but had now reached the last hours of their journey. Sir William's nephew, the Junior Counsel, rode beside the coach, which was accompanied by an armed escort as well as by a retinue of servants. Sir Giles Eyre had been obliged to raise his voice to dominate the rumbling of the wheels, the clatter of the horses' hoofs and the vainglorious cracking of the postilion's whips.

"I've never known Ferguson on the side of papists before," observed Williams in a more conciliatory tone. "Have they hired his pen, think you?"

"Most undoubtedly," declared Aaron Smith. "They'll not spare money—indeed we have already occasion to know that they have made ceaseless efforts to suborn our witnesses."

Williams looked up sharply.

"Nothing new, I suppose?" he said. "Nothing to tell against Lunt's testimony?"

"No, no," said Smith hastily. "But I thought well to send him down with Captain Baker and our solicitors and the other witnesses. They are well escorted."

"Mr. Lunt deserves every consideration," Gold observed.

Smith looked slowly from one countenance to another and then said emphatically:

"I trust, gentlemen, that we are all giving this case the extreme attention it deserves."

"Why, Sir, do you doubt it?" exclaimed the Justice. "Is not treason ever the blackest of crimes?"

Smith assented impatiently. "This case is peculiar in that we are all like to stand and fall by it," he said. "Let us not pretend to be ignorant of the disturbed state of the country. The Church has behaved most unthankful to the King's most gracious majesty. To think that so many of the bishops the late King sent to the Tower should prove non-jurors—'tis the blackest ingratitude. And hundreds of other clergymen have, of course, followed suit, pretending to equally tender consciences."

"But there is no need to stir up religious intolerance over this affair," cried Williams. "It is not exclusive to any one sect—'tis Jacobinical that's all. The adherents of the late King are scheming to rise in armed rebellion, and 'tis our duty to bring proof against the ringleaders."

"Laying stress upon the fact that their faction is essentially against the true Protestant cause," insisted Eyre. "Indeed, Sir John, I agree with you there. Such Church of England gentlemen as are involved are doubtless wickedly entangled with the papists, and vilely tending to Romish practices."

"Justice takes no notice of a man's private faith," protested Williams.

This scandalous assertion raised a clamour.

"Sir William, you are pleased to jest! Why, Justice is universally known to be the Keeper of the country's conscience!" exclaimed Naps, one of the Judges.

"I hope, Mr. Counsel, that you are not inclined to a lax temper towards these miscreants?" thundered Turton. "This is no case of minor misdemeanour which we are sent down to convict—"

"To try," interrupted Williams suavely.

"Certainly to *try*. There will only be a handful of prisoners 'tis true, but the affair is symptomatic. The mere fact of a pamphleteer of Ferguson's notoriety daring to take part against a Crown case shows the roots of dastardly treason go deeper than was at first supposed."

"'Tis true that though only seven arrests have been made, Lunt alleges that there is a widespread conspiracy," agreed Williams. "'Tis a pity, Mr. Smith, that we have no witnesses of better education and standing than Lunt."

"I have him wrote down as 'Gentleman'—he'll do very well," returned the Solicitor. "We have no lack of witnesses, but it is essential that the evidence be pressed home—that the Jury be left in no doubt. If this canker be not crushed in the bud, the whole country will be rent from end to end."

"No penalty can be too severe for men who have actually plotted the horrid murder of our noble, gracious King," said Hollis.

"And it becomes us to remember the outrageous attack planned upon our innocent children," chimed in Smith. "Besides confiscating the estates of all true Protestants the late King James intended to lay hold of all children under the age of ten, and bring them up papists by force."

"A spade guinea to a sixpence the solicitor wrote that into Lunt's confession himself," whispered Naps aside into Sir William Turton's ear.

"For shame, Mr. Naps!" murmured the Judge half aloud.

"I think we're all agreed to consider this case as the farmer does the crow he kills and hangs up to scare others from his wheat," remarked Justice Eyre. "The utmost penalty of the Law must be imposed—'tis necessary for the safety of the realm."

There was a murmur of agreement.

"The Protestant succession is in danger," declared Sir Giles Eyre. "This must be our rallying cry! Ah, there are the lights of our inn," he added, with a complete change of tone. "I sent on one of our rascals to make sure of an eatable supper. I hope you all have as good an appetite as I have."

"I see my clerk awaiting us," grumbled Mr. Smith. "What say you, friends, shall we postpone all business until tomorrow?"

"My fellow is here too," said Williams, getting out and stretching his cramped legs. "Well, nephew, what news?"

Young Mr. Williams, the Junior Counsel, had ridden ahead and, reaching Manchester half an hour in advance of the coachload, already knew all the clerk had to tell.

A little crowd had gathered to watch the arrival of the grand London Judges, but for the most part they stood staring in sullen silence. The only huzzas which had greeted the dignified cortège had emanated from sundry ragged boys, turning catherine wheels along the line of route in hopes of ha'pence.

When the nine portly gentlemen had made their way into their private room after a great show of politeness as to precedence through the doorway—young Williams burst out with his news.

"Feeling is running pretty high here!" he exclaimed. "Our witnesses would have been pretty rudely jostled as they rode in on Sunday had it not been for the strong armed escort."

"On the Sabbath too!" commented Smith in a shocked tone.

"Aye, they were greeted with groans and hisses and there were stones flying, by what I heard," answered the young man.

"Are the prisoners safe come?" queried Judge Eyre sharply.

"Yes, Sir Giles. They had a very different welcome, I promise you! Blessings and prayers instead of curses and hissing."

"Did Baker and his men make any arrests then?"

"Nay, Sir, the mob was orderly enough. But it seems Mr. Roger Kenyon is giving them his support—the Recorder for Wigan you know, gentlemen, a man who is monstrously looked up to in these parts—he is a member of the House of Commons and his son is the Earl of Derby's attorney."

"Never fear, gentlemen, we will soon show these rustical squires that they cannot revolt against the King and Queen's most gracious majesties!" exclaimed Smith. "I dare swear my lord Derby will make no move. His estates were pretty shrewdly nipped and sequestered in Cromwell's time—he'll not meddle in politics, I'll stake my soul."

"Politics, Sir?" interjected Sir William sharply.

"Aye, in my opinion High Treason is a crime appertaining to the domain of politics," replied Smith.

"Nevertheless it behoves us to take a completely unbiased view," declared Sir Giles Eyre sententiously.

There was a chorus of approving assent.

Aaron Smith's plea for a convivial evening untroubled by business interviews was overruled. Mr. Lunt waited upon the company as they were at supper, and drew the Solicitor-General aside as soon as he could do so discreetly.

"I left Taafe in town according to your wishes," he began breathlessly. "And I hope by now that he is safe in Newgate."

"I am very far from satisfied with the way in which you have conducted this affair," returned Smith sharply. "Who is this Captain Howard, for instance? I cross-questioned Taafe and he declared him to be an acquaintance of yours."

"He's a damned impudent liar then!" exclaimed the informer hastily. "Why, I never set eyes on Howard till Taafe brought him to me three weeks since."

"Take care, Mr. Lunt! You must not tell me anything different to what is set down in your affidavit," said Smith bluntly. "Where is Howard?"

"He rode down with Womball," answered Lunt cautiously. "And he is to meet us at the 'Phœnix' before the Court sits." He considered his patron slyly, wondering how much he dare tell.

"Well, but where is he now?" insisted the other.

"It seems he is somewhat over devoted to the fair sex," replied Lunt at last with a leer. "But, however, he is combining business with pleasure, for he undertook to visit all the houses at which he had previously left King James's commissions so as to be able to swear to them accurately at the trial."

"I don't feel sure of this man," observed Aaron. "What caused him to abandon the Jacobite cause? What reason had he?"

"Oh, the same as my own. He was not prepared to go as far as murder," returned Lunt glibly. "When the horrid plot for the taking off of King William was proposed to him—"

Smith interrupted him with an impatient gesture.

"Enough!" he declared brusquely. "He won't do." Sinking his voice to a whisper he added: "You must get rid of him."

"If you'll give me a warrant, I'll have him arrested with a commission in his pocket," proposed Lunt.

"But not here," rejoined Smith, after a moment's thought. "We are opposed by a very dangerous and bold gang, and I prefer you to get rid of this man at some distant place, where it will make little noise."

He gazed at Lunt very narrowly and added in a low, hard voice, "Do you understand me?"

"I believe that I do, Sir," responded Lunt cheerfully. "And I must tell you further that things fall out very opportunely, for there's a crazy weaver or scutcher come to town with a complaint that this Howard has made away with his daughter."

"We don't want a second low story of this kind brought against a Crown witness," said Smith sourly. "Howard must disappear. One of the Messengers must seek him out, and he can have a file of soldiers to assist him."

"And the dragoons need not be too squeamish if Howard resists arrest, I suppose, Sir?" inquired Lunt.

"I will not meddle with any such details," declared the Solicitor loftily. "'Tis for you to deal with, for 'tis you who brought the man into their Majesties' affairs, and," he concluded with sudden fierceness, "'tis you who will be answerable for him."

CHAPTER TWENTY-THREE

ON THE NIGHT of the Judges' arrival, Mr. John Lunt ordered a fire in his own room and sat by it in a wadded gown, his feet, in tarnished embroidered slippers, resting on the hob. A decanter and glass were at his elbow, and he eyed them askance from time to time, but still adhered to his resolution not to drink until he had thought out his plans. Mr. Smith's discourse had given him food for thought. It was a delicate situation, but he was well used to that: boldness and hard swearing had got him out of many an apparent impasse. Mr. Aaron Smith seemed satisfied with the original list of witnesses and was content to throw off Taafe, now doubtless safe in gaol, where he could conveniently be left until he perished. There remained the problem of Captain Howard. Properly manipulated, Howard might serve a double purpose, but here skill was more necessary than boldness. Lunt was accustomed to reach his end rather by dash and effrontery than by careful skating over thin ice such as would be necessary in this instance. He had asseverated to Smith that he knew every man in the plot, and as he was chief witness he must make this secure. It was not an easy thing to do. Womball was only really acquainted with Squire Standish, who had disappeared and was not in custody. It would certainly be satisfactory if the person to whom he applied for information could vanish from this globe once the knowledge was imparted. It all seemed to fit in most satisfactorily, and with a little dexterity it could be arranged without either Smith or Captain Baker becoming aware of the weak spot in the evidence of the chief witness.

"First," murmured Lunt to himself, ticking off the items on his fingers, "first I must contrive to get hold of Howard without arousing his suspicions. Then I must be sure of the identity of the prisoners and of two or three persons who are sure to be in Court. Yes, yes!" He nodded to himself—it would all work out most neatly and even agreeably, but it required careful timing. That little devil, Scutcher's Peg, would fall into his hands too, most likely, for Lunt knew enough of the girl to be sure she would come to seek her old father, who was safe under lock and key in one of the Messengers' houses. He had not forgotten Peg's rebuff, and thought it would be sweet to make the slut pay for it. A little smile curled the corners of his mouth and he stretched out his hand for the bottle.

Yes, dates and times must be carefully worked out. It would not do to loose Baker and his myrmidons until the right moment. Above all things Howard must not be arrested in the neighbourhood of Manchester. Sir John Trenchard had been a little testy about the warrant, which now lay snugly in Lunt's breast pocket. He was thin-skinned enough to have been annoyed at the stinging comments of Ferguson the pamphleteer, on a Secretary of State who issued blank warrants to Messengers which they could fill in themselves when they discovered a suitable subject for arrest.

Lunt reflected that he must have spies out to intercept Howard directly he returned to the town. Then when he, Lunt, had sucked him dry of every particle of information he possessed, Howard must be sent off on a fool's errand to Thornleigh perhaps, and after allowing him a sufficient start, Baker's men must be loosed at his heels. All this was plain sailing: there was just a little difficulty on the financial side: Howard would doubtless expect to be paid for work done and commissions delivered up to date. With any luck he would have such moneys on him at the time of his arrest, and it would be a sad shame if Baker and his crew retained them.

"I must bargain before handing over the warrant," decided Lunt, taking a pinch of snuff, and wishing that he held a woman's soft hand in his and could inhale the fragrant powder from a dimpled wrist. This one evening, alas, had to be sacrificed to business, but all deprivations should be atoned for later. Baker must be told that Captain Howard had stolen the cash from him, Lunt, but the dragoon was a greedy brute and not over nice about money matters. He would deny that Howard had any coin upon him as like as not. Yet he must give Howard money or his suspicions would be roused. Of course 'twas Government money, but anything that Lunt had a chance of appropriating seemed to him to be his already.

It was satisfactory that Captain Howard had pretended to be a papist and Jacobite among the country folk. If need be Morley might be schooled into making a passable affidavit to that effect. It all fitted in admirably and for the ultimate good of such sound patriots as Mr. John Lunt. These Dutch troops were not squeamish about a little violence, especially such as had been employed in Ireland. With each succeeding glass Lunt's complacency increased. There was no knowing what pleasures the future held in store. Forfeited estates meant ruined families, and pretty women cast upon the world. 'Twas said that Thornleigh, one of the prisoners, had a monstrous pretty daughter.

.   .   .   .   .

Mr. Legh Bankes and his colleague Mr. Pigott were sharing a bottle of mulled claret in a private room in a quiet tavern on the outskirts of Manchester. The jug stood between them in the hot ashes raked out of a generous wood fire. The wind was high and shook the shutters from time to time, or moaned in the chimney, but the two gentlemen were mighty comfortable and inclined to take a rosy view of life.

"The local Justices should be here tomorrow," remarked Bankes. "Baker and Lunt are already in town, I understand."

"Yes, they came down about the same time as the Judges and King's Counsels, but there's one thing that troubles me a little," said Pigott. "Taafe rid not down with the others. I sent a man to inquire for him privately from one of the Messengers and he would have it that Taafe was in Newgate."

"I hope that is false—indeed, I feel sure it is," returned Bankes, yet he was uneasy.

Pigott stirred the fire.

"Otherwise all goes well," he resumed. "More witnesses have come in, and one of them—Wilson—is own brother to the perjured wretch on the other side. I heard of him through Roger Dicconson, and he has sent in ten or twelve others from the country today. We owe the Shones to him too."

"Yes, my clerk and I had been busy enough," added Bankes. "But if they've put Taafe out of action—Lord, that were a sad loss."

"What could they send him to Newgate for, think you?" inquired the country lawyer, who was careful not to venture an opinion until his London brother had first spoken.

"'Twas said there were warrants out on a charge of corrupting the King's Evidence, but there had been no arrests as I know of when I left town. There were spies set about my chambers though, and I reckon Aaron Smith will stick at nothing for he stands or falls by this trial."

"They say if the case is won for the Crown there's scarce a man in Lancashire of any property that will not find his neck in a noose," went on Pigott, with gathering excitement.

"Lunt has certainly sworn to a list of over a hundred names— so Roger told me. See here, Mr. Pigott"—Bankes sat up vigorously. "If they've got Taafe, it behoves us to keep Dicconson as the apple of our eye. Lord bless us, we must find him and get him into safe keeping."

"They would not dare do away with him surely?" gasped Pigott.

Bankes took snuff: his shadow loomed fantastically large on the plastered wall as he leaned back, legs crossed, his wrist, half-veiled in his ruffled shirt-sleeve, elegantly lifted.

"H'm, we've scoundrels in office, my dear fellow, and they are no mean conjurers—they can make folks disappear."

"Were you—you weren't attacked coming down?" faltered Pigott. His feeling of comfort and security began to ooze away.

"No, I travelled in company. They'll hardly dare interfere with me, but witnesses—especially out in the country—that's another thing."

Mr. Pigott could not control a violent start when a tap on the door followed hard upon this statement.

A red-cheeked maid-servant thrust her head into the room and asked if they would be pleased to see Mr. Green, who was below inquiring for them.

"Certainly, show him up," said Bankes.

As the girl closed the door he whispered behind his hand, "It's Taafe—that's the alias we agreed on."

The two men had turned their chairs and were gazing eagerly at the door when Taafe came in and was duly presented to Pigott. He was pinched and blue with cold and stood at the fire, stamping his numbed feet and overflowing with his own grievances. Lunt had treated him in the most scurvy manner, he declared—he had given him the slip and had even had the meanness to make off with Taafe's own saddle and bridle.

"That's all of little consequence, Sir," cried Bankes, interrupting him brutally in full flow. "There's a rumour about that you were in Newgate. What gave rise to that, eh? Is the game up? Have they found you out?"

Taafe's countenance assumed an unbecoming yellow shade, and he glanced from one man to the other with a dropping jaw.

"I—no—I hope not," he stammered. His hands felt suddenly wet as he rubbed them together. "I hope Mr. Dicconson has not run me into danger."

"Have you seen him?" Bankes rapped out the question sharply.

"Not since he left London," owned the informer. His eyes flickered uneasily as he went on: "Baker sent for me before he left town and would have me tell him who this Captain Howard was. I answered that he was Lunt's acquaintance, not mine, and I desired him to ask Lunt."

"Well, well? What said he to that?" queried Bankes eagerly.

"Why, he perceived that I did but banter him," replied Taafe sulkily. "And he began to threaten me. 'The Law is very severe,' he says, 'upon all men that go about to put tricks on the King's Evidence.' So says I, 'I've not offended against the Law so the Law will not meddle with me,' I says. And then I told him if he would go with me to the Secretary of State, I'd justify myself."

"That was mighty bold," commented Pigott. "What said Baker to that?"

"Why, 'If the Secretary of State saw you,' says he, 'he'd commit you.' I took my leave then, and next morning they all went out of town without a word to me. I'd changed my lodging but had someone to watch at the old lay—the old lodging, I mean. And now you say the rogues are putting it about that I'm in Newgate?"

"Yes, Mr. Taafe, and you may be sure it is not Captain Baker's fault that the report is untrue," cried Bankes briskly. "You must keep yourself very private indeed, Mr. Taafe. Indeed, you had better remain here. We cannot risk your being arrested before you appear in Court."

"They will not expect me here," said Taafe with a return of his usual jauntiness, "for Lunt knew I had no money. I had trouble enough to get it too—six guineas it cost me, coming down post."

"Yes. We will not discuss your expenses till after the trial, Mr. Taafe."

"I take you, Sir!" responded the informer cheerfully. "Now where's Mr. Dicconson? If he were but here we should be a merry party. I think you would do well to keep him carefully also, Mr. Bankes—for lord! the Jury will think twice as much of my evidence if 'tis corroborated."

"Aye, to my mind Mr. Dicconson is the more important of the two," muttered Pigott in the Counsel's ear. "'Tis a name to conjure with in this country. It's mighty important to be able to produce Mr. Roger."

Mr. Legh Bankes got up and rang the bell.

"We must have some refreshment for Mr. Taafe, and then we'll retire," he announced. "Mr. Roger Dicconson is wise in keeping himself out of the way till the last moment. There's no great hurry. The indictment will not be read to the prisoners till Saturday, and no doubt both sides will challenge the Jury. There is no cause for alarm."

Taafe suddenly ran across the room and seized Mr. Bankes by the cravat.

His eyelids were reddened by the cold wind and want of sleep, for he had not been in bed for two nights, and sheer terror showed in his pale, flickering eyes.

"But you do not know Lunt! But you do not know Lunt!" he repeated feverishly.

His little high voice was not raised, but it suggested such a torment of fear that the thin, strained tone rang in Bankes' ears all night. If only Roger Dicconson were there! But the next day passed and he did not come.

CHAPTER TWENTY-FOUR

I**T WAS ONE THING** to discover persons able to give testimony in favour of the prisoners, but quite another to persuade them that it was their duty to appear in Court in a case of High Treason. The Lancashireman's innate sense of fair play was a strong motive, but had not Roger come armed with money to pay for their transport, few of the witnesses for the defence could have reached Manchester in time. Peg Morley was a most useful aid, and Dicconson found himself relying on her shrewdness and assiduity in sifting friend from adversary.

Captain Howard had appeared in Stonyhurst in character approximating to his own. He let it be known in secret that he was beating up witnesses to prove an alibi for one prisoner and to discredit the witnesses on the opposite side. Mr. Shirbourne was duly warned that this was no fit time in which to indulge in Jacobite proclivities, and the Priest was advised to keep himself concealed.

There was much to be done, and Roger roved ceaselessly about the district interviewing anyone who might prove helpful until Wednesday, the day on which the Judges were due to arrive. This date saw Roger also on his way to Manchester. Peg agreed to rejoin her father, who should by this time be in the neighbourhood of Thornleigh. She waited for Roger on the road, a bundle of heather brooms tied upon the crupper, determined to accompany him as far as their ways lay together.

"There's many a fine gentleman as wouldn't be seen riding with a broom-girl," she observed when he came up to her. "But you're not that sort."

"What sort am I?" inquired Roger, laughing.

"Eh, my lad, you're simple enough! I sometimes think me and unbethink me"—Peg broke off and pulled her horse into a walk.

Roger waited but she rode on with downcast eyes. The curly eyelashes were tipped with gold, and the gaunt, starved look had vanished from Peg's little face. The man turned his head away.

"I sometimes wonder," resumed Peg suddenly, "if thou meanest to spend all thy life beating at a closed door. Thou might mate low enough and have a little house and a warm hearth."

"I certainly am never likely to be able to afford more than that," returned Roger. "Shall we trot now?"

"Nay, lad, hear me out. I'm spoiled to look at by toil and starving, but I was a shapely child. I'm an honest wench too—I pray you believe me."

She hung her head humbly at the last words.

"I do believe you, child, and I pray God you may meet your match and marry him—"

"Don't be a fool," interrupted Peg. "You know well enough what I'm telling you." She dropped the familiar, tender "thou" and looked him full in the eyes. "You could have a croft on your brother's land and live on it well enough. Many a great man's younger son has done the like. You're only young once and love is sweet."

"My dear, this is no time to think of love. My mind is full of this life-and-death struggle for justice, and—you know—my heart is Bridget's."

"But she doesn't want you," said Peg bluntly.

"Well," Roger laughed awkwardly, "that's the pity of it."

"I'd be true to you," persisted Peg. "If they put you in prison for your share in this do, I'd come to you there."

"Hush, hush, child—"

"Now it's no use your trying to put me off," declared Peg. "You think it shame for me to speak, but I think no shame. 'Tis the truth—I love thee, and if you'll let me I'll warm thy poor cold heart, lad, and make thee happy."

"Oh, Peggy, my poor, kind child! It cannot be," he murmured.

"Nay, but it can. You're noan proud. I'll say no more, but when you're sick at heart, you can be thinking of me—and of the things all men need, a true mate and little childer."

"Peggy," he said in a choked voice, "I thank you from my heart, but think of this no more."

"Will you kiss me then?" she whispered, leaning towards him.

Light curls of hair twisted over the rough edges of her leather cap, the corners of her soft mouth drooped like those of a chidden child.

"No, I will not kiss you," said Roger, pulling his horse aside.

Peg burst into a wild fit of laughing.

"Nay, thou's afeared!" she shrieked triumphantly, and jerking the bridle, she galloped from him with the besoms bouncing on the back of her astonished steed.

The rest of the ride was accomplished for the most part in silence, but Peg sang to herself from time to time. They parted at the top of Parbold Hill: both were weary for they had pressed on rapidly. Roger had changed horses at Preston, but Peg had kept her tired mount and meant to sleep in a neighbouring cottage where she had an acquaintance.

Below them the two rivers shone out like faint paths of light in the darkening landscape.

"See the waters yon," said Peg, pointing. "They travel all that weary road, and yet they meet at last."

"All rivers flow into the sea, if you call that meeting," rejoined Roger, deliberately prosaic.

"Well," resumed Peg. "Have you no message for your love?"

Chapter Twenty-Four

Instead of answering Roger put a question in his turn.

"Peg," he said, "have you ever watched a fowler at his trade?"

"Oh, aye," she answered indifferently, surprised at the change of subject.

"In Italy they spread lime on twigs of trees," he went on.

"So they do here, and fasten up an owl for a decoy," returned Peg. "But 'tis not a trade I fancy. I'd sooner harken to a throstle in the hedge or a blackbird whistling on a tree-top at the dawn o' day than have 'em in a cage. Now I'll be going."

"Wait a moment," said Roger.

He was looking away from her and his face had a strange softened beauty, lit up thus by the low rays of the sun.

"Peg, I have a fancy at times that I'm a bird under the fowler's net. The mesh is drawing closer round me—I saw the great black strands of it last night between sleep and wakening."

"Hush, lad, that's not lucky!" exclaimed the girl in alarm.

"Oh, well, I do not believe in dreams," he said in a lighter tone. "And in a few days now we should be free of dread or— Yes, Peg, I will ask you to take a message to her."

"Or what?" demanded Peg harshly. "Or lying in a cell with a chain on your legs and a rope about your neck? Is that what you were going to say? Why don't you get out while there's time? Haven't you done enough for a brother and a faithless jilt?"

At every question she pressed her cob nearer until she was close beside him, her knee touching his. She peered up into his face, afraid that she might have angered him.

"My dear," he said, "I thank you for your kindness to me. I accept it from you like a child's love which is ever sweet. And I am going to trust you with something which I would give to no man living. If anything happens to me, will you bear this token to Mistress Bridget Thornleigh, and this letter? If any folk stop you, drop the little seal and tread it into the ground for it must not be found upon you."

"That couldn't betray—'tis too easy copied," said Peg. "I know folks that would make a counterpart in fifteen minutes."

Roger silently touched the spring and Peg started.

"I might have guessed it," she remarked, and then flung her head that he might not see the tears in her eyes. "Give it here then—I'll take it to her if need be."

"But, Peg—there's something more. I want you to be guided by Mistress Bridget—to let her provide for you."

"Oh, and do you! Well, I'm none of your mind," she retorted.

"If we should not meet again you'll remember it is the last thing I asked you, Peggy. I'd die easier—if I have to die—knowing that you have a home, and will not be walking the roads, half-starving."

"Or worse?" queried the girl with a hard laugh.

Roger did not answer for a long time: it seemed he was choosing his words.

"I have told my pure, proud, honest little lady that you are her equal there," he said at last. "Now here's the letter and the token. You'll say nothing, of course, of my foolish apprehensions and ill dreams?"

"That is for me alone," she agreed with mournful satisfaction, adding with a visible effort: "You called me a child just now, but I am no child, Mr. Roger Dicconson. I am a woman as would follow you to the gallows-foot."

"I'd rather you planned to dance at my wedding," said Roger with forced lightness. "Now good-bye, my little lass, and may you travel safe."

"You called *her* 'little' just now, but by all accounts she's as tall as a maypole," complained Peg, straightening her insignificant figure. "Take care you fall not between the high and the low and be left lonely in the end."

She turned abruptly down the little path which twisted between thorn-bushes to the cottage door. Roger had begun a protest but the words died on his lips. He sat on the fidgeting horse, gazing down over the wide plan to the smoky sunset: when at last he turned away and followed the muddy road towards Manchester, it seemed to him that he had turned his back not only on life's glories but also on more humble joys. Behind him somewhere below those rosy shafts of light was Bridget Thornleigh: here near at hand where the firelight winked on the tiny lattice he had turned his back on poor Peg and her love. Before him were angry rain-clouds and a dark road leading away into the night.

CHAPTER TWENTY-FIVE

T**HE LONG** rambling building of Thornleigh Hall was wrapped in a clammy sea-fog and anxiety reigned within. The little store of money, hidden in a cavity behind the bed of the master of the house, had long since been raided to provide for the prisoners in Newgate and for legal assistance. Old William had returned home immediately upon his release, travelling by coach to Chester to save expense. But the fatigue of the journey in such cold weather had brought on a return of his ague and he lay abed—shivering and feverish by turns—his condition made worse by his impatience to be at Manchester. Next morning his daughter-in-law set forth, leaving Bridget in charge. It was settled that she was to wait at home until the last moment, for the old man was obliged to surrender to his recognizances on Friday at latest.

Mother and daughter embraced as they stood beside the mounting-block in the cobbled yard.

"Ah, Bridget, God only knows with what a sad burdened heart I leave you," said the elder woman. "Who knows—"

"We'll not think of that!" cried Bridget, tossing her bright head. "We'll trust all to God—all, all!" she added to herself.

Mary looked at her steadily.

"Yes, but we must be ready. Now, child, quick before Dick brings the horses, say this prayer with me: 'My sweet Jesus, I accept the cross Thou dost destine for me.'"

Bridget's face whitened—she drew back sharply, but Madam Thornleigh kept her grave eyes fixed upon her.

"Otherwise how shall we be ready?" she asked. "All is in His hand—our home, our living, all those we hold dear."

"But we may plead for mercy!" exclaimed the girl passionately.

"For courage first to bear all for Christ," insisted the delicate pale lady.

Bridget, hitherto so courageous, was sobbing stormily, but her mother, whose tears lay usually so near the surface, was dry-eyed, and glanced at her almost impatiently.

"There is no time to weep now," she declared. "You have much to do, Bridget. Come, everything depends upon us women at these times. We may have to endure a further sequestration—you're too young to remember that in all its rigour. Look well that nothing is wasted in the house. The butter should be salted down this week—you must see to that. Grandfather must have nourishing broth—strew a few marigolds in it."

Bridget nodded, and dried her eyes hastily as the groom came up. It seemed almost heartless to think of such things as salt butter when dear ones lay in danger, but she knew her mother was right.

"We'll not mourn before it is time," said Mary. "But we'll leave no duty undone, my love, that can help the family."

She set her pale lips closely together and climbed on to the pillion behind Dick. The led horse carried their saddle-bags. At the gate she bid Dick stay and called back anxiously over her shoulder:

"You'll turn the big flitch today, child, and rub in a little more saltpetre? Tell Elizabeth to take the small ham from the chimney. It should be smoked sufficient, I reckon."

"I'll do everything myself," called Bridget. "Greet my father, Ma'am, and keep your heart up! Grandfather and I will be with you on Friday, God willing."

As the horses jogged away up the miry lane, Bridget ran back to the invalid.

"Sir," she cried as she entered his room, "I have but just discovered that my mother is a heroine, for I vow it takes greater courage to look to small duties in a calamity than to face sudden death with boldness. Perhaps," she added softly, kneeling to kiss the poor quivering hand, "perhaps to lie inactive takes the greatest courage of all."

The old man sighed.

"I had hoped to pass my latter years in peace," he declared, "but it was not to be. God willing, I shall be able to travel to Manchester and 'tis most essential I should do so. Let the Jury judge for themselves if such a shattered hulk as I could be a fit subject for the framing of a riot. Oh, Bridget, if we only knew exactly what the indictment was to be!"

"Mr. Dicconson has given us a good notion of it though," declared Bridget. "And I doubt not Mr. Bankes will be prepared. It isn't as if we had anything to hide."

"No, but you see, my poor lass, they may twist things sadly to their own ends. For instance, I have often visited my lord Molyneux as a neighbour and on business—" He broke off, and Bridget answered cheerfully:

"But you'll see, Grandfather, Mr. Dicconson will show it all up as an infamous plot against your lives and properties. You forget that we have Mr. Dicconson!"

"Nay indeed, child, else we were all as good as beggared. Give me the Douay Bible yonder, and go about your business— for I know your mother left your hands full."

"Yes," agreed Bridget with a little laugh. "Yet do you know, I feel as though ordinary occupations were an interruption. The servants would fain stand about all day discoursing upon our hard case, and I'm nearly as bad myself. But I'll mend, though there's an odd sort of consolation in it too."

"'Tis an unwholesome comfort, believe me," returned the old man. "But who am I to chide you? Why cannot I set myself with more energy to my prayers? Come, let us both be prompt to duty."

"Yes, Sir."

But all the same Bridget went away with lagging steps. Then she suddenly became a prey to feverish activity, rushing from buttery to salting-stone and hustling all the maids until everyone was in a bad humour. Conscience then compelled her to ask the old housekeeper's pardon for a sharp speech, a humiliation which Mistress Bridget found most unpleasant. Dinner was a brief and lonely meal, served by old Walter and punctuated by his sighs and dolorous prophecies.

Next day the Squire was so much recovered that Bridget made preparations for the morrow's journey, sending to neighbours to borrow a coach and hurriedly collecting such comforts and comestibles as he might need. She devoted that afternoon to the unpleasant work of salting down fresh butter and packing it into a huge jar—a greasy and tiring performance which she greatly loathed. On Friday morning Bridget was conscientiously pounding away with a wooden pestle, making certain that the butter was compressed into every curve of the last pot before the final layer of salt was laid on to seal it, when she was interrupted.

"There's a lass at the yard door, asking for you," announced Moll, the dairymaid. "She'll noan stir for all Mrs. Elizabeth says to her. A proper bold young madam, selling besoms if you please."

"Oh, Moll, I'm busy! Ask Elizabeth to give her some food if she wants any. We have no need of brooms just now."

"'Tisn't that," said Moll. "She will have it she must speak with you."

"Oh!" said Bridget. A sudden tingling shot through her. "Here—I'll come—don't let her go."

She wiped her hands hurriedly and followed fast on Moll's heels. But the small, squat figure leaning against the door-jamb was quite strange to her, and her eagerness departed. She had had the folly to imagine that Roger Dicconson might be visiting her in disguise.

The besom-seller noticed her change of expression.

"You don't know me," she cried. "But I know you, and a friend of yours too. Is he here?"

As Bridget did not answer immediately, she stamped her foot in its coarse, wooden clog.

"Is he here? Is Roger here?" she repeated.

"No," said Bridget. "Come with me," she added, and led the way swiftly back to the dairy.

"Now, what are you come for?" she asked, closing the door.

For a moment Peg faced her without reply. This abrupt, energetic lass, hard at work at the butter crocks, was not her notion of a fine lady.

"You are Mistress Bridget, I suppose?" she said uncertainly.

"Yes." For the life of her Mistress Thornleigh could not speak more graciously; there was something profoundly troubling to her in the presence of this ragged girl.

"Where's Roger Dicconson? Haven't you seen him?"

"I answer no questions to strangers," cried Bridget. "Who are you? Whence come you?"

"Eh, I can't be moidered explaining all that!" exclaimed Peg. "I'll be bound you're the lass as set poor Roger on this murderous game. And now he's dead as like as not, if he is not here."

"Dead!" whispered Bridget. She grew white as a sheet and her eyes widened. She strode up to Peg and seized her by the arm. "Quick! Explain yourself!" she cried.

Peg twisted herself away pettishly.

"I know all about your plan, and about Roger passing himself off as Captain Howard," she said. "I've been working for him up and down the country, and I can show you summat to prove I speak truth."

She jerked her clenched hand almost into Bridget's face and unclosed it, showing the little Jacobite seal, open, in her dirty, work-roughened palm. Then she snatched it away again and thrust it into her bosom.

"You've no call to look at me as though you could strike me. You've no love for the lad, and I'd—I'd give him my heart's blood."

"How did you get that token? But it doesn't matter," Bridget went on quickly. "Why do you think he is in danger? Have you a message to me?"

"Yes. I was to take this to you at Manchester and bid you provide lodging for me. And the little rose was to let you know I am in Roger's confidence and have helped him to find witnesses."

"I am travelling to Manchester with Mr. Thornleigh at noon," said Bridget stiffly. "And you may accompany us if you wish."

The besom-seller laughed rudely.

"I've been to Manchester, my fine Madam. And somebody has blown the gaff—I mean they have found out or suspect our Roger. There's a warrant out for him—aye, and a posse of Dutch troopers on his tracks that would think as little of giving him a crack on the head as they would of crushing a fly."

"But where is he?" asked Bridget, suddenly beginning to tremble.

"Aye, where is he?"

Peg let her bundle clatter to the floor, for the hand which held it had suddenly grown nerveless. "He were at Manchester this morning early, for my Dad saw him. He was with that villain Lunt, and stood naming the prisoners to him as they were brought out for exercise."

"Then your father spoke to him?"

"Nay, he did not. He was mad with him, and his head full of some make of nonsense about me. But he heard Lunt say that

Roger was to ride post to Thornleigh Hall and deliver a paper to Squire Standish as lay hid there—"

"That isn't true," interrupted Bridget.

"Nay, doubtless it was but a tale o' Lunt's. But Father says 'twas what he heard: 'We'll send a posse to take Standish,' says Lunt, 'and find the commission, and that will convince the Jury of all my information.'"

"And what did he say? Are you sure it was—he?" asked Bridget, still fearful of pronouncing Roger's name.

"Dad said he was sure 'twas the same," said Peg. "And that Roger recognized him, for he turned away and muffled up his face and spoke to Lunt in a feigned voice after. They had my poor old chap chained up there. He's a traitor and all, but there's just one thing he didn't give away—Roger's real name."

"Captain Howard will come here, then?" resumed Bridget, her face lighting up. "I see no danger in this."

"That's not all," declared Peg, rubbing her hand wearily across her brow. "I only went to Manchester yesterday, looking for my Dad, for he wasn't at his business over at the card-houses as he should have been."

"You must be very tired," said Bridget, more kindly than she had yet spoken.

"Aye, I've ridden from Manchester since daybreak, and 'tis thirty-eight miles if 'tis a furlong! But you don't understand! I saw my Dad with a posse of soldiers this morning—and I got speech with him and learned what I telled you—and more."

"What more?" whispered Bridget.

"Why, that they were carrying a warrant for Captain Howard's arrest—not for Standish at all—don't you see 'twas a trap of Lunt's? He sent Roger out o' the town riding post for here, and now he has loosed his blood-hounds after him! We mun find him, lass! Where is he? I made sure he'd come to you."

Bridget shook her head.

Chapter Twenty-Five

"You heard nothing of him on the road?" she asked.

"No. I didn't stay to ax questions. I came hell-for-leather and those —— troopers are at my heels—they'd be here now only for the fog."

"We must detain them then," said Bridget decidedly. "They can have done him no harm if he is still being searched for. I will detain them."

Peg's drooping spirits were revived by Bridget's confident tone.

"I'll send out folk I can trust to watch and warn Mr. Dicconson," went on Bridget. "But how will they know him? Alas, none of them knows him by sight."

"It must be my job then," said Peg. "Are you jealous, Mistress?"

"Nay, but you're so exhausted," protested the young lady, a brilliant, angry colour springing into her cheeks.

"I'll make shift to watch, howsomedever, for the lad I love. Aye, Mistress, I'll take him from you if I can, I warn you. I see now you're bonny—but you haven't the love for him that I have."

"You lie!" said Bridget.

The words sprang from her lips unbidden. She could add nothing to them; she had stooped to take up the challenge flung down by Scutcher's Peg. Was this proud Bridget—the heart so difficult to win?

"You have come down to my level, I see," commented Peg with grim approval. "Well, if he can live this week through, he can choose between us."

Her hand kept playing with her kerchief as she spoke, for beneath the linen folds, thrust down against her heart, lay Roger's letter. She triumphed inwardly at the sight of Bridget's perturbation.

"He's not dead yet," she cried, obstinately stifling her qualms of conscience. "He's not dead yet!"

Chapter Twenty-Six

Peg's heart was heavy as she sat by the fire in the huge kitchen eating the meal which the housekeeper set before her. She longed to distinguish herself in Roger's service, but could hit upon no good plan. Bridget had promised her the farm pony to ride, and she resolved to change into her boy's clothes. The fog thickened as she stuffed down the food, disdaining the knife—two-pronged forks were reserved exclusively for the dining-parlour.

"Like as not those rascally dragoons have gone astray," she muttered, as she hurried into the yard, where the pony was munching a heap of hay.

Perhaps it might be possible to persuade the troopers to accept her as a guide. Fatigue vanished in the excitement of this thought, and Peg flung her besoms into a corner and scrambled into the saddle determined to be away before the great coach with its four heavily harnessed horses moved from the front door. She was familiar with the roads and was able to take several short-cuts, leaving a trail of open gates and remorselessly battened gaps behind her. Dragoons were a noisy lot, and she was bound to hear them a long way off, for Peg had the sharpest of ears, and it was now the troopers whom she was determined to intercept, not Roger himself. It was so long before she fell in with them that she began to fear that they had already seized their prey and were returning to Manchester with their prisoner.

Knowsley Park was fenced with a deer pale, and Peg had to go round it. She made inquiries as she passed through the village of Prescott, straggling on either side of the long hill, but there was no news of the dragoons there or even at St. Helens and she began to fear that she would drop asleep in the saddle. The track—for it was little more—skirted a piece of wild moorland—a spur of the great untilled tract known as Barton Moss where folk went to cut peat.

A rider appeared coming towards her at this point; she noticed that he bestrode an unshod horse and led two others. Peg called eagerly:

"Are you a brother of Pharaah Lee?"

He clattered past, then checked his three beasts in masterly fashion and wheeled them round to face her.

"I'm Peg-the-Scutcher!" she cried.

"Greetings, my girl, but I cannot stay now. There are red-coats out and about, and I'm bound to take these beauties to a safe place."

"Wait and I'll give you news. Tell me first, where are the soldiers?"

"Up yonder, drinking at the ale-house, with their sweating beasts tied in the cold wind. The poor red-coat fools can't see in this weather."

"Stay, lad." Peg drew a long breath and whispered: "Know you the place where it is all quagmire, down yonder—and a sort of island like with a clump of bushes i' the midst? There's a way in—and a way out—for them as knows it."

"Maybe I do," said the man.

"Well, don't put your horses there," said Peg, "because I want it myself. I'll lead the dragoons there if I can. And hark you, if Phary be with you, pray him to come to me."

The gipsy nodded and slipped into the fog, his horses' hoofs drumming dully on the heather as he moved rapidly away.

Peg hurried on, much exhilarated by this encounter. She soon came to the ale-house, with the saddled horses tied up outside, and hung about the door for a few minutes nerving herself for the ensuing interview. At length she tied her pony to a ring and walked boldly in, trying to imitate the heavy rolling gait of a country yokel.

"Which of your honours is the leader, please you?" she inquired, pulling her forelock and making a leg, awkwardly enough.

The King's Messenger looked up from his pot.

"Because my master—that's t' parson at Moorbrow, heerd as how you was held up here by t' fog, and he sent me to ax did you need a guide to St. Helens for I can act as such."

"Where's your master?" inquired Tomkins abruptly.

"He's gone whoam," responded Peg. "But I have to ride on to Prescott tonight, to fetch back our young lady tomorrow."

"Prescott, that's on our way," cried the Corporal. "Art sure thou knowest the road, eh?"

"If I don't I'll get a drubbing," returned Peg with a grin. "But I mun ha' a pint before we go."

The Messenger flung a penny on the counter and Peg quaffed off her glass without waste of time. It made her feel rather light-headed when she got into the air. The dragoons mounted with a great clatter of bridle chains and jingle of spurs, and Peg's heart began to beat rapidly as she jogged ahead of them through the open gateway on to the moor.

"Halt there! That's not the road!" exclaimed the Messenger.

"'Tis all the road there is," returned Peg. "You're not the first to travel it."

She waited till he came up and then pointed to fresh hoof-marks running alongside the sunken track deeply scored by the wheels of turf wagons.

"Curse this for a savage country—lead on then," called Tomkins.

Peg struck the pony and went forward at a canter. It was difficult to calculate the miles once the turf stacks were passed.

The troopers, who had crossed the big moss that morning, followed unsuspiciously. At last the group of bushes all wreathed about with travellers-joy came in sight. Peg glanced back: the soldiers loomed very large, strong and fierce behind her.

"There's a bad bit here—you had better let me try it first," she called back, pressing on the pony.

"Keep in sight, at your peril!" shouted the Messenger.

Peg looked over her shoulder again with a grin and proceeded at a walk.

"Come on—it's sound enough," she cried. "But follow behind—go not wide of my track."

She led the way slowly round the bushes, then suddenly jerked her pony, hit it smartly, and urged it into the copse.

"Good-bye now! You're safe till morning!" she shouted mockingly.

She had marked down what she thought to be the safe way out, but now when she came to the place, cunningly screened by the bushes, the pony floundered, sank in the wet ground to his knees, and then struggled snorting back to firm land. The angry troopers were crashing through the bushes. Peg slipped down, whipped the pony till it galloped off in one direction while she ran away like a lapwing in another, trusting to the fog to hide her.

Here was the path by which they had entered. She flew along it, rejoicing in her noiseless steps. The troopers were blundering into each other, with frightful oaths, one horse plunged into the bog and rent the air with screams, which sounded almost human. The men could not find the path again, and in another moment Peg would be in safety.

A shot rang out and went wide, ricochetting over a long pool of water and stirring the wild-fowl to flight with loud clamour.

There was a second shot. The earth seemed to rise up and smite Peg on the chin. Then she found herself crawling under thick whin bushes in the cold, wet grass.

"It's a shame," she sobbed. "A shame! It wasn't worth it—no man is worth it—and yet—I'm glad."

.   .   .   .   .

Meanwhile, on the morning of this same day, Roger had ridden out of Manchester, choosing the lane which skirted Barton Moss in preference to the highway to Warrington. Recent heavy rains had spoilt the roads earlier than usual this season. As a rule the main thoroughfares were passable up to Christmas: after that the sound of wheels was heard no more, until the road-plough was produced from its niche under the church porch in spring, and applied to furrow up the deepest ruts.

Travellers on horseback and foot had as usual broken into the fields on either side of the road, and Roger followed their example. Lunt had proposed to lend his own horse—a good one, which he had calmly purloined from its owner when accompanying a search-party a few months earlier. Roger had prudently declined the offer, and bestrode his own Noble, moving along at a brisk pace, engrossed in wondering what sort of reception he would get from Mistress Bridget. Could it be true that Squire Standish had taken refuge there? It seemed a most unreasonable risk, but he knew the loyalty of Catholics to friends in trouble, and no doubt if Standish had appealed for shelter at Thornleigh it might have been accorded to him.

Mile succeeded mile, and nothing arose to break the monotony of the journey. The day was mild and foggy, and though Roger met with several stout farmer's wives, jogging into Manchester to sell their butter and fowl, there seemed no one travelling in the same direction as himself. He had traversed nearly half the distance when his horse laid back its ears and quickened its pace nervously. Roger glanced round, but there was no one in sight. Still, it was evident that the animal had heard something, and its demeanour gave him the uncomfortable sensation of being trailed. It was open country, but there were thick hedges about the fields, and the day was so foggy that it was impossible to distinguish a moving object at more than a hundred yards.

He crossed the road at the first gap, galloped down a grass field on the farther side, and halted to listen. His horse flung up its head, its ears flickered, and Roger, too, heard something this time—the rhythmic thudding of galloping hoofs. A mounted figure loomed through the mist, and paused when it perceived him to be stationary. Roger moved off at a trot, one hand caressing the pistol in its holster—doubtless a highwayman was hanging about him. He was indignant at the thought, for it was the boast of the district that there were no such miscreants within the hundred. He trotted on briskly, while the unknown still dogged him. He could hear another horse upon his right and seemed to distinguish a certain creaking of leather and rhythmic jingling and clinking to the rear—sounds usually associated with mounted troops.

Taking advantage of a sudden declivity he struck southward across the great moor, confiding in speed to elude his pursuers—if pursuers they were indeed! Presently hearing nothing more, he slackened speed and proceeded at an easy canter. The air was heavy with the scent of wet earth and rotting leaves, and the fog which had darkened the sky ever since he had left Manchester now began to rise round him in ever-thickening billows.

"I must get back to the road," thought Roger, "'twill never do to lose my way. I should have gone by Warrington."

He guided his horse towards a line of trees which he supposed marked the thoroughfare, but when he reached the fence it was to find that it bounded a tangled copse, full of ferns and briars. What he feared had come to pass—he had lost the right direction, and now stood still listening. A thrush sang intermittently in spite of the weather and innumerable tits were chirruping to each other as whole families explored the crevices of a tall larch. Otherwise all was so still that the water could be heard dripping from twig and thorn. Roger turned and very slowly endeavoured to retrace his steps; he had no desire, however, to fall in with the men who had seemed to be in pursuit of him, and there was something strange about their appearance which harassed his mind. The more he thought about his mission from Lunt, the less he liked it. The Squire of Thornleigh would have to surrender to his recognizances that very day, and it was quite likely that a party would be sent to escort him. It would be ridiculous—even for an informer—to endeavour to plant a commission under the circumstances, and Lunt must have wondered that he had made no protest. Was it a test? Was it a trap? Could the riders who had followed him be seeking to arrest him?

Roger had spent the previous week in the saddle: he had been as far as Lancaster to secure the attendance of the under-gaoler who had assisted in branding Wilson in the hand, and was aware that physical weariness had rendered his brain less alert than usual. His thoughts had been foolishly fixed on the pleasure of seeing Bridget—for though she was so cold to him there was a tormenting joy in being near her—and he had not sufficiently examined Lunt's motives. In any case "Captain Howard" was at the end of his career. Roger decided to return to Manchester and to lie hid until such time as he could appear in Court in his true colours as a witness for the defence.

He rode slowly up and down for an hour or two, little guessing that Peg had passed within a few miles of him. In the afternoon the air cleared a little, and the sun appeared, hanging in the mist like a white wafer. If Roger was supposed to be proceeding to Thornleigh his pursuers should be far on their way, and it ought to be safe to return by the road on which he had started that morning.

The position of the sun allowed him to make a rough calculation of his position, and he retraced his steps without much difficulty. As he drew near the highway he heard the clatter of plunging horses, the shouts, creaking of harness and cracking of whips which betokened a very ordinary winter accident, namely a coach stuck fast in the mire. Roger's first thought was to proffer help—his second that any intercourse with strangers might be dangerous. He hung back therefore until the sound of a girl's voice, raised high above the din, reached his ears.

"Stop flogging the poor brute, you fool! Stop it, I say! You must get a spade and dig the wheel clear."

Roger leaped the hedge and rode over to the coach, hat in hand, his face eagerly flushed. Bridget was standing in the mud, the postilion and coachman stared down at her, while old Squire Thornleigh peered anxiously out of the window and the horses trembled and sweated.

"You'll break the axle if you—why, Roger!"

Bridget's angry voice changed in a trice as her eyes fell on the newcomer. There was a warmth and tenderness in her tone as she pronounced his name, which struck the man dumb with joy. She ran to him, splashing through the puddles, and glanced up anxiously into his face.

"You must not linger here! Have you not been warned?" Her voice dropped to an urgent whisper. "They have a file of dragoons out looking for you with a warrant."

"A warrant for whom?" he asked. His breath came thickly; he felt as though he were drowning as he held the gaze of her blue eyes.

"For Captain Howard— Oh, dear love," breathed Bridget, "put yourself in safety."

"Can you get us a couple of labourers with spades, Sir? I should be infinitely obleeged," called the old gentleman.

"I believe a few bushes will do the trick, Mr. Thornleigh," said Roger. "Will you hold my horse a moment?" he added to the girl, not yet daring to call her by her name.

There were hazels in the hedge and he slashed them down with fingers that trembled, wild rose-bushes too, set with little yellow leaves, which showered about him as he hacked with his knife at the thorny stems. The postilion came to join him, while the coachman soothed the horses. When the bushes had been laid under the wheels, Roger harnessed his own horse with tackle produced from the rumble. The five steeds were encouraged with shouts and cries, and their united effort heaved the cumbrous vehicle into motion and dragged it on to firm ground. Bridget followed, climbing along the bank, and Roger ran back to meet her.

"You don't really know me," she began unexpectedly. "And no doubt when you do, you will not like me so well. All the same, I'm yours, Roger! And I'm racked with fear while you are in danger."

"I'm ready to die now," he said incoherently.

They forgot the waiting coach, impatient grandfather, possible witnesses. Young love transformed the muddy lane under the pall of fog into a garden of paradise.

"Bridget!" called the old man.

It was the voice of duty: their hands fell apart and they came towards the coach together, their faces still flushed with joy.

Silently Roger opened the door, let down the step, and handed Bridget in.

"You will be wise, I think, to ride on ahead of us, young gentleman," said the Squire. "Our company may be dangerous."

"Yes, Sir, and mine no doubt equally perilous to you. But we shall not meet again save in Court and I have a secret counsel to impart."

He leaned into the coach and whispered very seriously into the old man's ear. William repeated the message.

"Must I do it, think you?" he queried.

"Sir Roland, I fancy," answered Dicconson after a moment's thought. "Yes, I think Sir Roland is quite safe."

He was very near Bridget as he leaned across her, his coat all beaded with the mist. How young and strong he was, she thought proudly.

Making a great effort, Bridget said as Roger withdrew:

"That girl—the besom-seller—is out searching for you."

"Oh, Peg can take care of herself," he answered easily. "They have clapped her father in gaol on some pretext."

He sprang on to his horse, glanced back once and again, and soon disappeared under the dripping trees.

Chapter Twenty-Seven

HE PRISONERS were gathered together in a small, dark room at the back of the Sessions House in which the trials were to be held. Several gaolers were present and the gentlemen were forbidden to converse or to consult one another. Their Counsel and Solicitors were already in Court, though they were not allowed to take any part in the proceedings. The loud rumbling tones of Sir Giles Eyre could be heard haranguing the Grand Jury and giving the charge respecting High Treason. Every now and then he raised his voice for some particularly spicy phrase or epithet, which was regularly greeted with clamour by the crowded audience.

"Our occasion of coming together at this unusual time, armed with this Commission, is from Informations received of the treachery and treasonable practices against the Government of their present Majesties, in which Protestants of the Church of England, as they call themselves, are mingled with papists as the iron and clay in Nebuchadnezzar's image, and have jointly conspired for the subversion of the good and quiet Government."

This flight of fancy produced a prolonged burst of applause which might have been in part ironic.

In the prisoners' room Lord Molyneux, who was stone deaf, remarked in a loud voice that it was plaguey cold. A gaoler jostled him rudely, bidding him be silent, but the old man continued his grumbling.

"What, must you seize me in bed, and devour my substance with your foreign mercenaries and their women—such folk as never before crossed my threshold, I promise you! And must I be starved with cold to boot? Why, the foulest cut-purse couldn't have been worse treated than I was on the road to London—"

"Hold your peace, you old fool," remarked the turnkey.

"It's all to get money," continued the Baronet. "I know your informers, Wilson and Barker, and it is all because I would not recommend Barker to be Post Master of Warrington—"

His voice was drowned in the noise occasioned by the rising of the Grand Jury.

"What happens next?" whispered William Dicconson to old Squire Thornleigh, who had been accommodated with a small stool as he was unable to stand.

"Why, the Jury will have to read the bills—that is, the information sworn to by the witnesses for the Crown. We ought to have a chance of challenging the Jury, but they won't give it us unless they bring in a bill against us."

"And then we plead 'Not Guilty,' I suppose?" pursued Dicconson.

"Aye, and pray for time to prepare our defence. There's the Court adjourning—the Judges are going to dinner. Now, neighbours, what say you?"

He nudged Mr. Dicconson with his elbow, and unclosing his gnarled old fingers, showed him a rosary hidden in his palm.

Presently the prisoners divided into two groups: the papists drew close together, each man held his right hand thrust into his pocket and their lips moved though no words were audible.

"At this rate we shall not get to the real business until Saturday," whispered Thornleigh at length, "and that is Our Blessed Lady's day. Keep your heart up, neighbour Dicconson."

In the afternoon the Jury considered the bills in the company of Mr. Winter of the King's Bench office, who acted as clerk of the arraignments. They returned a bill against Sir William Gerard.

"Have you Sir William Gerard in your custody?" demanded the Judge of the gaoler.

"I have," he responded, and turned to escort the prisoner to the Bar.

Mr. Winter read the indictment in English. The substance of the charge was:

"That he the first day of February in the third year of the reign of our Lord and Lady King William and Queen Mary over England, falsely, wickedly and traitorously did procure, obtain, receive and accept a commission from James the Second, late King of England, constituting him Sir William Gerard to be a Colonel of Horse in an army to be led by him and other their Majesties' enemies raised with intent to levy war in this Kingdom under colour and pretence of restoring the late King James."

The indictment was very long—for who should trouble to shorten it when the cost of setting it forth was imposed on the prisoners? Sir William looked covertly about the Court as he listened in apparent impassivity. The witnesses for the Crown looked bold and self-important, hawking and spitting on the floor as though the whole place belonged to them! There was her ladyship, gazing anxiously towards him, and surrounded by her own kinsfolk the Cliftons. That nervous-looking group behind her must be the witnesses for the prisoners—yes, there was Taafe in the midst, and Legh Bankes in his wig and gown. He could not see Roger Dicconson and, to gain time, requested that the bill might be read again in Latin. While this was being done, he glanced more openly about the Court, but still in vain. His Betsy must not notice his dismay. He caught her tearful gaze and looked back fondly, but his hands played nervously with the herbs with which the dock was strewn. The sweet pungent scent rose up in his nostrils and he remembered with an unexpected twist of fancy that 'twas in the simple garden at Lytham that he had courted his wife—aye—the first kisses had been exchanged over the rosemary bushes! He picked up a sprig of the little grey herb and thrust it into his sash: trust a woman to notice the gesture: she would understand!

He examined the crowd again while the clerk's voice gabbled on: no, Mr. Roger Dicconson was not in Court.

At last the time came to plead.

"Not guilty!" said Sir William loudly. "And, my Lords, I pray leave to have a copy of the indictment and of the panel."

Sir Giles Eyre raised his head indignantly at such a presumptuous demand.

"A copy of the indictment is not allowable by law," he returned shortly. "And neither—what?"

His clerk and Mr. Winter whispered urgently from their seats below him. "Oh, very well, then. Mr. Sheriff, the Court desires you to supply the prisoner with a copy of the panel—before eleven tonight," he added reluctantly.

The prisoners' friends turned to each other in dismay. The Judges were to sit again at seven on the following morning—they had only the dark hours of the night in which to consider which of the Jury it would be well to challenge—no time to make inquiries or verify information or produce acceptable reasons! But meanwhile business was going rapidly forward. The Jury brought in more bills and the other prisoners entered the Court. Five were arraigned and charged:

"That whereas an open war and notoriously public between the most serene illustrious and most excellent Princes our Lord and Lady William and Mary by the grace of God of England Scotland France and Ireland King and Queen Defenders of the Faith—"

Roger had entered between Legh Bankes and his friend Mr. Beresford. He was well though plainly dressed, and worked his way forward until he was just behind Bridget. He wore a full black wig and a wide-brimmed hat, and his cloak concealed the lower part of his face. Bankes, glancing at the little knot of peruked gentlemen, considered him indistinguishable. He had set men to watch and they reported that the dragoons had not yet returned to their barracks. In another few hours, if things went well, all would be safe.

The clerk was now naming the prisoners.

"One Sir Roland Stanley late of Hooton Baronet, Sir Thomas Clifton late of the parish of Kirkham in the County of Lancashire Baronet, William Dicconson late of the parish of Eccleston in the County of Lancashire aforesaid Esquire and William Thornleigh late of the Parish of Sefton aforesaid, gentleman—subjects and each of them being subjects of the said Lord the King and Lady the Queen...the premises well knowing and each of them knowing—the fear of God in their hearts not having—nor any of them having neither weighing...the duty of their allegiance but being by the instigation of the devil moved and seduced and each of them being moved and seduced as false traitors...devising the government of this Kingdom of England into an intolerable and most miserable bondage to bring and enslave to the aforesaid French King Lewis..."

Further, the prisoners were accused of having "falsely maliciously diabolically and traitorously have compassed imagined invented devised and intended the said King and Queen William and Mary off and from the regal state...to depose throw down and altogether to deprive and them the said King and Queen to death and final destruction to put and bring—"

The indictment continued, accusing with bringing in the French King and his army in order to procure the "miserable slaughter of the faithful subjects of the King and Queen throughout this whole Kingdom."

The pages of vellum clattered as the clerk turned them one by one; he seemed to roll the legal repetitions unctuously over his tongue. Four of the prisoners listened with pained attention, trying to note the dates on which they were supposed to have formed an unlawful assembly—the fifth, deaf Lord Molyneux, gave it up, and turning aside, was intent on studying the Jurymen.

The lawyers and their clerks were scribbling like mad in their note-books—February 1st, 1691.

"God bless thee, Roger!" murmured Bankes, wiping the sweat from his brow. The room was cold enough, but it had been an anxious quarter of an hour. "Only for him," he added to Pigott, "these poor folk would have had to answer for every action of a day three years past without the slightest preparation or time to reflect."

"There's nothing new—we're prepared for all," whispered Pigott in Madam Thornleigh's ear.

The indictment was read in Latin. Then Mr. Walmsley was also arraigned and charged with receiving a commission. He protested that he was named in the indictment as of the "Parish of Church" whereas there was no such parish.

The Court made short shift of this. If he insisted on his plea he should do it at his peril, they announced.

Stanley, Clifton, Dicconson, Langton and Thornleigh were then told that it was proposed to try them all five together if they would but challenge thirty-five of the panel peremptorily. They agreed to this after a short consultation, and were bidden to prepare for their trial next day. The prisoners were taken out of Court, a mournful little procession, two hobbling on sticks, and all pale and worn from their recent confinement. On Mr. Aaron Smith's motion the Court ordered the Sheriff immediately to summon forty more householders for the panel.

"'Tisn't legal, we should have a week's notice," grumbled the solicitors for the defence. They dared make no protest. The Judge directed that no subpœna should be granted for summoning witnesses for the prisoners, but that a copy of such witnesses' names must be given to Mr. Aaron Smith.

The Court then adjourned, and the officials filed out. It was a gorgeous procession: the four Justices in trailing robes of scarlet and ermine marched slowly along, followed by the local Judges; then the King's Counsel in their crisp white wigs and rustling silk gowns, Mr. Aaron Smith and a host of clerks and gentlemen; the prisoners had made a poor show in contrast. Bridget's eyes were full of tears; the angry epithets still rang in her ears as she helped her mother to adjust her mantle. They waited while the crowd poured into the street, and then went forth, surrounded by their friends. There was a little damp garden, planted with clipped yews, behind the Sessions House, and Roger pointed it out to Bridget, while her mother stood gazing doubtfully at the seething mass of humanity which filled the public square facing the building.

Bridget laid her finger on her lips and tiptoed through the gate.

"Only one minute!" she murmured.

"Look at me!" besought Roger. "Are you indeed my own?"

Scarcely were the words breathed than Bridget leant towards him, but before their lips touched they were hailed by words which parted them like a sword.

"Are you Captain Howard?"

A gipsy had approached them silently and now pushed between them, his black eyes staring curiously from face to face.

"Don't answer!" whispered Bridget in terror.

"Why, it's Pharaoh!" cried Roger, recognizing the lad. "Wait a while—I'll speak to thee presently."

"I can't wait," he answered. "'Tis a question of life and death."

"Dare you trust him?" queried Bridget.

"I'll follow you in an instant, my dearest," declared Roger, his voice still trembling with emotion. "Here is Mr. Beresford, who will escort you home. Now, Pharaoh, what is it?" he added impatiently as Bridget moved away.

The gipsy instead of answering put a little packet into his hand.

Roger unwound the rag from a soiled envelope, and then uttered a startled exclamation.

"Whence had you this? Quick—what has happened?"

"They took it from her breast," said the gipsy. He spoke steadily and his bold black eyes were dry, but as he read the consternation in Roger's face, his own began to work.

"There's blood on it!" gasped Dicconson.

"Aye, I reckon hoo's dying. Hoo wants to see you and I swore you should come."

"Peg dying! What villain can have harmed her?" asked Roger.

"Thou art the man!" answered Pharaoh.

As Roger stared uncomprehendingly, he added: "'Twas for love o' you. She went in boy's rig and guided the troopers into a marsh. Aye, she tempted them to follow her, pretending she was leading them to your hiding-place. One was nearly drowned, and the Corporal fired at her. We picked her up in a ditch! She cannot last out the night."

Roger paused for one moment, glancing first after Bridget then at his own letter with its deadly stain. He measured Pharaoh with his eyes.

"Lead the way, I'll follow," he said. "Have you horses?"

Pharaoh nodded.

Bridget, looking back, anxiously watched the two figures in the waning light. Their colloquy only lasted a few moments, then the gipsy led the way down a side alley and Roger followed him without a glance for her; nay, he seemed to be gazing at the letter in his hand as though it had blotted all thought of her from his mind.

Chapter Twenty-Eight

A FEW DIRTY BLANKETS, bent over twisted hazel fronds, made a low shelter under which Peg lay on a heap of hay. A smoky fire burnt outside and hot stones, wrapped in rags, had been placed round the dying girl.

"Yon chap who is with her is some make of surgeon," whispered Pharaoh, holding Roger back for a moment. "But he's one who likes to keep himself quiet, so you'll noan split, eh?"

"You can trust me."

Roger had ridden fast, but now that he was within a few yards of his goal he hesitated. Peg had been so full of life and vigour only three days ago! He dreaded inexpressibly to see the gay, childish creature stricken with hopeless pain.

The makeshift tent was illumined with rays of firelight, and as he stood staring at the trampled ground the man, kneeling within, spoke softly and clearly:

"So you see, my poor child, we must offer all for the greater honour and glory of God."

Roger started violently. It was strange to hear the famous Jesuit maxim enunciated at such a time and place. Could it be accident or was "the sort of doctor" also a member of the Society?

"I'll believe it," said a trembling voice, "if he comes—if Roger comes before I dee."

"I'm here," said the young man.

He drew near and sank on his knees in the rimy grass, but even though so near he could not see Peg's face.

"Art thou frettin'?" asked the girl tenderly. "Eh, lad, that's not for me?"

He drew nearer silently and the stranger moved a little and raised his lantern so that the light fell upon the bed.

"It is all fair," went on the faint, labouring voice. "I have but my own self to thank. I gave thee my love, thou knows, Roger, and now I give thee my life—and I'm—fain—"

"Oh, Peg!" murmured Roger, and then choked.

"Yo' see he liked me!" announced Peg, with a certain triumph, turning her head towards the man in the dark cloak. "Now listen—oh, I'm tired!"

The stranger moistened her lips.

"There's something she wants to say to you," he declared. "I'll go outside for a moment, but there's very little time."

"Are you—" began Dicconson, then he checked the query and made the sign of the Cross. "Are you a member of the College of St. Aloysius?"

The stranger bowed his head without speaking; as he withdrew Peg began to whisper urgently.

"Look you, my lad, you mustn't seek to bring the red-coats to justice. 'Twas my own doing—I 'ticed 'em into the bog and they were in their rights to fire. I want you to promise as you'll do nought—you can tell the truth if you are axed and if you're not axed you'll let it be."

"Oh, that is too cruel—"

"Nay—'tis best. Promise! And, lad! You'll look after my old Dad?"

"Yes, Peg, I promise you I will. Are you in pain, my little lass?"

"Not now," she sighed, and added with a frightened cry, "You won't leave me? Promise you won't leave me?"

"No, I'll stay—I won't leave you," repeated Roger.

He took her hand in his, and she sank into a half-conscious

state. The priest, wrapped in his cloak, prayed and slept by turns, and the gipsies came and went about the fire.

Roger laid the girl gently down and sat beside her until broad day. She still breathed, and he thought that at any movement of withdrawal her fingers strove to close round his.

Pharaoh had sobbed himself to sleep: the other gipsies went about their morning tasks, bringing fuel, feeding their horses and leading them off to water.

The Jesuit came in presently and looked at his patient. He shook his head and presently the two men began to talk in low voices.

"It seems you are concerned in this trial, Sir?" said the priest. "I must warn you that this poor child may live some hours. The bullet is lodged in the lung, I believe, and the loss of blood was great before these good people found her. The pulse is very faint," he added, touching her wrist.

"Can any help be sought? Could anything more be done?" asked Roger.

The other shook his head.

"Useless," he said. "I gave her conditional baptism. No earthly aid can reach her now. I think she will go without waking."

As time wore on Roger became tortured with anxiety as to what might be happening at the Sessions House, but he did not stir.

It was an hour or two past noon when Peg sighed and said faintly:

"Oh, Roger, lift me up!"

He slid his arm under the improvised pillow and raised her gently until her tousled yellow head rested against his shoulder.

"How sweet the whin smells!" she said thickly. And then: "I'm noan afeared!"

Chapter Twenty-Eight

"Will you come, Sir?" called Roger.

"I mean no harm," murmured Peg, with a little upward glance as the priest came in. "Oh, lad, she's bonny! You'll bury me at th' owd chapel at Wrightington in the sun, and get—one of your priests—to bless the grave to keep off boggarts?"

"Peg," said Roger, "this is a priest, here beside you."

A startled look crossed her face and then she looked up at Roger, saying trustfully:

"If thou says it's reet—it's reet for me."

The Jesuit leaned forward quickly and made a sign of benediction, for Peg, with this simple profession of faith, had breathed her last.

.   .   .   .   .

"Where is young Dicconson? Where is Roger?"

Periwigged heads swayed together with the anxious query. Legh Bankes was scarcely on speaking terms with Mr. Beresford: had he not allowed the most valuable witness to be wiled away without a single protest?

Legh Bankes was receiving company after supper, and the room was crowded with folk whose names were on the roll of witnesses, and neighbouring squires and the ladies who had come to inquire how the case was going.

Four gentlemen had come over from Paris with a safe-conduct from King William: Sir Henry Wingfield, his tutor Mr. Perkins, Mr. Widrington, brother to Lord Widrington and Mr. Martin Buckland. Legh Bankes halted before the last-named with an inquiring frown.

"Mr. Buckland, I believe? But I understood, Sir, that we decided you should not appear here? We decided that in view of the fact of your—acquaintance"—he would not name Colonel Parker and Mr. Crosby more particularly—"it would be wiser for you to be entirely dissociated from my clients."

"You decided, Mr. Bankes," declared Buckland jovially. "But since that time I have come to an accommodation with my father. The old gentleman wishes to marry again and has provided for me very handsomely."

Bankes tried to interrupt. "Nevertheless, Sir—"

"And whereas and moreover! Good friend, spare me your legal jargon. I have a notion that one of your clients at least will be glad to see me."

The little lawyer stiffened perceptibly at this fatuous remark. He was acutely anxious about Roger's disappearance but determined to show a bold front to friends and colleagues.

"I cannot conceive, Sir, of whom you are thinking," he said. "And I have an appointment—I must leave you."

"If 'tis to wait on the Thornleighs I will go with you," suggested the beau.

"Infinitely obliged," murmured Bankes, his face the picture of vexation. "But the ladies are receiving no one."

"They might make an exception for me," insisted Buckland.

"Well, you can try if you like," returned the other ungraciously. "But I wait upon them on business and therefore necessarily alone."

When later that night Bankes was ushered into the company of the ladies who had gathered together for mutual comfort, he mentioned Buckland's name.

"We refused to see him," said Madam Thornleigh, and her daughter struck in sharply, her blue eyes flashing fire:

"Why does he come here? He can do us nought but harm."

.   .   .   .   .

The Court was crowded next morning and a noisy crowd had assembled in the street outside. The envoys of the Crown had rallied their supporters in large numbers, and there was the usual contingent of folk who came to feast a morbid curiosity, and those of neutral mind who were attracted by any show. Here were brave folk in gilded coaches, with scarlet apparel, drummers, bombardiers and dragoons! The grand London gentlemen were yawning aggrievedly as they took their seats—it was but seven in the morning—and five of the prisoners were brought to the Bar.

The hall was lit with smoky flares and little piles of sweet herbs had been freshly strewed on the Judges' table and in the dock.

Mr. Roger Kenyon, the member of Parliament for Manchester, was present, as legal adviser to Mr. Walmsley; he was conferring anxiously with the other lawyers.

Presently Legh Bankes, who had been anxiously examining the hall through his quizzing glass, whispered to Pigott:

"Send out more messengers, man. We must find Dicconson. The Secretary has brought signed warrants with him and the executions are to take place three days after the trial—if we fail."

Bridget, who was sitting close behind them, heard these dreadful words. This, then, was what Roger had kept from her in London! A qualm of deadly faintness shot through her, and she clenched her hands in her muff till the nails bit into the palm. The gipsy might have been a decoy and Roger might have fallen into Lunt's hands after all.

"You're ill, Ma'am!" murmured Bankes, full of concern.

She shook her head impatiently and stood up, forcing her cold lips into a smile, for Grandfather was looking towards her.

The business of challenge and counter-challenge now began, but here as usual the Crown had the advantage as it was allowed to challenge without showing cause. At length twelve men were selected and sworn, the Jury charged by the Clerk of the Crown, and the indictment opened by the youngest Counsel in the same terms as before. Mr. Gold, the King's Serjeant, spoke next and confidently promised to prove the guilt of the prisoners, dwelling particularly on the supposed fact of an intrigue to bring a French Army onto British soil.

"Gentlemen!" he exclaimed, "we shall go further with you and prove it to you by those very persons that were their agents, how that arms were bought and soldiers listed and actually quartered upon you."

His triumphant voice echoed round the room, the Crown witnesses stood up, but before they were called the prisoners put forward a petition.

"We would ask," they declared, "that the witnesses may be examined apart."

"It should be so with all my heart," returned the Judge hastily. "That is to say, if the King's Counsel assent thereto. But I must say I never remember any instance of it, especially in such a criminal fact."

"Not allowed, not allowed!" muttered the Counsel.

"The Court decides," announced Eyre, "that the prisoners' petition cannot be allowed."

The Crown witnesses glanced at each other with furtive smiles, and John Lunt, the first witness for the King and Queen, was produced and sworn.

"Do you know all the five gentlemen, prisoners at the Bar?" inquired Williams, the leading Counsel.

Lunt turned his hard stare slowly from face to face.

"Certainly, Sir, I know them all," he answered boldly.

"Now," whispered Thornleigh to his next neighbour.

Sir Roland Stanley leaned forward.

"Which is Sir Roland Stanley?" he demanded, raising his voice for the benefit of the public.

Lunt advanced a pace or two and pointed his finger to Sir Thomas Clifton, who stood at the end of the row.

There was instant uproar among the onlookers, shouts of laughter, mingled with booing.

"Mr. Lunt," exclaimed the Judge testily. "Take one of the officers' white staves and lay it upon the head of Sir Roland Stanley."

The witness, no whit taken aback, seized the Crier's staff.

"This man is Sir Roland Stanley," he cried, and laid his wand with great composure on the head of Sir Thomas Clifton.

There was a renewed outcry, and when Mr. Thornleigh inquired which was Sir Thomas Clifton, Lunt indicated Stanley.

For some moments nothing could be distinguished through the jeering clamour of the crowd; when the Sheriff's officers obtained silence, the Judge inquired:

"Had you ever seen these two gentlemen, Mr. Lunt, before the time you brought them their commissions?"

The informer was quick to take the cue.

"Why, no, never in my life!" he asserted roundly.

"Then there is no such mighty matter in the mistake," declared Sir Giles Eyre. "Being told that these were the two gentlemen, you diversified their names, taking one for the other. It's no such mighty matter," he repeated.

Thus encouraged, Lunt proceeded with his accustomed audacity, and swore that Sir Roland Stanley gave him five pounds.

"Two guineas, that is, and the rest in silver," he cocked his eye at the Jury as he thus elaborated his statement.

"Yes, and Sir Thomas Clifton at his house of Lytham gave me ten pounds to buy arms," he went on. "It would be about February in 1690. And before that Sir Roland had given me four pounds. Then in July or August 1691 I was at Standish with Sir Roland Stanley and Mr. Dicconson and Mr. Thornleigh—and—and"—for the life of him he could not remember the name of the fifth prisoner—"and Mr. Lameton and others, and was by them sent into France to acquaint King James with their forwardness."

Bridget sat listening, not only to the evidence brought against the prisoner, but anxiously to every noise in the rear. If

Roger came now could he ever fight his way through the crowd, she wondered? When she turned her head she was sickened by the sight of hundreds of eager faces, all staring as though at a stage play. Grandfather was being tried for his life, and the life of her father, now in prison, virtually depended on the same verdict. And where was Roger? Every past unkind word and glance she had meted out to him rose in her memory and tortured her heart. How could she ever have been misled to seize upon the shadow as she had done? For Buckland had indeed proved to be a mere outward show of manhood; whereas Roger— Oh, if he would but come!

Bridget now bitterly regretted her candour in declaring to her lover that she was not all he thought her. Perhaps he had believed her! Perhaps in his disappointment he had turned to Peg who offered him the charm of uncritical devotion! Then again she chid herself—Roger was not the man to look back once he had set his hand to the plough—something more tangible than a check in love had kept him from his place among the witnesses.

Meanwhile Lunt proceeded with his evidence, his voice growing more and more assured as he instanced the different times he had taken part in treasonable gatherings at which all the prisoners "and a great many more" were invariably present. He was glib enough in stating the names of London merchants on whom the prisoners had given him bills of exchange, for the enlisting of men and the purchase of arms. He did not, however, produce any written account nor yet the names of the fifty men whom he had engaged on Mr. Dicconson's behalf. He swore that in February 1691 he was at Dunkenhalgh, where Mr. Walmsley produced a commission from King James, appointing him Colonel of Horse and Commissions for Mr. Dicconson and Mr. Langton to serve under him, and he presented these commissions in Lunt's presence.

"The gentlemen very humbly accepted them upon their knees, kissed them, and drank King James's health and that of the Queen and Prince." He paused a moment and then added: "Mr. Legh of Lyme was there too, and they did all declare they did not question to be well prepared against the King's landing in the spring."

Mr. Dicconson here craved leave to speak, and inquired with some heat:

"And why, may I ask, Mr. Lunt, if you knew all this three years ago, did you not declare it sooner? Or indeed why did you discover it at all, since your sympathies were all for King James?"

The informer strove to take on a modest and penitent air which became him singularly ill.

"There were some things put on me which I could not do," he announced.

And he turned up his eyes and laid his hand on his heart, at which the Court politely begged him to explain himself further.

"When I was last in France," said Lunt with gusto, "there was a design on foot to kill King William. The Earl of Melfort asked me if I would do it, and I answered that I would."

Aaron Smith frowned: the man made this announcement in far too blithe a tone: he had been particularly warned to allow the admission to be drawn from him with apparent reluctance.

"I came over to England intending to do it," resumed Lunt. "But then as I was travelling the country I met a friar—a Carthusian friar, 'twas—and he assured me when I went to Confession that 'twould be willful murder, and I thereupon made the discovery."

There was a stir in the audience and an ironic clapping of hands, mingled with laughter. This oft rehearsed scene was not going at all as well as Smith had anticipated. He glanced at the leading Counsel and noted that he looked vexed and perturbed.

John Womball, carrier, was called next and gave evidence of having brought arms from London, "horse-loads of them," and seven packs he took in the night to Standish Hall, where he saw all the gentlemen at the Bar except Sir Roland Stanley.

The next witness, also a carrier, proved a disappointment to the officials. He swore that he had carried three boxes to Mr. Dicconson's house but did not know that they were arms. The next, another carrier, sworn witness for the King and Queen, stumped into the box, gazed about, and then declared roundly:

"By fair yea and nay, I know nought on't!"

Two more witnesses appeared and made long rambling statements of having purveyed arms, but without mentioning what kind, where purchased or how paid for. Captain Baker finally swaggered into the box, his sword clattering, his spurs jingling, and improved matters somewhat by a few decided statements. He had gone with a search-party to Standish Hall in July last and had discovered thirty-nine saddles, a good many bridles, and one buff coat. This lost interest by the fact that Standish was not in custody.

There was now a prolonged pause while the King's Counsel and Solicitors consulted among themselves. At last William Dicconson, speaking for himself and the rest, inquired if that was all the evidence there was against them.

"If you have more, we move that you give it all together," he declared.

Sir William Williams hereupon stood up.

"To deal plainly, we have no further evidence to give," he said. A clerk tendered a paper to him, but he dashed it aside. "Unless," he added, "we have occasion given by what may fall from the prisoners' evidence."

There had been a good deal of noise going on in Court, in spite of the efforts of the ushers, but now a sudden silence fell and Sir Roland Stanley was plainly heard.

"My Lords, we are not able to make our observations upon all the improbabilities and incoherence of the evidence given against us, but we are well assured your Lordships' Justice will do it for us: there has been great industry to conceal from us the particular matters we are charged with. All the discoveries we owe to the Providence of God, who protects the innocent—we shall satisfy your Lordships and the gentlemen of the Jury that this is a bloody conspiracy against our lives for the sake of our estates carried on by indigent and necessitous villains."

The prisoners were given leave to call their witnesses. The first was gaoler at Lancaster and swore that in 1690 Lunt was a prisoner in his charge, poor and shabby. Two others swore that Lunt had been a highwayman and had invited them to join him in robbery, a fourth swore that Lunt had sold a horse to three different people on the same day, and another that Lunt told him of the plot and invited him to be a witness against the prisoners but he refused him.

Mr. Legh Bankes came next. The excitement grew as he described his meeting with Mr. Taafe, and stepped down to give place to Taafe himself.

Taafe's story suffered from the same disadvantage as Lunt's —it was obvious that the narrator was a man of no principle who had betrayed each side in turn according to his own advantage. The Jury, however, began to listen with a much greater interest when he described his visits to Legh Bankes and Madam Dicconson, and how finally Mr. Roger Dicconson had been introduced to Lunt.

"Evidence of no value, lacking corroboration," muttered Justice Eyre to his three colleagues. "There's Brown and Wilson to call yet for our side."

"As for Roger Dicconson—I can't find that he exists," murmured Aaron Smith. "My fellows can find no trace of any such person. They must produce him! You'll see they won't be able to produce the rogue! And yet, if they do, I have a cousin of the family who'll swear against him."

"Next witness for the prisoners, Mr. Roger Dicconson, gentleman," proclaimed the clerk, reading from the list rendered to him by Legh Bankes overnight.

There was no answer. The witnesses turned themselves about, looking at each other inquiringly. Bridget sat rigid: the prisoners' hands, resting on the edge of the dock, closed convulsively on the wood, worn with the previous clutch of many desperate fingers.

"Mr. Roger Dicconson, gentleman," repeated the clerk.

"Present," replied a voice hoarse with weariness, and a man, splashed with mud from his riding-boots to his crushed linen collar, began to force his way from the door.

There was a buzz of astonished talk: the ushers, unbidden, went to make a way for the witness, and another gentleman, attired in the height of the fashion and diffusing an agreeable fragrance of jasmine water, seized the opportunity to follow him into Court.

Lunt had been leaning back in his seat with a supercilious expression, but as the witness marched into the box he sat up abruptly and uttered a startled oath.

Womball, Wilson and Baker gazed at each other and then at Lunt with almost ludicrous surprise.

Meanwhile Roger was taking the oath.

"I swear to tell the truth, all the truth, and nothing but the truth, so help me God."

CHAPTER TWENTY-NINE

RIDGET JUMPED to her feet at the sound of Roger's voice; her eyes were bracketed on him and she did not at first notice his companion.

He did not intend to be disregarded, however, and elbowed his way vigorously towards her while Roger went to the witness-box.

Lizzie Dicconson jerked Bridget's sleeve.

"Look, look!" she whispered. "It is Mr. Buckland."

Mistress Thornleigh's blue eyes dwelt coldly for a moment on her whilom lover, then she turned her shoulder on him and devoted all her attention to the witness.

Roger gave his evidence in firm, unfaltering tones and in the most business-like manner, emphasizing the fact of the false commissions, and that Lunt was personally unacquainted with several of his would-be victims.

"We shall call witnesses to prove that Mr. Walmsley was not at Dunkenhalgh in any part of the year 1690, as Mr. Lunt has sworn, and therefore he could not have delivered a commission to Mr. William Dicconson there at that time nor to any of the other gentlemen. At my first encounter with Mr. Lunt, I took steps to ascertain if he knew the prisoners by sight," he related. "I alluded to Mr. Legh who is a fair, very young man as old and tottering and swarthy, and Lunt agreed with my description. I asked him if he knew Hugh Dicconson of Wrightington, and he answered that he did and had delivered a commission to him in 1691. Now my father, Hugh Dicconson, has been dead these six years. I made myself out to be a hungry, necessitous fellow of the name of Howard and declared I would not join with him unless there was a fortune to be made."

"In fact," interrupted the Chief Solicitor, "you tempted Mr. Lunt to give you employment? You tempted him to give you money?"

"I represented myself to be the sort of person of whom he declared himself to be in need," replied Dicconson composedly. "He promised I should make my fortune and told me he was tired of acting with a parcel of beggarly mechanics who could not produce any evidence unless he first taught it them by rote. He told me that he had received money from Mr. Aaron Smith to pay the charges of bringing up George Wilson from Lancaster, whereas the said George Wilson was all the time chamberlain at an inn in Holborn and had never been in Lancashire at all."

"An inn! What inn?"

"The 'Bear and Ragged Staff' in Smithfield," returned the witness promptly. "Lunt gave Wilson and Baker some of the money but retained the greater part. The whole plot is a question of money and so I examined this side of it very closely. Seeing my apparent dissatisfaction, Lunt told me that this present trial was in the nature of an experiment; if it was successful we were to go through the whole of England, indicting innocent gentlemen and seizing upon a third of their estates for ourselves."

He went on to explain in detail each meeting with Lunt and related the business of Lunt's deposition which had been amended by Aaron Smith and rewritten in consultation with Captain Baker by his clerk, Mr. Ellis. That Captain Baker had chambers in the Temple which he called his office, where he and his brother, a man in the service of Sir William Godolphin and the famous Mr. Dockwra were accustomed to meet. "It appears these gentlemen claim they have an order for the discovery of recusants' estates, and are to receive a percentage of all sums levied on such estates.

"I asked Lunt," he concluded, "if he knew Roger Dicconson. Lunt said he knew him well. I therefore assured him that I was ready to swear against Roger Dicconson, and would not fail to be in Court."

He raised his eyes and looked full at Lunt, but the informer's bold gaze did not falter. He stared back, and then glanced malignantly at Smith. The Crown witnesses would have to be protected at all costs, lest they drag down too many administrators in their downfall, but it seemed that the money profit from this affair was like to be nothing better than a beggarly pension from Government.

The whole atmosphere of the Court seemed to have altered with Roger Dicconson's testimony. As he proceeded, Mr. Aaron Smith was observed to change colour, he asked for a glass of water and one of the attendants opened a window. As Roger stood down, Mr. Smith declared in a faint voice that he was taken suddenly ill and craved leave of the Court to withdraw.

Bridget was the next witness upon the list. Grandfather was gazing towards her from the Bar to give her courage, but as she stepped across the floor the girl thought only of the moment when she and Roger must pass each other. It would perhaps be discreet to keep her eyes downcast, but love was stronger than prudence. She approached quickly and smiled at him, making a hardly perceptible pause. Roger stood aside with a little bow, and when she had reached the box and looked for him again, she could no longer distinguish him among the crowd.

Her hand trembled as she took the oath, her voice faltered at first, but she soon pulled herself together.

"When my grandfather's house was searched on the day of his arrest, George Womball stole a sum of money," she announced. "It was one pound eight shillings and sixpence, and 'twas found upon him, and the King's Messengers paid the money back."

Walter Thelwall corroborated this statement, and all the other witnesses gathered together by the prisoners marched up boldly and gave their evidence in turn. The Shones repeated Brereton's curses uttered against Stanley and Legh in their ale-house, and a sedate old gentleman in a black gown, Doctor Williamson, declared that he had been present and had heard the words: "Damn Sir Roland Stanley—I'll have his blood."

Four witnesses deposed that Sir Roland Stanley was not at Croxteth or anywhere in Lancashire at the dates named, but that he had never left his house at Hooton. Even the Ensign who assisted in Sir Roland's arrest testified to the same, as he had had occasion to search the house several times during that period. One by one each of the gentlemen brought witnesses to prove alibis as to the dates and places of the supposed unlawful assemblies until he came to Mr. Thornleigh's turn. The old gentleman had a most charming smile which lighted up his blue eyes as he spoke.

"My Lords, I have not the same advantage as the rest of the gentlemen to disprove Lunt's testimony that I was at Croxteth in June or July 1689; for, my Lords, I live a neighbour to Croxteth and I must own I have visited Lord Molyneux as a neighbour. But any person can pledge how unfit I am for such a command as Mr. Lunt would put upon me—I am lame of both my hands and feet and cannot get upon a horse without help."

"But were you on horseback you could ride," declared Mr. Justice Eyre acrimoniously.

The prisoners had now concluded their evidence, and the Judge inquired of Sir William Williams if he had not further witnesses to call for the King. To which the King's leading Counsel replied almost violently:

"No, my Lords, I refuse to call any more witnesses."

Eyre looked considerably taken aback and leaned forward to urge him further, but before he could speak, Williams jumped up again.

Chapter Twenty-Nine

"I decline to sum up the evidence to the Jury," he declared.

"We also decline," cried Squire Thornleigh promptly. "And we refer it all to the Court."

"Sir, Sir!" pleaded the clerk, pulling importunately at Sir William's sleeve. "There's Wilson has not spoken—evidence against Taafe—Agnes Barker, too—"

He received no reply save a savage look, and Mr. Justice Eyre was obliged to sum up the evidence for both sides in a lugubrious tone, concluding at length to the Jury:

"Gentlemen, there has been an iniquity on one side." He pronounced these words with great emphasis.

"Hear! Hear!" called someone from a gallery.

The Judge frowned.

"Yea," he continued. "If we believe the evidence for the King it is plain there hath been a great contrivance to bring in the French among us and that these gentlemen were actors in it." He paused again and gazed earnestly at the Jury, but could read nothing from the expression of their countenances.

"But *if* you believe that this is a contrivance of Lunt and the rest to ruin these gentlemen at the Bar and take away their lives and estates, hoping to enrich themselves thereby—as the witnesses for the prisoners have declared, then"—he hesitated—"then—well then—the fault will lie more upon the accusers." His voice dropped to a mumble. "If you do believe it to be so—the gentlemen are innocent—and you must acquit them."

There was dead silence in Court, not a foot shuffled, not a movement was made.

Mr. Justice Eyre resumed:

"Gentlemen of the Jury, this is a matter which deserves great consideration. We will adjourn for two hours and then come into Court again. Meanwhile you are to consider how credible the testimony is which has been given against the witnesses for the King."

A bailiff was sworn to keep the Jury but the foreman announced sharply:

"My Lords, we need no time."

The members of the Jury then turned themselves together with their backs to the Court while the same deathly stillness prevailed. The prisoners had maintained an unperturbed appearance till this moment, but now in this agonizing hiatus between the struggle and the verdict, they were observed to change colour, now paling, now flushing, as their lives and all they held dear hung in the balance.

Bridget's rosary, clasped inside her muff, broke in the clutch of her icy fingers. The shadow of death lay over Roger also, and her father. If the verdict went against the prisoners, they, too, would perish.

"My Lords, we are agreed," announced the Jury.

It seemed to the anxious spectators that the business of calling over the Jury would never be done. At length the prisoners were summoned severally to the Bar.

"Sir Roland Stanley of Hooton, Baronet, guilty or not guilty?" inquired the Court.

"Not guilty."

A sound like a giant sigh ran through the hall, as hundreds breathed relief. Almost immediately the crowd outside the door began to cheer.

"William Thornleigh of Thornleigh, Esquire, guilty or not guilty?"

"Not guilty."

"Sir Thomas Clifton, Baronet, guilty or not guilty?"

"Not guilty."

"Mr. William Dicconson of Wrightington, guilty or not guilty?"

"Not guilty."

"Mr. Philip Langton, guilty or not guilty?"

"Not guilty."

The roar of cheering without broke into Court like a great tide. Only the first sentence of the Judge's address to the gentlemen acquitted could be heard through the din.

"You see under what a merciful and easy Government you live: you are sensible now that it is tender of the lives of papists as well as Protestants..."

"Hurrah!" shouted the good people of Manchester. "Acquitted! Acquitted! Hurrah, hurrah! Down with informers! Down with the bloody plot-mongers! Hurrah! Hurrah!"

.   .   .   .   .

"Bridget, my child, we must sit still while the Court is being cleared," said Madam Thornleigh. Some of the ladies were sobbing, others were on their knees.

Bridget bowed her head. She felt suddenly too tired to speak, almost too tired to feel.

Through the mob two men were forcing their way towards her: one so handsome and gay that it was a pleasure to look on him. The outgoing crowd bore him towards her while the other man was battling against it, struggling from the opposite direction.

Buckland arrived first.

"Triumph!" he cried, waving his little plumed hat. "Dearest lady, I have come into an independence and now I can at last in honour lay my heart at your feet."

Bridget, after a glance, scarcely seemed to attend to him.

"Lay my heart," he repeated, in surprise. "Alas, Mistress Thornleigh, have you no word for your own faithful Buckland?"

The girl hastily put him by with her hand. Roger was coming, he was searching for her with those heavy, weary eyes of his!

"I had nothing to offer you until this moment," continued Buckland eagerly. "The family estates—"

Bridget stood up and pushed him out of her way with the full strength of her vigorous young arm. She hardly knew what

249

she was doing, she was only aware that Roger was coming to her: poor, shabby, muddy, travel-stained Roger.

"Oh, Roger, love, my own love!" she cried, and heedless of the bystanders, she cast herself upon his breast.

.   .   .   .   .

There was a house upon the Wrightington estate, known by the odd title of "Paradise Farm": the land below it sloped sunnily to the south.

"Only a poor man's house, Bridget," whispered Roger, as they sat together hand in hand. The room was crowded with excited Lancashire neighbours, come to offer congratulations on the glorious acquittal, and to bring the news that the King's Counsel, Sir William Williams, had already set forth to return to London, while Aaron Smith was like to die of fright and spite, and the Judges had been hissed and booed in the street.

"I'd be wasted on a rich man, Roger," answered Bridget happily. "I can make butter and bake and brew, you know. Indeed I'm a notable housewife."

But even as she uttered the words recollection smote her. The dairy at Thornleigh! Scutcher's Peg!

"Roger," she faltered, "where were you all that time? And have you—have you news of the girl? Where's Peg?" she insisted, as he did not answer immediately.

"She died to save us, sweetheart. She intercepted the dragoons."

"Died!"

"Aye, she led them astray." He held Bridget in his arms while he told her the end of the pitiful story.

"But there is still a warrant out against you then?" panted Bridget.

"No, dearest, only for Captain Howard. We shall hear no more of that."

"Roger, let me see to her burial. I owe it to her, poor brave child. Roger," she confessed, hiding her face, "I was bitter jealous."

.   .   .   .

Scutcher Morley was set at liberty that night and showed no surprise or displeasure when he found Roger Dicconson waiting for him in the street. His feeble mind had groped its way back to his first arrest and release, and he greeted Dicconson as his benefactor.

"Eh, but to sell your horse! They'm telling me you sold your horse!" he said.

Roger endeavoured gently to break the tidings of his daughter's death, but the scutcher seemed unable to take it in. Even when he was conveyed next day, accompanied by Madam Thornleigh, Bridget and Roger, to Wrightington Hall, to see Peg for the last time, he hardly seemed to realize that the still, childish form, wrapped in white, could be his merry, bustling, laughing Peg. Mr. Cuerdon laid her in the spot she had chosen, in the shadow of the ruined chapel. The parish authorities wrote down that "a vagrant had died by misadventure," and concerned themselves no further.

Farmer Leather undertook the care of Morley under Roger's supervision. The man was happiest when at work, but he would break off every hour or so to shamble to the gate "to see if our Peg was coming."

"You may tell him the poor lass is dead forty times a day, he takes no notice," Mrs. Leather would remark. "He's turned silly, you know, but he's happy enough."

The good woman tended him as she did her own children, and he often left his wool to play marbles with the little boys.

On Monday morning the Court sat again, no witnesses were called, and the remaining three prisoners were acquitted.

Mr. Buckland took his rebuff very quietly: he made a formal call upon the whilom prisoners with the other gentlemen from France, who had given evidence in Court, and with them he left Manchester, though he was very careful to separate from them after the first day's journey. It was said he joined the Jacobite Club, initiated a few years later by Sir William Watkins Wynn, and helped to devise the uniform which was held to become him vastly.

Mr. Legh Bankes was indeed triumphant at the victory of right over might, and set it down entirely to his own good management.

The Lancashire gentlemen arranged before they parted to sue Lunt, Womball and Wilson for perjury at the next Assizes, and it may here be stated that they did so, and won their case.

The day after the Thornleighs' triumphant return to their home, Roger Dicconson rode over with his brother and the Thornleighs' own cousin, Sir Roger Bradshaigh. It was a merry meeting, for Bridget refused to allow the gentlemen to renew the request for her hand in form, it reminded her too painfully of the first occasion. She came into the parlour clinging to the old Squire's arm and announced that she and Roger had fixed the day with Grandfather's approval, and she trusted her honoured father would grant his consent.

Mr. Thornleigh supposed he had better not withhold it, as such saucy young people seemed ready to do without it! And then Bridget begged his pardon very prettily, and called her mother and knelt down hand in hand with Roger for her parents' blessing.

Walter Thelwall came bustling in, wreathed in smiles, with a flagon of the best French wine, but he was pushed out of the room again for there was still some business to be discussed before health drinking began. William Dicconson had brought the title deeds of Paradise Farm and such messuages and parcels of land as would make up Roger's heritage, and Bradshaigh had come to offer him the post of overseer to his new mine-shafts and coal-workings at Wigan, with a share in the profits.

"I must have an honest, ingenious man to study these affairs," he declared. "And though I would greatly wish to please neighbour Dicconson out of gratitude," and here he wrung Roger by the hand, "I know very well that I shall be the great gainer by the bargain."

·   ·   ·   ·   ·

Early in January the simple wedding took place, with Lizzie as solitary bridesmaid. Mr. Cuerdon conducted the ceremony and the Parson of Sefton was paid marriage dues and raised no question.

The young pair rode towards Paradise Farm, whither their baggage had preceded them, but when they reached the summit of Parbold Hill, Bridget drew rein.

"I want to go to the old chapel first," she said.

"Shall we not go tomorrow?" he asked, fearful of sad thoughts on their wedding day.

"No, now," she returned, with something of her old imperiousness.

It was after sunset when they reached the spot, tied their horses to the gate, and walked through the long grass and bushes to the new grave, on which the sods had not yet joined. They said a prayer together and then Bridget turned to her husband. She had meant to make him a little speech to the effect that she wanted to love him with Peg's self-sacrificing love, but she could not do it. She could only murmur over and over between quick little kisses.

"Oh, I love you! Indeed I love you, Roger!"

The gate of Paradise Farm stood wide, wreathed with greenery and decked with lanterns. The servants and neighbours waited a long time, but at last the clatter of horses' hoofs was heard, a lusty cheer was raised, and Roger sprang down to lift his wife over the threshold.

Presently the neighbours tramped off to the suppering at the big house, misty winter moonlight fell over pasture-land and neglected garden, and Roger sat before his own warm hearth with "the thing called Bridget" in his arms.

THE END

OTHER TITLES AVAILABLE
FROM ST. AIDAN PRESS

View sample chapters from each title at www.staidanpress.com or on Amazon. com.

SCOUTING FOR SECRET SERVICE
by Fr. Bernard F. J. Dooley

Frank and George are going to spend their summer vacation in the Adirondacks, thanks to Frank's uncle Ed. But once they get there, they realize something fishy is going on. Can they trust Pete, their Indian guide, or is he mixed up in it too? And is Frank's mysterious uncle really behind it all?

$9.95 — available at www.amazon.com

THE HAPPINESS OF FATHER HAPPÉ
by Cecily Hallack

Shingle Bay did not know what to make of Fr. Savinius Happé. He was a cheerful, rotund Franciscan, a famous author of books on everything from Etruscan civilization to Alpine meadows to beetles, and someone who had never quite mastered the English language. His jovial demeanor concealed a wisdom that alternately bewildered, astonished, but ultimately won over the people of Shingle Bay.

$8.95 — available at www.amazon.com

CON OF MISTY MOUNTAIN
by Mary T. Waggaman

"It had been a long night for Con. Just what had happened to him he was at first too dazed to know. Dennis had flung him into the smoking-room with no very gentle hand, turned the key and left him to himself. And, sinking down dully upon a rug that felt very soft and warm after the hard flight over the mountain, Con was glad to rest his bruised, aching limbs, his dizzy head, without any thought of what was to come upon him next."

$9.95 — available at www.amazon.com

The Anchorhold
by Enid Dinnis

Editha de Beauville had all that the world could offer: wealth, wit, and beauty. Yet a chaplain's sermon drove her to give up all this, and enter the religious life. But could a proud, strong-willed noblewoman accept and embrace the poverty and self-abnegation of the religious life, particularly that of full seclusion in an anchorhold? A difficult path lay before Editha. Read on to learn how she fared, and how her life affected those around her, including Sir Aleric, her erstwhile suitor, now a crusader knight; Fr. Nicholas, a young priest who was quite bright, and thought so too; and Fiddlemee, the witty yet wise court jester whose past held a surprising secret.

$9.95 — available at www.amazon.com

The Shepherd of Weepingwold
by Enid Dinnis

The church at Weepingwold has lain abandoned for years, but change is in the wind. The Luffkyns, former peasants who have made their fortune, have purchased the manor house from the noble but impoverished de Lessels. Humble Brother Kit from nearby Bycross Priory soon finds himself plucked from the cloister and made the parson of Weepingwold. Is he up to the task? And is there really a witch in the parish?

Meanwhile, young Petronilla, heiress to the de Lessels family, hopes to regain possession of the manor she considers rightfully hers. Her guardian, none other than Robert Luffkyn himself, has other ideas; he places her in the care of the Abbess of Gracerood, with the admonition that she is to become a nun. Will she?

$9.95 — available at www.amazon.com

www.ingramcontent.com/pod-product-compliance
Lightning Source LLC
Chambersburg PA
CBHW020315200626

46814CB00006BA/2259